SEPTEMBER HEAT

James rapped softly on the door. "I hope I'm not interrupting anything. I'm a little thirsty— could I have some water?"

"Of course you're not disturbing anything!" Brandy nearly tripped over the box labeled "dishes" to get to him. "Come on inside." She opened the door and told him to follow her to the kitchen.

"James, I really appreciate all of your help." Brandy smiled as she watched him drink the water.

"It's no problem. I'd do anything for a friend of Tricia's." He winked at her and kissed her on the cheek.

Was that electricity she felt? *No,* she told herself. *It must be the September heat.*

"Brandy," James continued. "We have to go out some time. I know you're busy, so when you get time, call me."

Brandy smiled. "I'll definitely call you. I want to repay you for helping me move."

"You don't owe me anything, Brandy." He paused for a moment to drink in her spirit. She was the picture of perfection and he suddenly longed to hold her. "I'm here for you."

ENJOY THESE ARABESQUE FAVORITES!

FOREVER AFTER   (0-7860-0211-5, $4.99)
by Bette Ford

BODY AND SOUL   (0-7860-0160-7, $4.99)
by Felicia Mason

BETWEEN THE LINES   (0-7860-0267-0, $4.99)
by Angela Benson

Eternity
Neffetiti Austin

PINNACLE BOOKS
KENSINGTON PUBLISHING CORP.

PINNACLE BOOKS are published by

Kensington Publishing Corp.
850 Third Avenue
New York, NY 10022

Pinnacle and the P logo Reg. U.S. Pat. & TM Off.

First Printing: September, 1995

Printed in the United States of America

10 9 8 7 6 5 4 3 2

Setting suns reveal footsteps
which lead directly to me—
my love, my confidante.

My beautiful best friend quenches
parched lips with kisses of passion burning—
with him there is no yearning.

Secure in his walk with God,
no fear of losing his way,
committed to us, planning to stay.

One

"Good morning, Ms. Curtis, how was your weekend?"

This Monday morning greeting came from the doorman, Mr. Robinson.

The tall, distinguished African-American man was in his late sixties and had worked at the Wells Fargo Building for twenty-eight years. The building was thirty years old. In the 1960s, it was a ten-floor, light gray cement building with a newspaper stand in front of it. There were tiny, waffle-shaped windows all over the building and a forest green and gold awning that covered the main entryway. In the late 1970s, the city of Santa Monica voted to restore all of the buildings along Ocean Avenue. The Wells Fargo Building was no exception. The new design included an ocean view from every office. Light gray cement blocks gave way to smokey marbled walls, picture windows, underground valet parking, a gift shop and a sidewalk cafe. When it was sunny, which was most of the year in Southern California, tables and chairs were set up outside for the customers to enjoy the warm weather. The awning remained, though it too had been replaced with a new one.

Brandy liked to talk to Mr. Robinson because his easygoing self-confidence reminded her of her grandfather.

"Oh, it was okay. I spent most of it here in the office."

"Girl, is that all you do, just work?"

"Yep. That's all I seem to have time for," she said with a smile that didn't quite reach her eyes. Brandy's oval face was a softened version of the Egyptian sphinx. Where the statue's eyes were piercing, hers were soft brown feline eyes surrounded by long, curling lashes. They were sultry eyes that revealed her innermost feelings. Under naturally arched eyebrows and those telltale eyes sat slightly flared nostrils sprinkled with freckles. Brandy's shapely lips parted to show two even rows of white teeth. Her smile could brighten any room, and often did. Her dark reddish skin coloring was reminiscent of a vintage bottle of E&J Brandy— her father's favorite drink, for which she'd been named.

All her life, she had wanted to be an attorney and work in a large law firm. She set goals for herself early on, and so far had achieved all of them. But now, four years later, the partner track wasn't as fulfilling as it once was. Today, her office with an ocean view from the thirty-second floor, her convertible black BMW with personalized plates— *BJCSQRE*— her three-bedroom townhouse, weren't enough. In four short years, Brandy Janae Curtis had gone from a vibrant, socially conscious, "fight-the-power," upwardly mobile woman to a poor little rich girl.

"When you get tired of hiding behind your work, I'll introduce you to my grandson. He's a fine young man," he smiled. "You have a nice day now and don't let those people work you too hard."

The elevator doors opened before Brandy had a chance to ask Mr. Robinson why he thought, as did the rest of her family, that a man would be the answer to her problems. That was such an old school way of thinking. It was a shame that in 1995, a woman was still "nothing" without a man.

Men found her attractive, as Mr. Robinson's flirtation

proved. Brandy's flawless complexion gave her the look of a twenty-three-year-old. She prided herself on looking younger than she actually was. Maybe it was her hairstyle that made her look twenty-three instead of twenty-eight. She wore her thick chestnut colored hair in a bob, parted down the middle. It was just professional enough to be fashionable. At five foot eight inches, Brandy was a shapely package of curves, proving that not one ounce of her 125 pounds was wasted.

She had moved to Marina Del Rey two years ago. After Brandy was hired as an associate attorney in the litigation department of Lloyd & Lloyd, she put herself on a budget. She lived frugally for two years, even after her salary jumped from sixty-five thousand dollars per year to seventy-two thousand in the first year of her employment with the firm. Finally, two years from her first day at the firm, October 1, 1991, she had enough for a down payment. What a glorious day that had been! In a matter of months, she found her dream home and moved in.

The Marina, as it was affectionately known, was replete with pricey restaurants, ritzy hotels, and a dock with yachts, sailboats and motorboats. But what really sold Brandy on the location was the short walk to the beach; she loved the sound of waves crashing against the sand in the early morning and late evening, and the smell of the ocean breeze.

When the elevator doors opened again, Brandy was greeted by the receptionist, Shirley Lawson. Shirley was the only other African-American woman who worked at Lloyd & Lloyd. Shirley possessed a down-home easiness that made clients and attorneys alike feel immediately at ease with her. Though she was easy to get along with, Shirley was no pushover. She was quick-witted and funny, but she didn't hesitate to let people know when they had crossed her.

Shirley was a full-figured, almond-colored woman who never missed an episode of *All My Children*. She was capable of doing three things at once and had the greatest phone voice in the world. It was low and smooth like a Lincoln Continental, yet slightly nasal. Unless one listened closely, one could miss the Mississippi in her voice. She wore her hair in a sassy short cut, tapered on the sides and curly on the top. In fact, she referred to herself as the Anita Baker of Lloyd & Lloyd.

Though not a flashy dresser, Shirley had a huge collection of multicolored scarves to match each outfit she owned. She was a sucker for shoulder pads, because she once read in *Essence* that shoulder pads made large hips look slimmer. Shirley's cocoa brown eyes, high cheekbones and dimples complemented her flawless complexion. Brandy thought that Shirley was an attractive woman; she might have been the woman the Commodores had in mind when they sang "Brick House."

Shirley, who had started working at Lloyd & Lloyd in 1986, was the eyes and ears of the office. She made it a point to befriend all of the African-Americans who worked in the office, feeling it her responsibility to school the new employees on the ins and outs of the firm. Unfortunately, not enough African-Americans had remained at the law firm once they passed through the oak double doors.

"Hey, girl! What's up? Here's your mail." Shirley removed the rubber band from Brandy's mail with the grace of a magician.

"Thanks, and I'm doing fine." Brandy flipped through her mail and made a mental note to call Stephanie Myers, who was the opposing counsel for a new case she had been assigned on Friday. "How was your weekend?"

"It was great! My youngest son, Billy, turned five. He

had a Batman birthday party on Saturday and on Sunday his grandmother took him to Disneyland." With slender fingers and nails polished to a high gloss, Shirley deactivated the voice mail system.

Brandy looked up from her stack of mail and smiled. "I hope you guys took pictures." André had inherited his mother's dimples.

"Girl, we've got pictures and a videotape of André's party. I'll bring them to work just as soon as Michael gets them out of the shop." Whenever Shirley talked about her husband or her son, she got very excited. "Girl, the kids were *sooo* cute! You should have seen them. Michael rented an air jump and hired a clown to entertain the kids." She paused and laughed deeply at the memory.

"I'm sure you guys had a great time."

Shirley waved her hands in the air and took a deep breath so she could talk. "Wait— do you know that André cried every time the clown came near him?" Brandy laughed. "You know, Brandy, André is just like his daddy, he runs at the first sign of trouble!"

"Ooh, Shirley!" Brandy playfully admonished her. Michael was Shirley's husband. Brandy wasn't ready to settle down, but she was happy for Shirley. "It must be nice to have a family."

"Yes. It's hard work, but there's nothing like it in the world." Shirley leaned forward conspiratorially. "When are you getting married?" She was very sweet, but a bit on the nosy side.

Brandy smiled wistfully. She used to think about getting married all the time. Now all she did was work to keep from thinking about it. "Me? Get married?" Brandy laughed a hearty but false laugh. "How about the day after never?"

"I don't believe you." Shirley shook her head.

"You're so pretty and smart. You'd make a great partner to someone."

"Well, that remains to be seen." Brandy gathered her mail and headed to her office.

The receptionist's desk faced the lobby, which spoke of old money and an old boy network. It was conservatively decorated with an almost life-size oil painting of the firm's founders. A mahogany table, with a bric-a-brac china vase full of fresh white orchids, amber tiger lilies, lavender carnations and numerous hybrid violets stood next to the wall beneath the painting. The walls were paneled in a dark wood, and the mahogany wing chairs with studs at the seams looked comfortable but cold at the same time. The hardwood floors, decorated with expensive Oriental rugs, were polished to perfection, and showed no signs of Lloyd & Lloyd's seventy-two years, nor the wear and tear of the wingtips, Cole-Haan's or Bally's preferred by the men and the clients of the firm.

As Brandy trudged down the hall to her office, she heard a familiar voice.

"Hey Bran, it's 8:05 a.m. and you just cost the firm $200! You're slipping." The voice belonged to Bradley L. Stevens. Bradley, or Brad, as he liked to be called, was clean shaven and lanky. He had bright red, curly hair and red eyebrows that covered squinty emerald green eyes. His voice was as high and squeaky as if he had never left puberty. To compensate for his high voice, Brad talked fast and walked with his chest puffed out like a peacock.

His father was CEO of the country's largest skateboard company. Brandy disliked Brad more than any of her other colleagues, although he had qualities the firm liked. He was white, self-assured and rich. He got the position with Lloyd & Lloyd after his father played a game of golf at the Century City Men's Club with a former classmate, Richard Lloyd, Jr., the firm's hiring partner. While Brandy had to admit that Brad was bright, he was not the genius he thought he was and could have used a few lessons in how not to be a jerk.

Thinking of the devil, Brandy noticed Mr. Lloyd walking in her direction. The younger Lloyd looked very distinguished in a navy blue Brooks Brothers suit. "Good morning, Brandy. Good morning, Bradley." Lloyd smiled warmly.

"Good morning, Lloyd," Brandy said. Mr. Lloyd, Jr. was a well-tanned older man with grayish-blue eyes. In his mid-fifties, he regularly worked out four times per week at the gym, giving him the sexy physique of a thirty-year-old.

"Lloyd," Brad interrupted, "I was just asking Brandy if she will be representing our firm in the Los Angeles Marathon 2000: Race Against Urban Poverty."

Brandy witnessed Richard Lloyd smile. Unlike Richard Lloyd Sr., Lloyd Jr. was an advocate for the homeless, the poor and the disenfranchised. He was extremely charming and the reason why Brandy had chosen the firm.

She'd thought that she was joining a firm that had a legitimate interest in improving the conditions of the city. Lloyd had represented that much to her during interviews four years earlier. Brandy had looked forward to doing pro bono work in the African-American and Latino communities. What she learned, however, was that the younger Lloyd's sales pitch for the less fortunate was the older Lloyd's way of winning the token associate from the other big firms in Los Angeles. It took too long for Brandy to realize how naive she was.

"Well, Brandy, will you be running in the marathon again this year? Those long limbs of yours have always made the firm so proud." Lloyd waited for her to answer.

Brandy smiled at Lloyd and then at Brad. Her heart was screaming in her ears. There was no way she was running the marathon this year, or any other year, for that matter. Brad was trying to get the best of her. What he didn't realize was that Brandy was a pro at masking her true feelings.

"No, Lloyd, I will not be running in the marathon this year," she answered sweetly, yet sternly.

"But, Brandy, you always run," Brad prodded.

"Yes, I know. This year I plan to contribute differently. Instead of participating in that one activity, I plan to give my time and money directly to the people in my old neighborhood that day and the rest of the year." She smiled again. She had done it. She had said "no" to the old boy network straight to its face.

Three years ago, even one year ago, Brandy would never have dreamed of telling her employer "No". She thought she had to accept every invitation and attend every function to keep her job. Now she knew better.

Lloyd seemed surprised by Brandy's answer. Lately Brandy had seemed distracted, even unhappy. He made a mental note to look further into it.

Turning his attention back to the ongoing conversation between Brad and Brandy, Lloyd said stiffly, "Well, Brandy, I respect your decision. I'll go break the news to the other partners. They'll be so disappointed that our star runner won't be participating this year." With that he smiled and continued down the hall to his office.

"Yeah, Bran," Brad whispered in her ear, "you've got the hottest pair of legs. I'll miss seeing those powerful legs glisten with sweat this year."

Brandy turned sharply to face Brad, eye to eye. "Brad. First of all, my name is Brandy. And second of all, if you ever make another sexist, racist comment about me

again, I will sue you for sexual harassment!'' Brandy
stormed away.

Halfway to the bathroom, Brandy realized it was only
8:35 a.m. Already she felt like she had been at the office
all day. ''Damn,'' she said out loud.

Two

"I can't teach if I can't eat!" was the caption under the picture of the article entitled "Teachers' Strike Turns Physical" in the *Los Angeles Times Magazine*. Brandy was poring over the article early one Sunday morning. The article had caught her eye because many of her friends were teachers, and she was concerned about how the strike was affecting them. The teachers were having an extremely rough time with the school board. In addition to increased hours, the pay cuts had reached an all-time high of 40 percent and the educators and administrators were tired of it. Teachers had been laid off, and others had been switched to substitute teacher status, which meant no health insurance, no vacation and penalties if a teacher refused to sub too many times. Many administrators were sent back to the classroom and still received pay cuts. Because jobs were so hard to come by, these demotions were welcomed.

On day thirty-seven of the peaceful yet bitter walk-out, a fight broke out. There had been at least three of them. In the first fight, a shouting match broke out between a tenured teacher and a teacher's aide. The teacher blamed his pay cut on the aide. He accused the aides of being parasites on the school system and the sole cause of his decreased salary. The aide, who could scream just as loud, told the older teacher that his pay was going to be cut whether or not aides were paid. He also pointed out that the school board was spreading rumors like the one the teacher believed to take the pressure off of themselves. The aide said it was a plot to divide teachers, administrators and aides so that the strike would lose momentum and fizzle out. The elder told the aide that he was full of shit and to stay out of his way.

The second fight was between a husband and wife teaching team. The husband refused to strike, because he felt that his family needed the money. They had two kids in college and a third in high school. The house had been mortgaged twice and his mother was hospitalized for breast cancer. The wife, on the other hand, chose to strike because she believed that teachers, like other professionals, deserved to be paid their worth. Since teachers spent more time with students than most parents, the future rested on the information passed on to students from their teachers. It was a domino effect. If the teachers were happy, the students were happy. If the teachers were upset, then a nation of upset, undereducated children would be let loose into society. It angered her that the powers that be continued to treat the teaching profession like a step-child when, for many children, the teacher was the only parent/counselor/praiser/provider/disciplinarian they would ever have. Her fight was about principle and her husband simply didn't get it.

Brandy didn't remember what the other fight was about. She kept abreast of the teachers' strike through the newspaper and her best sister/friend, Simone, an elementary school teacher. Simone loved her job, but hated the bureaucratic red tape that came with working for the public school system. She also hated the strike. She missed her students, and most importantly, she missed having her own money, although her husband, Phil, was a civil engineer, and they were still financially comfortable.

Simone, Phil and their three children lived in Ladera Heights, a mixed, upper middle class section of L.A. Their children attended parochial school. Simone, who had attended public school her entire life, wanted to send the children to the local public school. But the school system in Los Angeles wasn't what it used to be and she had no choice but to send them to school on the West Side.

Since Simone was one of the leaders of the strike, she held weekly meetings at her home. The meetings were mainly business-oriented, but they also served as an outlet for her colleagues who were in dire financial straits. Brandy had attended a couple of the meetings, giving free legal advice about creditors, mortgage payments and even divorce in a couple of instances.

That night was one of her volunteer sessions at Simone's house. There she had met William Johnson, another teacher. He was trying his best to keep up the morale among the teachers, even offering money to several teachers who were minutes from filing for bankruptcy. Aside from the obvious generosity and compassion he showed for his colleagues, he was gorgeous. Brandy guessed he was about 6'2" and 190 pounds. He was very dark— no, he was black. Jet black, and Brandy couldn't stop staring. He had black curly hair and a thin mustache, a deep voice and a beautiful smile. No earring, no beard and no wedding ring. His hands looked powerful and smooth, hands that could caress and stroke. Brandy wondered how his hands would feel when they touched her.

"Hello." Brandy heard the African king speak.

Startled, she responded barely above a whisper. "Hello, how are you?" She cleared her throat and extended her hand. "My name is Brandy Curtis."

"I'm William Johnson." He looked at her and smiled. "I've never seen you before, where do you teach?"

"I'm not a teacher. Simone asked me to stop by and give legal advice." Brandy felt like a fool. Here, the most beautiful man in the world was talking to her and her hair was in a ponytail, her nails were not done, and her lipstick was smeared, because she had eaten it off during dinner.

"So you're the lawyer who's been handing out free advice." William sort of laughed as he looked her over. She felt as though she were on display.

"You sound disappointed." Brandy was starting to get irritated.

"Disappointed? No. It's just that I expected to see . . . I don't want to offend you, but I expected to see . . ."

Brandy finished his sentence. "A man." Her tone was dry and her attitude had changed. He was just like the others, sexist, chauvinistic and intimidated by her title.

"No, I expected to see a woman. I just didn't expect to see someone so pretty. I'm embarrassed, and I apologize for thinking you would be anything less than beautiful, just because you're a professional. I hope that I haven't offended you." William seemed sincere and Brandy couldn't help but laugh.

"Contrary to popular belief, many African-American female attorneys are quite beautiful." Her initial assessment of William had been wrong and the irritation that she felt earlier vanished.

"What grade do you teach?" There was something about William that caught Brandy's attention. He gave off a positive vibe and she wanted to know where it was coming from. Just as he was about to respond, a woman interrupted them and informed William that she was ready to go home.

"Terry, this is Brandy Curtis. She's the attorney Simone's been telling us about. I believe she's Simone's sister." After he made the introductions, William smiled warmly and asked Brandy if she was going to come to the meeting the following week. Brandy told him that someone else would be coming.

"I didn't know Simone had a sister," Terry said.

"Well, we're not real sisters, but we've known each other since grade school. We grew up together," Brandy explained.

"It was a pleasure meeting you and I hope to see you again," William said.

Brandy handed him her card. Jokingly, but seriously, she told him, "Take this in the event the strike turns ugly and you or some of the other teachers need to be bailed out of jail." This time Brandy smiled, and then she excused herself and went into the kitchen.

Simone was in the kitchen looking for garbage bags to put the trash in. She was wearing a denim shirt, faded jeans and black flats. Three kids later and Simone was still slim. In fact the biggest thing on Simone were her cheeks. She had large brown cheeks, slanted eyes and a pointy nose. Her jet black hair was curly and reached the middle of her back. For years she had wanted to cut it, but she knew that if she did Phil would have a heart attack. Also, a short haircut meant regular visits to the hairstylist, which she didn't have time for. Between three kids, her job and her husband, ponytails and French rolls had become her signature hairstyles. On this night, it was twisted into a French roll.

"Simone, I just met the most beautiful man," Brandy said with a faraway look in her eyes.

Simone straightened up. She was five foot eight inches, about the same height as Brandy. "Who?" Simone could not think of anybody in particular.

"William. William Johnson." Brandy's dreamy look reminded Simone that in addition to law, Brandy had a flair for the dramatic.

ETERNITY

Simone smiled. She wasn't surprised that William had caught Brandy's eye. From what Simone could tell, William was a very warm and supportive person. Unlike some people who taught because they had nothing else to do, William taught because he liked shaping young minds.

"Oh, yes, Mr. Johnson. He is so fine!" Brandy and Simone exchanged high fives in the kitchen.

"Simone, you've got to help me. I think I want him to father my children." Brandy was quite serious.

"I thought you said that you weren't having any children," Simone teased.

"I lied. Anyway, girl, why have you been holding out on me? I mean, who is he? What's his story? And how long have you known him?"

Laughing, Simone answered, "Slow down! One question at a time. First, I don't know him very well, but I do know that he transferred from another school district."

They were interrupted by Terry, who needed her coat. Simone led her out of the kitchen and into the hallway, where she embraced Terry and shook hands with William.

"Who was that?" Brandy said when they'd left. She knew she sounded ridiculous, but after her fiasco of a relationship with James, she made sure that she got every man's pertinent details up front.

"That was Terry. I think they're related."

What a relief, Brandy thought.

Slowly the meeting broke up and Simone and Brandy started cleaning the living room. While they were emptying ashtrays and dumping paper plates and cups, Simone resumed the rundown on William.

Simone didn't know much, but what she did know, she shared with Brandy. He was from the South, had one sister and she lived wherever their parents lived.

Terry was his cousin. William was down-to-earth and a Southern gentleman in every sense of the word. He had a master's degree in elementary education and was currently working on his doctorate. Simone didn't think he was married, but she wasn't sure about that. He didn't appear to be a womanizer, but again, she didn't know for sure. Her daddy had always cautioned her about the shy ones and she gave Brandy the same warning. In the six months that he'd worked for Simone's district, she'd heard nothing but good things about him.

The women worked in quiet until Brandy broke the peace. "Simone, I saw James last night." Brandy tried to sound as if their meeting was no big deal. "We went to dinner."

"You did?" Simone was happy that Brandy was finally speaking to James. "Why didn't you tell me sooner?" She got the vacuum cleaner out of the closet.

"Well, I didn't think about it." Brandy took a deep breath. Their dinner hadn't been at all what she'd hoped it would be. His arrogance overwhelmed her. "There's really nothing to tell. He's still a pig and we will not be getting back together."

"That's it? What happened?" Simone swallowed hard. This was the moment that Brandy had been waiting for. James was trying to reconcile.

"Nothing." Brandy checked her watch. It was almost two in the morning. She needed to go home. "I shouldn't have mentioned it." Brandy went into the kitchen to get more trash bags.

Simone knew better than to pry. There was something Brandy wasn't saying. Whatever it was, Simone would have to wait; Brandy would tell her in her own time. She hoped that Brandy and James would be able to work things out. It was a shame that two people who loved each other couldn't be together. Simone remembered how their relationship had blossomed. They were so right for each other! Brandy, the superstar attorney, and James, the charismatic, upwardly mobile professional. But then, out of the blue, James froze. Simone wondered if he knew how much he had hurt Brandy.

Brandy had to be at the office by nine, so she grabbed her purse and keys and headed for the door while Simone was still vacuuming. Phil, who had been taking care of the kids during the meeting, watched Brandy get into her shiny black BMW from the doorway.

On the drive home, Brandy couldn't stop thinking about the smooth-talking, tall, dark-chocolate dreamboat who called himself William. She had a good feeling about him. Brandy knew that she was hard to get close to; her defense to potential suitors was to play a very indifferent role. This tactic worked well at screening out the riff-raff. On the flip side, Simone told her that she had thrown away some good brothers by being so cold. Brandy tried to explain to her that she wasn't being cold, she was just being cautious. To this comment, Simone would respond that she would end up alone if she kept being so mean to every man who entered her life. Brandy would just laugh or roll her eyes. Some days she agreed with Simone's prophesy. Other days, she could care less.

Tonight, however, Brandy was ready to shed her ice goddess persona. It wasn't a real part of Brandy's personality. It was a put-on, like putting on a hat or a jacket. Brandy always let the situation dictate how she would or would not respond to a man. She considered herself to be an excellent judge of character, and figured that when the right one came along, she would be nice.

For the first time since her break-up with James, Brandy wanted to be nice to someone. James. Brandy didn't want to admit that she had made a bad call. He was everything she had ever hoped for, but he disappointed her. Brandy guessed part of her would always love James.

Brandy thought back to the night before, when James had called her and asked her to meet him at The Fountain. Something told her not to meet him for dinner, but he'd persisted and she reluctantly agreed. The Fountain was the site of their first date two years before. The decor of the restaurant was tropical and the menu was Mexican. The chairs were rattan with light orange cushions. Each table had miniature candles, white cloth napkins and magenta-colored tulips in the center. The tiled floor was a Spanish red color, and there were murals of lovers on every wall. The two-tiered fountain sat in the middle of the room in a gold, tiled pool, with blue and pink lightbulbs at its base. This caused the water to look lavender as it spouted from the fountain. Mariachis sang quietly in the background.

James was waiting for Brandy at the door. He inhaled sharply when he saw her. "Brandy, you are still the most beautiful woman in the world!" He leaned down and kissed her cheek.

She wasn't ready to let her guard down, but she smiled anyway. "Thank you," she responded, and took his outstretched hand. Brandy watched him from the corner of her eye. Though he looked debonair in a rust-colored turtleneck and black slacks, something wasn't right. James was too young to be shrinking, but Brandy could have sworn that he looked shorter than his six foot four inches. It was clear to Brandy that he hadn't been sleeping. Brandy enjoyed the fact that he was looking haggard, but she wanted to reach out to him. Oh, how she missed massaging James' broad shoulders when he came home from work, feeling his hard muscles soften under her hands. His five-o'clock shadow was going on eight o'clock, and the rims of his sweet bedroom eyes were red.

James led her to their table. "I made sure that we sat in the same place we did the first time we came here. You remember, don't you?" He looked at her with longing.

"How could I forget?" Brandy looked down at her hands. He was making her uncomfortable. "Why are you looking at me like that?" She felt her back stiffen.

"I can't . . . I just can't take my eyes off of you." James reached across the table and grabbed her hands. He stared lovingly into her eyes while he kissed her fingertips. She allowed her fingers to linger and savor the softness of his lips. "I really miss spending time with you."

Brandy looked up. "I miss you, too." His smile was melting her. Why couldn't things be like they were? When had it come to this? Why did it all have to happen, when everything was so perfect?

She found herself melting. He was charming her like he always did when he was in trouble. She was determined not to let him off the hook without an apology or, at the very least, an explanation. Brandy cleared her throat. "James, I've got a lot of work to do tonight. I wish you would get to the point."

"Brandy, I asked you to dinner because I wanted to talk to you."

She leaned forward. "I'm listening." There was a mounting excitement in the pit of her stomach. *Here it comes!* He was going to ask her to come back to him.

He began to speak authoritatively. "I think you overreacted."

"Excuse me?" Aware of her surroundings, she kept her voice low. *"I overreacted?"*

James continued. "Yes, Brandy, you did overreact. You know how I feel about you. Of all the people in the world, you know that I would never do anything to hurt you. I was going through a rough period and you left me. How could you do that to me?" He spoke with sincerity.

For a moment, Brandy considered his words. Was he right? Had she left him when he was in a crisis? Maybe she had overreacted? *Wait a second!* He was the one who hadn't been ready for marriage, not her. He was the one who'd needed space, not her. "James, I cannot believe that you have the unmitigated gall to look me in my face and tell me such nonsense!"

A puzzled look came over his face as Brandy continued.

"You know that's not true. I tried to be there for you, but you shut me out. What was I supposed to do? I sacrificed my job for you and that wasn't enough. You began to pull away from me, one small step at a time. I guess you thought I was so lovestruck I didn't notice."

Brandy caught herself. He didn't need to know how much he hurt her. She reached for her purse and stood up. "I don't need this." She was so mad, she felt tears welling up in her eyes.

Brandy's mind jerked back into the present as she turned onto her street. There were two other cars at the red light beside hers. The car on the right was a navy blue Rolls Royce, Silver Spur edition. That was her favorite car and one day she hoped to own one. The other car was a smoke gray Jaguar XJ19. It wasn't so much the car that caught her eye as it was the man behind the steering wheel. He looked like James. She wasn't sure though, because the last time she saw him he was driving a baby Benz. Well, she wasn't going to hurt herself trying to see if it was him. James was just someone she used to know and right now William was the *homme du jour.* Two minutes later, Brandy was safely in her townhouse. After a quick shower, Brandy wrapped her hair and did a Superman dive into the bed. She fell asleep saying her prayers.

The man in the smoke gray Jaguar had caught a glimpse of the convertible BMW as it made a right turn in front of him. For a moment his heart froze.

"Hey, isn't that Brandy?" his buddy, Keith, asked him.

James shook his head, "No, man, that wasn't her."

Keith insisted that it was Brandy and told James to follow her. They were returning from a party at the Double Tree Hotel in the Marina.

"Keith, I'm not following that woman, whoever she is. It's ten after two in the morning." As James continued to drive, he started talking about the NBA finals. Keith, who was an expert on basketball, took the bait and proposed a theory on the new breed of basketball players. He proposed that many players, like Dennis Rodman, concentrated on rebounds and less on making thirty points per game. While Keith rambled on about who had the most rebounds, James thought about Brandy. It was almost one month to the day that she left him. He knew he'd messed up. She knew it, too.

He also knew Keith was right . . . that had been Brandy in that car.

Three

The rising California sun woke Brandy up. It was six-thirty in the morning, but she wasn't going into the office until nine, so she pulled the covers over her head and tried to go back to sleep. After ten minutes of listening to the birds sing, Brandy reluctantly admitted that she was fully awake.

Brandy closed her eyes and took several deep breaths. She mumbled the Lord's Prayer to herself and then opened her eyes. She could tell today was going to be "one of those days" and she felt the need to have a long talk with God. She sat up in bed and the conversation began.

"God, I met the most beautiful man last night and I had another dream about James. I'm trying so hard to be strong and have faith, but it's really hard to forget about James— "

James Collins was the cousin of her classmate and study partner, Tricia. Whenever the legalese got too deep, Tricia would call on her favorite relative, James. Since he traveled quite a bit, he was frequently in Washington, D.C. He never complained and generously took them wherever they wanted to go. James was a stockbroker at Tyler Securities, and liked to go to dinner, plays, the movies and museums almost as much as they did. He was a person who loved being on the go and could be ready at a moment's notice.

Sometimes he brought dates and other times he didn't. Brandy and Tricia noticed he never brought the same the woman twice. When he did bring a date, she was usually strikingly beautiful. From what Brandy could recall, James' dates were usually light-skinned, tall and athletic. They generally came with faces full of make-up, expensive clothes and lots of small talk. James had a fetish for short hair and nice cars. He dressed like a fashion model and required his women to look like they had just left the runway. These women were not the kind of women to challenge James. They usually let him do all the talking and nodded in agreement to whatever he said, no matter how ridiculous he sounded. Though they seemed to be nice women, most of them were void of personality and about as exciting as bumps on a log.

James had often marveled at what attracted him to Brandy. She definitely did not fit his mode. She was shorter than most of the women he had dated, had long hair, wore very little make-up, was extremely feminine and loved to argue. She would debate with James into the wee hours about everything from jazz to politics to literary criticism. She tested him every step of the way and refused to allow him to change her opinion when her mind was made up. For this, James respected her. She opened his mind and forced him to see the world as she saw it.

Brandy looked great when she had a meeting or when she was working. During her off time, however, she lived in sweats, jeans and tennis shoes. In the beginning James thought that he would never get used to her casual attire; later, he learned to love it. There was a realness about Brandy that never changed no matter what she wore.

When Brandy graduated from Georgetown Law Center and moved home to Los Angeles, she went to work right away. Tricia remained in Washington, D.C., and James was promoted and given a primary office in Los Angeles. He still traveled frequently, but his home office was in the mid-Wilshire district of Los Angeles.

After six months of living with her parents, Brandy needed space. She found an apartment in Culver City, a one-bedroom with a loft in the Fox Hills area of Los Angeles. The area was full of apartments and condominiums. It was bordered by a shopping mall, a park complete with a jogging trail, tennis courts, a baseball field and swings for children, a cemetery, a small business district, a grocery store, and the freeway. Predominantly African-American, Fox Hills was the perfect spot for Brandy, who loved the convenience of having all of her needs met within a one-mile radius.

The big day for her to move arrived and Brandy asked James to help her. He agreed without hesitation. Her father and brother were at her new place waiting for her furniture to arrive. Her mother, Lena, and Simone remained at the house and helped her pack her things. Brandy had hired movers, but James insisted on assisting them anyway.

Brandy could remember her moving day with unbelievable clarity. She tried to ignore the images rushing into her mind, but she couldn't avoid the thoughts of James.

At eight o'clock sharp, James rang the doorbell. Brandy answered the door, because her mother was in the bathroom and Simone was in the kitchen. The front door of her parents' home had two large cut-glass windows in the frame. The glass was designed for the person on the inside to be able to see out, but the person on the outside could not see in. Brandy could see James through the glass. Even in a Bob Marley t-shirt, jeans and hiking boots, he looked handsome. She thought of her own appearance— an oversized white t-shirt, yellow sweat pants and tennis shoes with no socks— and almost didn't open the door.

"Hi, James. Good morning." Brandy was genuinely happy to see him.

"Good morning to you, sweetness." James smiled broadly and kissed her on the cheek. "I see the movers have arrived." Brandy followed his gaze and saw two men get out of a U-Haul truck.

Brandy felt herself blush, but then she caught herself. "Good, they're right on time." She stepped back from the doorway. "Come in. Can I get you anything? Coffee? Juice?"

"No, I'm fine, thanks." Looking at Brandy made James feel like he could do anything. And he wanted to do anything and everything for her. All she had to do was ask. James was surprised at how he felt. Though he always appreciated her intellect and thought she had a great personality, she had never struck him the way she did at that moment. "Just tell me where to begin." Brandy pointed to three stacks of boxes.

"They're all yours, James."

He tugged on his Raiders baseball cap. "No problem. Don't worry about the movers, I'll give them instructions." James said this over his shoulder as he surveyed the three stacks in front of him.

Brandy was amazed at how helpful he was. "Okay, you're in charge."

An hour later Lena noticed James. "Brandy, who is that with the movers?" Her mother was peeking through the off-white chiffon curtains which draped the living room window. The window took up most of the wall.

Without looking up, Brandy responded. "That's James." She was labeling boxes so that when she got to her new place, she wouldn't have to look for things.

"James who?" Her mother ran slender finger through her salt-and-pepper hair. Lena was a shorter stockier version of Brandy. She was a friendly woman who knew everybody in the neighborhood. She loved her children and wished Brandy would hurry up and get married so she could have some grandchildren.

"James Collins, Tricia's cousin." Brandy stopped writing and stood up. Her brow was damp with sweat and her fingers were stained with felt black marker. "He's the one who used to take Tricia and me out when we were in law school."

Lena turned her attention to James. "You ought to get him to take you out now." She stepped back from the curtains and pulled Brandy in front of her. James was working up a sweat. His biceps bulged under the weight of the box he was lifting. The box looked heavy, yet he lifted it effortlessly. His Bob Marley T-shirt was wet and his face glistened in the morning sun.

Brandy had an opportunity to admire him from afar. She liked seeing James in jeans. He wore them well, not too tight, not too loose. They hugged his butt perfectly. His cap was turned backward and they could see his face clearly. "Brandy, he's cute!" Lena had a naughty look on her face.

"Mama, I know that look and I ain't interested."

Simone entered the room. "Ain't interested in whom?"

Before Brandy could reply, her mother spoke up. "Simone, Brandy is telling me that she is not interested in James. I don't see why not." Lena faced Brandy. "The whole time you stayed here, you only went on three dates." Lena shrugged her shoulders. "Not that I'm counting or anything."

Brandy rolled her eyes. "Mama, I only had time for three dates. If you remember, I spent half of those six months studying for the bar, the other two looking for a place to live, and I started my job at Lloyd & Lloyd." She looked to Simone for support.

Simone had joined Lena and Brandy at the window. "Don't look at me, Brandy, James is fine and I don't know what you're waiting for."

"You guys are impossible!" Brandy couldn't help but laugh. "I know what you two are doing, but I can pick my own dates, thank you very much."

It was only nine-fifteen, and James was thirsty. They had been transporting boxes from the house to the U-Haul van since eight o'clock. He was dog tired, but his day was far from over. When he left Brandy's parents' home, he had to take a quick shower and meet the boys he mentored at the YMCA. Today was the first boxing tournament. They had been practicing every Saturday for the last two months. James, a natural competitor, was excited and looked forward to a victory. It was almost time for him to leave. He definitely wanted to say good-bye, so he decided to go into the house and ask Brandy for some water, even though he had bottled water in his Mercedes.

James rapped softly on the door. "I hope I'm not interrupting anything. I'm a little thirsty— could I have some water?"

"Of course you're not disturbing anything!" Brandy nearly tripped over the box labeled "dishes" trying to get to him. "Come on inside." Brandy had headed toward the kitchen when she heard, "Um-um." She caught the admonition in her mother's voice for not introducing her to James before taking him into the kitchen. "James, this is my mother Lena Curtis and my best friend, Simone."

James shook their hands. "It's a pleasure meeting both of you." Brandy noticed that his eyes sparkled when he spoke. "Mrs. Curtis, I see you are the reason Brandy is so beautiful." This caused Lena to blush.

Not wanting her mother to respond, Brandy rushed James into the kitchen. "James, I really appreciate all of your help." She smiled at him and watched him gulp down a tall glass of ice water.

"It's no problem. I'd do anything for a friend of Tricia's." He winked at her and lightly kissed her on the cheek.

Was that electricity she felt? *No*, she told herself, *it must be the September heat.*

"Brandy, we've got to go out sometime."

She refilled his glass. "You're right." Brandy bit her bottom lip trying to think of a day when she would be free. Something made her look up. "What?" James was staring at her.

"Oh nothing, I was just watching you think." Brandy was beginning to feel self-conscious about her appearance. She hoped he didn't notice the ink stains on her clothes.

"I'm going to have to call you about a date. My appointment book is somewhere in this mess." Brandy gestured toward the many boxes.

James shook his head. "Look, I know you're busy, so here's my card. When you get time, call me." He reached for the pen by the telephone and wrote the numbers to his pager and cellular phone on the back of his card.

Brandy accepted his card and smiled. "I will definitely call you. I want to repay you for helping me move."

"You don't owe me anything, Brandy." He paused for a moment to drink in her spirit. Brandy's eyes looked tired but he could feel her soul dancing all over the kitchen. She was the picture of perfection, and he longed to hold her. He locked his gaze into hers. "I'm here for you."

Brandy moved her eyes away from his. He was making her nervous. Without further conversation, he left.

* * *

Brandy had chosen black and white as the decor for her new apartment. Her mother said that those colors were masculine, but it was all Brandy could afford for the time being. She decided to dress up the black and white with mauve accents. Her sofa was black with pink pillows. Her prize possession was a beechwood dinette set that doubled as both a kitchen and dining room table. Her kitchen was small but it was equipped with a dishwasher. The living room faced the east and this allowed sunlight to creep in over the balcony. Spiral stairs led to the loft where her bookcase and desk were located.

Two weeks after moving in Brandy called James and invited him to her new place for dinner. She nervously fingered James' business card as she waited for him to answer the phone. She expected his machine to pick up, but to her surprise he answered.

"Hello?" He sounded like he was in a hurry.

Brandy took a deep breath. "Hi, James, it's Brandy."

"Hi, darlin', how are you doing?" He was on his way out to play tennis with his best friend, Robert, but her voice stopped him.

"You sound like you're on your way out the door." She was relieved because she didn't want to worry about making conversation.

"Actually, I was, but that's okay." James checked his watch. He was going to be late. "What's up, Brandy?"

She felt the tension easing up. "Nothing much, I just wanted to formally thank you for helping me move last month. I thought that I would cook dinner for you."

"That sounds like a plan." He set his racket down. "When and where?" James was intrigued.

Feeling comfortable, she responded, "My apartment,

next Saturday at seven-thirty." Brandy liked the way "my apartment" rolled off her tongue.

He paused for a moment to mentally check his calendar. "Next Saturday will be perfect."

"Do you have any requests or favorite dishes?"

"Brandy, whatever you cook will be my favorite." James grabbed his racket. "I eat anything and everything."

Brandy was happy to hear that he was not a picky eater. "In that case, I'll make my specialty, spaghetti à la Brandy."

James half chuckled. "That sounds interesting. Do you need me to bring anything?"

"No, just yourself." Brandy surprised herself by her sweetness. She gave him her address and directions to her apartment.

"How 'bout I bring the wine?" James was determined to bring something. After all, he was a gentleman.

"Sounds good." Brandy crossed the date off in her book. "It's a date. I'll see you next week."

"Take care, Brandy."

Before Brandy knew it Saturday had arrived. James was excited and happy that Brandy had not forgotten about him. He stopped at the store and bought a bottle of Cabernet Sauvignon. He knew that she was cooking spaghetti and thought that red wine would be the perfect complement.

Brandy did not normally cook, so it took her hours to prepare the spaghetti. If she was cooking for herself, she would have grabbed the Prego and called it a day. Since James was coming, she decided to experiment by adding bell peppers, fresh garlic, onions, mushrooms, black olives, and strips of rosemary chicken sausage on top. She fixed a spinach salad and baked a loaf of garlic bread in the oven. For dessert, she bought a Sara Lee strawberry cheesecake from the grocery store. Brandy took out her best plates, which was an old set of china given to her by her mother. She set the table and waited for him to arrive.

The aroma of garlic greeted James as he exited the stairway onto the second floor of Brandy's building. He wasn't starving but after smelling the food, he suddenly realized that he was hungry. In one hand he held a bottle of red wine, and in the other he held three large sunflowers.

Prior to James' arrival, Brandy had agonized over what to wear. She finally settled on a casual outfit. After all, this wasn't a date. It was a thank you dinner, and she didn't want James to get the wrong impression.

When Brandy opened the door, James' eyes swept over her. He smiled approvingly and entered the apartment. "Umm, it smells good in here."

"Thanks." She reached for his coat. "Did you have trouble following my directions?"

He winked at her. "No, they were perfect." She was trying to hide her figure under a loose cotton, button-down shirt with matching baggy pants. The pale teal shade of her outfit accentuated her skin tone. Her freshly styled hair lay softly on her shoulders. The lamp by the door made it easy for him to see the outline of her body. Once again, he smiled approvingly and handed her the flowers.

"Thank you." Brandy was impressed. James certainly knew how to treat a lady. He set the wine on the table.

Once James was settled in she gave him a tour of the apartment. When they left the loft, she took him to her bedroom. "This is my second favorite room to be in."

He understood why she liked her bedroom. It was spacious, with a platform bed in the center of the room. It was definitely a woman's room, with a flowery comforter and matching pillows. It smelled of perfume. He thought the scent was Red Door by Elizabeth Arden. "May I ask where your favorite room is?"

"My office, of course," she said matter-of-factly.

"Spoken like a true workaholic." James respected her ambition.

Leaving the bedroom, they returned to the living room. "Would you like something to drink?"

James shook his head. "No, I'll have my drink with dinner."

"If you're ready, then we can eat." James walked toward Brandy and pulled her chair out for her. After she was seated he joined her. He took her hand and gently squeezed it as he bowed his head and blessed the food.

"You made this all by yourself?" James was teasing.

Brandy feigned annoyance. "I most certainly did." They both laughed. She proceeded to fix his plate.

Dinner conversation centered on Brandy's new job at Lloyd & Lloyd. She was thrilled about her new career and revealed her plans to become a partner in six years. James listened attentively, interjecting from time to time. He was pleased to have finally met a woman who was happy with herself. He admired anyone who not only followed their dreams, but made them a reality.

After dinner, James offered to wash the dishes. Brandy readily agreed because she hated housework. James also hated housework, but he enjoyed being close to her. When the dishes were done, Brandy and James went into the living room and sat on the couch.

"Brandy, where are your photo albums?" He looked around the room.

She pointed to the floral photo albums on the bottom shelf of her entertainment center. "They're right over there, just beneath the VCR."

"I'll get them." James stretched the length of the floor and retrieved them. "Ah-hah, I bet these books

contain the secrets to your past." He smiled mischievously.

"I bet I don't have as many secrets as you do." She
took one final swig of wine.

James gave her a "we'll see" look and opened the
first book. After learning the family tree, James was
hungry again. Brandy cut him a slice of strawberry
cheesecake and poured him a cup of coffee.

"My boys had a boxing tournament the day you
moved."

"Boys? I didn't know you had children." She didn't
remember Tricia mentioning any children.

He laughed at the shocked look on her face. "I teach
boxing at the YMCA."

"That's interesting." Brandy was impressed to learn
that he thought it was important to share his time with
young men. "How did the tournament go? Did your
team win?"

He puffed his chest out with pride. "My boys pulver-
ized the other team."

She liked his bravado. He was easy to talk to, and
before they knew it another hour had passed. Not wanting to overstay his welcome, James thanked Brandy for
the lovely dinner.

She walked him to the door, where he hugged her
lightly before departing. She closed the door and lingered for a moment.

"James. What a nice name." Brandy didn't know
when she would see him again, but hoped it would be
soon.

Another year of casual dating passed without Brandy
thinking of a serious relationship with James. Tricia and
Simone had been telling her for months that he was interested in her, but between the bar and trying to impress

her new colleagues at Lloyd & Lloyd, she really didn't have the time to pursue it.

Brandy had no intentions of making the time until the night she locked her purse and keys in her car. To make matters worse, she had backed over a bottle earlier that evening and a tire was flat. Locked out of her car, Brandy had no choice but to walk two blocks in the unseasonably cold night to the service station to use the pay phone.

When she got to the gas station, she tapped on the window. The attendant nearly jumped out of his seat.

"Excuse me, can you help me?" The attendant ignored her. *"Hello,* can you hear me?"

"You go away. No begging. Go!"

"Begging? I'm not begging for money, I need help."

"You get away! I call police! No money! *No money!"*

Puzzled and angry, Brandy caught a glimpse of her reflection in the grimy window. She was wearing gray biker shorts, a sweaty T-shirt, and dirty tennis shoes; she'd been on her way home from the gym, when she decided to stop at Legal Aid on Manchester and Broadway. She didn't have a jacket and her hair was windblown. She couldn't blame the man for being suspicious. For all he knew, her accomplice was waiting around the corner to rob him.

"I need a phone. Where is the phone?"

The attendant pointed to two phone booths on the corner. It was eight o'clock and people had already started to emerge from the shadows. Brandy acted as legal counsel to the poor and working class people in this part of South Central Los Angeles. It was a forgotten section of town with few conveniences like drug stores, movie theatres or even a grocery store with reasonable prices. The residents were primarily African-American and Latino, good people who did the best they could with what they had. Because the court system was designed for those who had enough money to beat the system, many people, especially the youth, wound up in jail before they realized what hit them.

Brandy was working on behalf of a young woman named LaDonna Washington. LaDonna was twenty years old facing three years in jail for writing a bad check. She was attempting to purchase diapers and milk for her three young children. The district attorney's office insisted that she had committed a violent felony and should be put away. While Brandy did not condone LaDonna's actions, she recognized LaDonna's determination to feed her children. Brandy had gone to Legal Aid that day to see how her job interview went. She figured that if LaDonna found a job, the judge would see that LaDonna was a productive citizen who had made a mistake trying to take care of her kids. LaDonna's trial date was coming up and Brandy needed to make sure that everything was on target.

LaDonna was by no means an exception among the residents of South Central. She was one of many who worked hard, despite the lack of opportunities available to her. There were some, however, who internalized this rejection by the city and victimized others. These young men and women had given up hope. They wore their rejection like a badge of honor. This enraged and scared Brandy at the same time. She hated being afraid of her own people, but so many of them just didn't care if they lived or died. She cared, however, and had to get out of there.

To her irritation, the first telephone was broken. The second booth had a working phone, but the stench of urine made her nauseous.

Brandy called Simone, but there wasn't an answer. She even called her brother, Byron, but of course he wasn't home. Byron was a junior at San Diego State University. He was majoring in math and "Macking 101." Though he normally only came home on the weekends, every now and then he came home during the week. She called him anyway, knowing that he probably wouldn't be there.

"Excuse me, can I get some change?"

Brandy jumped. She hadn't heard the homeless man come up behind her.

"No, I'm sorry, I don't have any." Brandy thought about her purse locked in the trunk of her car.

"Okay, sistah, bless you anyway."

In a flash Brandy called James. The phone rang three times before he answered.

"Hello?"

"Oh James, I'm so happy you're home! It's Brandy. Are you busy?" Brandy began to eye the passers-by with concern.

James, who was standing in his kitchen, looked into the connected living room and winked at his dinner guest. The huge room had a vaulted ceiling, hardwood floors and an L-shaped black leather sofa. There were two matching armchairs, and a glass table in the center that faced a fireplace. Sliding glass doors opened out to a sun deck.

"Uh, what's up?" James began to open a bottle of white Zinfandel.

"James, I can't hear you. I'm at a pay phone."

He set the bottle on the kitchen counter. He spoke loudly into the handset. "What are you doing at a pay phone?"

"I've got a flat tire and I locked my keys and purse in the car."

"Where are you?"

"What?" The intersection was jam-packed with cars and people. The street was especially crowded that night. Children were running up and down the street, adults yelling after them, but no one seemed to be listening to one another. A car drove by Brandy and

stopped. Three young men were sitting in the car passing marijuana between them and drinking. The music was on full blast and the "boom-boom" from the radio was making the phone booth shake.

"Where are you?" He was trying not to yell, but he couldn't hear her.

His date was starting to get impatient.

The air was cooling rapidly and Brandy was starting to shiver. "I'm on the corner of Manchester and Broadway."

"What are you doing over there by yourself?" James was concerned.

"Wait, a plane is going over my head." Brandy put her hand over her ear. "Okay, what did you say?"

"I'll ask you when I see you."

"What?"

James didn't hesitate. "I'll tell Triple A to meet me there. I'm on my way."

"Thanks! I owe you one!" Brandy hung up.

James went over to the CD player and turned off the music. "Lisa, I've got to run out for a minute."

"Who was that?" She was clearly irritated. This was her third date with James, and things seemed to be going pretty well between them.

"I'm sorry, but a friend of mine is in trouble."

"Are you really going to leave me to go to rescue some other woman?" She folded her arms across her chest and pouted.

James knew that it looked bad, but he couldn't leave Brandy all alone. "If you were in trouble, I'd do the exact same thing for you. I'll be right back. You can watch TV if you want. I promise I won't be too long." James kissed Lisa on the cheek and ran out the door.

Lisa was pissed off. How dare he leave her! They

hadn't even eaten yet! She waited one hour and then went home. James would definitely hear about it in the morning.

On the drive over to meet Brandy, James couldn't help but feel excited. This was the first time in a couple of months that they had spoken to one another. Brandy was very dedicated to her work, and prided herself on helping others in need but he worried about her going to such a bad neighborhood by herself. He was flattered that she called him to help her. By the time James reached Brandy, Triple A had already arrived.

While Brandy was waiting for James and Triple A, she walked back to her car and sat down on the trunk. She tried to think about the unfinished cases she had to work on when she got home but found herself thinking about James. She wondered for the first time in months what he had been doing.

"That was fast," Brandy said when James pulled up, giving him a quick hug.

Seeing Brandy made James' heart leap. Though it had been months since they last went out, it felt like it was just yesterday. "I couldn't leave you out here by yourself, now could I?" He gently touched her chin.

"I hope I didn't pull you away from something." James was more attractive than she remembered. He was clean shaven and he smelled good.

James thought about Lisa, but he shook his head. "No, I wasn't busy." He was lying, but it was worth it. He reasoned that the Lisas of the world were a dime a dozen. Brandy, on the other hand, was a precious flower that only fully bloomed once in a lifetime.

After rescuing her from Manchester and Broadway, James had followed Brandy back to her apartment. They were standing by her car, now safely parked.

"James, thank you, but you didn't have to follow me home." Brandy reached into her purse and grabbed

twenty dollars out of her wallet. She hugged James and
tried to press the money into his hand.

"Brandy, you don't have to pay me." He put the
money back in her hand. "What kind of man do you
think I am?"

"I'm sorry, I wasn't trying to insult you. This is just
a little something for your trouble."

"Oh please, you didn't cause me any trouble." James
took her gym bag and escorted her up the stairs to her
apartment. When they got to the door, Brandy invited
James in.

"I'm sorry my place is a mess, but I haven't been
here for a couple of days."

Brandy was adjusting the pillows on the couch.

"So, I guess your boyfriend keeps you pretty busy."

Brandy stopped what she was doing. "Excuse me?"
She was on the defensive.

"I mean, I just assumed that you were with your
man."

Brandy shook her head. All men were the same. "You
can sit down now." Brandy motioned toward the couch.

James felt foolish. "I'm sorry. It's none of my business
to know where you've been." He knew he was out of
line, but he wanted to know who had been loving her.

"If you really want to know, James, just ask." Her
tone remained defensive.

"Never mind." James stood up. "I just wanted to
make sure you got home safely. I'm going to go home
now." He was embarrassed for being so obvious.

Her tone softened. Brandy had not seen James in a
couple of months and wanted to spend time with him.
"You can't leave now, I haven't even offered you something to drink or eat." She moved right in front of him,
so that he would have to go around her to get to the
door.

He avoided her stare and mumbled, "That's not necessary." That was Brandy's cue to go into the kitchen, which connected to the living room. She went over to the refrigerator and opened it. Since she lived alone, she didn't do much cooking. "Well, I have some left-over yams and baked chicken from Aunt Kizzy's Back Porch, two eggs, three pieces of bread and some lunch meat."

James followed her into the kitchen. He looked down into her eyes and something inside of him stirred. "Please don't get mad, but that doesn't sound too ap-petizing." James looked around the small kitchen. "You've got all this gourmet cookware and no food in your refrigerator." He laughed a deep, smooth laugh. Brandy liked the way his eyes closed when he laughed.

"We could go out and grab something."

"That sounds good." James got excited just thinking about gazing into Brandy's eyes over candlelight.

"I hope you're not too starved because I need to take a quick shower." Brandy remembered her attire. "Make yourself at home, I'll be right back."

James stepped back and let Brandy pass. He took his jacket off and placed it on the couch. He thought about Brandy standing before him in her biker shorts. She had nice thighs and smooth legs. James thought she looked her best when she was dressed casually. That thought made him laugh because if Brandy was any other woman, he wouldn't be caught dead with her dressed in sweats. Tonight, Brandy's wind-blown hair had sparked a fire deep inside of him. He knew she was changing clothes for his benefit, and he almost wished she wouldn't. Funny, women never really knew how beautiful they truly were.

He picked up the giant African art book on the coffee table and flipped through it. "African people are so beautiful," he mused to himself. Then he looked through her compact discs. Frankie Beverly & Maze,

Teena Marie, Luther Vandross, Janet Jackson and at least one hundred other titles stared back at him. James hit the button on the amplifier and CD player. In seconds, her living room was flooded with the sweet sound of "Baby Come To Me," by Regina Bell.

Brandy couldn't believe what she was doing. Ordinarily, she would have let James leave after his comment about her being at her boyfriend's house. What boyfriend? She hadn't been at home because she was working a marathon week with fourteen- and fifteen-hour days. She would come home to sleep and then head back to the office. Funny, he hadn't asked her where she had been when he had the chance. Oh well, she'd let him think that she was carrying on a torrid love affair with Mr. Right, whoever that was.

After a quick shower, Brandy put on jeans and a cream-colored cable knit sweater. She brushed her hair and left it down.

"Hey, that sounds nice," Brandy said as she entered the living room.

James was startled. He hadn't heard her come up behind him.

"Oh, I hope you don't mind. I was starting to get a little lonely out here."

"I hope I didn't take too long."

"No, no, I was enjoying myself." James looked her over. "You look very pretty."

"Thanks. Are you ready?"

"Where are we going?" James turned the music off.

"It's a surprise."

Brandy took James to a little taco resturant in Inglewood. "They have the best shrimp tacos in the world."

"Shrimp tacos?" James swallowed hard. "I never had those before."

"You'll love them." They sat at a table in the small restaurant.

"Sus ordeneres?" asked the man behind the counter.

"Dos tacos de camarones, cilantro solo. James, do you want the works?"

"Yes."

"Para el, un taco de camarones y carne asada con todo."

"Bebidas?"

"Si. Pepsi y— James, what do you want to drink?"

"I'll have what you're having."

"Dos Pepsi's."

"Gracias." He left silently.

"I didn't know you were bilingual." James was pleasantly surprised.

"I majored in English as an undergrad and had to take a language."

"But you've been out of college five years. I thought that if you didn't speak it, you would lose the fluency."

"That's true, but I speak it whenever I can."

James smiled. "That would explain those Luis Miguel CDs in your collection."

Over tacos they talked about everything from economics to basketball to Shahrazad Ali's controversial book, *The Blackman's Guide to Understanding the Blackwoman.* James called Shahrazad an embarrassment to the African-American community. He also said that she was doing women a disservice by promoting such archaic views as men hitting women to keep them in their place. Brandy was pleasantly surprised to learn that James was a progressive African-American man who believed that a woman's place was wherever she chose to be. That was one of the things she liked most about James, his ability to share new aspects of his personality every time he was with her.

It was midnight when Brandy dropped James off at his car. He walked her to her door for the second time that night. On tiptoes, she kissed him lightly on his cheek. He hoped that she would ask him in. Not for sex, but just so he could be close to her. No such luck. Brandy closed the door and he just stood there.

James walked slowly to his car in an effort to savor the moment. "Brandy. Hmm. She is definitely a possibility." When he got into his car, he received a reality jolt when he saw Lisa's jacket on the passenger seat.

He knew she was pissed, so he didn't bother to hurry home. With any luck, she would be gone when he got there.

Brandy shook her head and cleared her mind of the reverie. She stretched her bare hands out on the floral comforter before her. Looking down at them, she sighed and said, "James thought he was the one. I did, too."

Feeling somewhat resolved, Brandy jumped out of bed. She knew that there was nothing she could do about James or William so she decided to go to the gym to take her mind off both of them.

The next day Brandy arrived to the office at nine a.m. sharp. She was dressed in navy blue slacks, a pale pink silk blouse, navy blue suede loafers with a gold chain across the bridge, and her hair was pulled into a bun. Though it was not office policy to dress up on the weekend, she knew that she could never go work in sweats, no matter how much they cost.

"*Buon giorno*, bella." David Gratani, who could have been a *GQ* centerfold, stood in the doorway of her office. He was an attractive man with jet black wavy hair, gray eyes and olive skin. David was in his mid-thirties, single and had worked at the firm for the last seven years. He was the quintessence of elegance and kissed Brandy on both of her cheeks whenever he saw her.

"Bastante." David reached for Brandy's briefcase and opened the door for her. "Thanks, David."

"No problem." After he set her briefcase down, he sat down. "I wanted to tell you the other day that I agreed with you about not running in the marathon this year."

"I see that you've read the office gossip pages." Brandy grimaced.

"No, but you know how quickly good news travels." David crossed his legs and shifted his weight in his seat. "Bella, I'm not one for gossip, but something did cross my desk that I think you should be aware of." He dropped his voice. "Without naming names, Brandy, you're being watched. There are people in this office who don't want you to make partner."

"David, I'm two years from even being considered for partner."

"True. But Brandy, the partners may not start evaluating you even in your sixth year. But they're the least of your worries, for now anyway."

"Okay. Could you stop speaking in code and get to the point?" She was already frustrated and this tidbit of news was pushing her closer to the edge.

"The point is, there has never been an African-American partner in the firm's seventy-two years. The partners hope that you will be the first. There are some associates, however, who feel differently."

"I see." Brandy turned this thought over in her mind.

"Do you?" David had uncrossed his legs and was leaning forward. He was staring hard at Brandy.

"Yes. Thanks for—"

"I'm only telling you because I care about you." David stood up and ran a manicured hand through his thick black hair. Brandy rose from her seat and leaned, cheek first, across her desk. David kissed her cheeks and embraced her. *"Perché non usciamo per pranzo insieme qualche giorno. Ciao,* bella."

Brandy smiled despite the bad news he gave. "I don't speak Italian, David. What did you say?"

He stepped away from her. "It means that I want to have lunch with you."

"Oh, I'd like that."

David shut the door behind him. Brandy sat down and thought long and hard about what he had said. She took her hand mirror out of her desk drawer. Although still youthful looking, the last four years were beginning to show on her face. Tiny lines around her eyes and mouth were beginning to show. Though her hair was pulled back, she knew that beneath the Let's Jam lurked gray strands. "I'm too young for this!" she moaned into the mirror. Brandy put the mirror away. She was professionally drained and not sure that she was up for the fight that lay ahead of her.

Four

Brandy was the love of his life. It was as if God had made her just for him. James had never been so happy before. Yet, before meeting her, if anyone had even suggested that he would fall in love and want to marry Brandy, or any other woman, he would have laughed until he cried. James was a stockbroker. He enjoyed working with numbers and watching money grow. In his profession, he didn't run into too many women. He made up for this dearth by being active in his fraternity and attending various functions around the city. There had been many women in his life, but none who had been able to keep his attention. Brandy was different. She was special. Brandy was educated, articulate, professional, she had her own money and was beautiful. In short, Brandy could bring something to the table. That was a standard prerequisite for any woman who entered his life.

Whenever James thought of Brandy, he smiled. He tried to be a nineties man— sensitive, caring, giving and in favor of women having careers. But he knew that beneath his pro-feminist stance, he had a large ego that needed to be stroked.

Brandy, however, made his ego take a back seat. She didn't do it with words or attitude, she did it with her sweetness. He loved her disposition and positive outlook on life. Where he was pragmatic, she was idealistic.

Where he had scrooge-like tendencies, she was generous with her time and her affection. She made him weak. He had to get her back.

He turned his swivel chair so he faced the window in his office. He couldn't concentrate. He loved Brandy and missed her. He needed her. He stared sightlessly out the window as he remembered one of the last parties they attended.

Every year James' fraternity hosted a fund-raiser to increase awareness about the need for African-American bone marrow donors. It was a formal affair held in the Crystal Room at the stately Biltmore Hotel in downtown Los Angeles. James was chair of the event in 1994. Brandy had looked devastatingly beautiful in a black satin tuxedo dress, while James wore a white dinner jacket and black pants. He was busy working the room when Robert and Keith spotted him.

"James, what a great turnout," Keith said.

"Thanks, we completely sold out the tickets." This annual event was a source of pride for James.

"We've been looking all over for you," Robert said. He and Keith were also members of his fraternity, and chairs of other committees.

"I've been networking and I have one more side of the room to go." James fingered the business cards in his tuxedo jacket pocket.

Robert said, "I'm having a shin-dig in my room when this is over. You and Brandy should come up afterwards."

"We should come where?" Brandy was at James' side. She too had been networking, while trying to keep an eye out for James.

James put his arm around her and kissed her left temple. "Honey, Robert's having a party in his room later, and just invited us to come."

"Hi guys." Brandy shook hands with Robert and then

Keith. She cocked her head to the side and smiled seductively at James. "Sweetheart, I thought maybe we'd have our own private party for two in your room." She winked at him.

He tried to remain neutral because Robert and Keith were watching him, but there was no way he could turn Brandy down. "Robert, thanks for the invite, but I think Brandy and I are going to turn in early." He pretended to yawn. "You understand, don't you?"

"Yeah man, I understand. I'll get back to you later." Robert was visibly not pleased, but James didn't care. He knew that he was in love with Brandy because he involuntarily turned into silly putty whenever she was around. He felt this now, in front of his boys. He eventually stopped hanging with them, and if he went to a club, he rarely danced. He started comparing other women to Brandy, and when he discovered that there was no one like her, he revised his standards. He was so sprung at one point that if Brandy looked like she wanted something, he bought it for her. He knew then that Brandy was the one. He knew now that she was the one he wanted to take care of, forever.

Five

Though he had attended integrated schools, William was a firm believer that an African-American alternative school would be the answer to improving the education of African-American children. He made this belief the focus of his dissertation. He chose cities that had a high density of African-American students attending school in the inner city. In researching this topic, William traveled to New York and Washington, D.C. to study current alternative school programs. William then traveled to Oakland so that he could compare the West Coast models and teaching style to those on the East Coast.

In Oakland, his last stop before returning to Los Angeles, William visited one school and observed two different teachers teaching the same subject with one predominately white class and the other class completely filled with African-Americans. In the first class, a white male teacher in his early forties had a lively discussion going on over gays in the military. The "Don't Ask/Don't Tell" bill had recently passed both houses of Congress. The bill restricted the military from asking a prospective soldier his/her sexual orientation and, in turn, that prospective soldier could not tell what his/her sexual preference was. The debate the students were having was pretty sophisticated considering the kids were in the sixth grade. When William asked this teacher why there were no students of color

in his class, the teacher explained that there was one
student, but that he was absent that day. He further
added that he was glad the student was absent because
he would have slowed the discussion down. At that comment, the veins in William's neck tightened. Noticing
this, the teacher said that he did not mean to offend
him, it was just that black students were only interested
in rap music and baggy clothes. William figured that
the teacher saw what he wanted to see, because before
class started the teacher confiscated three Walkmans
and two boom boxes from ten white students who were
also wearing baggy clothes.

William concluded that African-Americans would
have to take education into their own hands.

"It's been three weeks and William hasn't called. I
don't think he's interested in me." Brandy said these
words out loud to herself.

*I can do this, I can do this. It's the '90s and women ask
men out all the time. I can do this.*

Brandy picked up the phone and dialed William's
number. Then she hung up. Simone had given Brandy
William's telephone number the week before. "You're
being stupid," she told herself. Brandy picked up the
phone a second time and called her sister Simone.

"Hello?"

"Simone, it's Brandy."

"What's up? Have you and Billy Dee Williams gone
out yet?"

"His name is William and no, we haven't."

"No? Why not?"

"Well, we just met and he hasn't asked me."

"Why can't *you* ask him out, or is that against one of
your many principles?"

"Asking a man out used to be on the list, but not anymore."

"Brandy, you're lying. You have never asked a man out!"

"I have."

"Name somebody, and don't say Oscar Mitchell or Troy Walker 'cause they don't count."

"They do too count. I wasn't going to name them anyway. It's someone you don't know, so it doesn't matter."

Laughing, Simone said, "I knew it."

"For your information, miss woman of the world, I called him," Brandy finally confessed.

"What happened? I want all the details."

"There are no details, because I hung up after I dialed the number."

Simone started laughing again, this time uncontrollably. Her sister/girlfriend could be so shy, it amazed Simone that she had become a lawyer. Brandy had always been very sensitive. But if she was pushed, she retaliated viciously. For the most part, Brandy was an even-tempered, passive-aggressive individual. She was wise beyond her years and that probably explained why not too much fazed her. This was perhaps her best attribute; it allowed her to be very focused. Simone wished she had inner direction like that. Unlike Brandy, who had pursued her career, she had finished college and married her college sweetheart all in the same month. Their parents weren't particularly pleased, but they got over it. Phil was good to her, but she wondered if she had jumped too quickly.

Although Brandy had gone straight through school, lately she had started showing signs of discontentment. Simone figured that Brandy had finally realized that she needed a man. James was the only man so far who had managed to get past Brandy's self-erected ivory tower. Simone could only imagine what he went through to prove how much he loved Brandy. Unfortunately, that didn't work out. James suffered from a classic case of cold feet, but in the end it was clear that James loved Brandy and Brandy still loved him, though she would never admit it. Brandy didn't return his calls. And even when she changed her phone number, he managed to get a hold of it.

Simone told Brandy that if she continued to be evil to every man who even looked in her direction, she would end up old and alone. Brandy's comment was typical: "I'd rather be alone for the right reasons, than to be with a man for the sake of having one." Brandy's ultimate defense was that she worked and didn't have time for a man. That logic was faulty. It was possible for Brandy to have a career and love in her life; she just needed to decide what she wanted. Simone predicted that as soon as work and that whole bourgeois lifestyle got old, Brandy would see the error of her logic. That time had come.

"Simone, stop laughing at me. I feel stupid enough as it is."

"Brandy, you should feel stupid. A grown woman hanging up on a man. He's going to know it was you when you call back."

"No, he won't, 'cause I ain't calling him back," Brandy declared.

"Do you talk like that at work?" Simone asked laughing.

"When I'm at work, I put on my professional voice. I pronounce all of my vowels and consonants. When I'm at home or in the street, I speak in code." Brandy was serious. "You know black people live behind a veil."

"Yes, Brandy, I know. Anyway, I wish you'd stop being so silly. If William could be the centerfold for *Ebony*

Man and still be down to earth, he'll accept your invitation."

"You don't think I'm being too forward?" Brandy knew Simone made sense, but had started to panic anyway.

"No, asking a man out is not being forward. You know, for someone who likes to blaze trails, you seem to be right at home playing helpless."

"I am not playing helpless. This just isn't my department." This made the second time that Simone was right. In a minute, she was going to hang up on her and ask someone else for advice.

"Brandy, where are you planning to take him?"

"I've got season tickets for the Lakers and they're playing the Bulls."

"Basketball?" Simone moaned. She forgot that Brandy was a consummate basketball fan.

Brandy could hear Simone yell to Phil that she was taking William to the game. "Do you have to tell him everything?" Brandy asked. "Well, what did he say?"

"He wants to know if you have a third ticket so he can go."

"He can go," Brandy offered.

"No, he can't." Simone's voice was firm.

"Anyway, Simone, what's wrong with basketball?" Brandy thought it was a good idea. She had seats in the third row behind the press.

"Brandy, you can't look cute at a basketball game."

"Simone, you know me better than that. My days for getting dressed up for a man I hardly know are over. At this point in life, I doubt if I'd get dressed up for a man I know well."

"You and basketball." Simone was through. Brandy was crazy.

"Simone, I need some help. What if he's married or has a girlfriend?"

"What if nothing, Brandy Janae Curtis. Call tha man, ask him out, then call me back and tell me wha he says."

"But Simone . . ."

"I'm hanging up now. 'Bye."

Click. The dial tone could be heard all over her room She couldn't believe Simone had hung up on her. Brandy was excited, even though she would have rathei gone to the basketball game with James. In fact, she hadn't felt this giddy since she had asked James to have Thanksgiving dinner with her and her family two years earlier.

James' family was having Thanksgiving at his great aunt's house in Las Vegas that year. He opted not to go because he had to work the day after Thanksgiving, so he accepted Brandy's invitation instead.

"Brandy, who have you been sneaking around with for the last two months?" Simone was giving Brandy her famous I know-you're-up-to-something-*Ms. Thang*-look.

"Sneaking around? I haven't been sneaking around, what are you talking about?" She was playing dumb.

"Yes, you have! I call you, you aren't home. I call your office and they tell me that you're either out of the office or in a meeting. C'mon, out with it, what's his name?"

A big smile spread across Brandy's face. "Ooh. His name is James."

"James?" Simone's eyes lit up. "You dated him a couple of times before, right? The man who looks like Mario Van Peebles?"

"Yes, James, that's him." Brandy couldn't believe that one year later they would be together.

"In that case you are excused. I'd sneak around with

him, too." Simone shook her head in pleasant reverie about the man who was so fine that she almost missed her mouth when she took a sip of water. "How long have you two been dating?"

"Oh, about a month. I'm sorry I'm just now telling you, but girl, I've been working my butt off. Last month I billed one hundred and seventy-five hours. Girl, I had to cut back. I wasn't getting any sleep. Do you know I even went two weeks without getting my nails or my hair done!"

"Hmm, you have been busy, 'cause we both know that you get your hair and nails done re-*ligiously* once a week." Simone touched her own hair. "So, how'd you start dating more seriously?"

"I got a flat tire on Manchester and Broadway one night on my way home from the gym. No one was home except James. He came and got me and I've been seeing him ever since. That was also the last time I've been to the gym."

"You don't need to lose any weight." It was always the women in excellent shape who fussed about going to the gym.

Brandy slapped her right thigh. "I know, I just wanted to get toned." She stood and sucked her stomach in.

"That was nice of him to come get you."

"It was. He told me later he had a date. He left her to come get me."

"What?" Simone asked incredulously. "I bet his date was mad."

"I'm sure she was, especially since he didn't leave my house until midnight." Brandy knew that if James had left her to get another woman, she would have been furious. Because he came to rescue her, she was able to excuse his behavior.

"What time did he come get you?"

"Eight."

Simone winced. "He was asking for trouble." She leaned forward with both elbows on the table. They were having a late lunch at her house. "Tell me more about him."

"He's very charming, very sweet, a bit on the egotistical side, but very generous— he won't let me pay for anything."

"That's good. The woman isn't supposed to pay for anything."

"Simone, I've got a job and my own money. I don't mind paying. Tricia said that he's used to women doing things for him, but he doesn't act that way around me. This may sound silly, but he makes me feel like a princess when I'm with him. I have his undivided attention and he hangs onto my every word. James really listens to me and he even argues with me without getting intimidated!"

"Now, I know you love that! Any man who can stand up to you will win your heart." Simone was getting excited. Brandy had finally found a man who was on equal footing with her.

"You got that right, I love a man with a backbone. Did I mention that he's a great kisser? He's got the softest lips in the world." Brandy's eyes turned soft at the thought of him holding her.

Simone waved her hands in front of Brandy's face, "Hel-*lo?* Earth to Brandy."

"I'm here." Brandy blushed.

"So counselor, is he Mr. Right?"

Her voice took on a serious note. "I don't know about all that. I've got to stay focused on my career. I want to make partner before I even think about getting married."

"By that time, you'll be thirty." Simone looked horrified.

"So? Thirty's not old."

Simone rolled her eyes. "Career sma-reer. What about love, Brandy? Can't you just pencil it into that expensive organizer of yours?"

Brandy was laughing. "Yes, Mom, I can. I just don't want to."

"I'm through with you." Simone threw her hands in the air.

"James is a very good friend. I don't know what tomorrow will bring, but let's just say that he's Mr. Right Now."

"We'll see." Simone smiled. She didn't say it out loud, but Brandy was on the verge of falling in love whether she wanted to or not.

Brandy dialed William's number again. This time not only did she let it ring, but he answered it.

"Hello?" She heard a rich bass at the other end.

"Hi, this is Brandy and I'm calling for William." She hoped she didn't sound nervous.

"This is William."

"Hi, um, I'm not sure that you remember me, we met at Simone's house during the teachers' strike."

"Oh, yeah, I remember you. Actually, that was almost a month ago. Why are you just now calling me?" Brandy was taken aback by this question.

"Excuse me?"

"I lost your card and I didn't remember your name. I figured you would have called by now." He wondered what took her so long to call.

He was a little too sure of himself, thought Brandy. She didn't quite know how to respond so she just said, "Oh."

"But I'm glad that you called. Since we didn't really

get to talk there, I was hoping we could go out and talk."

Brandy couldn't believe her luck. "I've got two tickets to the Bulls-Lakers game. Do you like basketball?"

"Any team that can give M.J. a run for his money is my team. I'd love to go— when's the game?"

"Next week."

"That'll work, I just hoped to see you before then."

Brandy was speechless. Was he for real? He was not a man to waste time. While his aggressiveness was a welcome change from the games she was accustomed to playing with other men, he was coming on very strong.

"What are you doing on Saturday?" William really wanted to see her.

"What time on Saturday?"

"In the afternoon."

She knew she had meetings on Saturday, but went through the motions anyway. "Hang on a second, William. I need to get my daily planner."

Brandy set the phone down on her nightstand and went into the living room. Her briefcase was in its usual place, to the left of the front door beneath her coat stand. She grabbed it and went back to the phone.

Brandy ran her finger down the page. "Hmm, I've got a meeting until 2 p.m. and another at 2:30. I won't be free until about 6. I'm free on Sunday."

"You're busier than I am! It's obvious that Saturday isn't good for you and Sunday isn't good for me. What about Monday afternoon? Are you free for lunch?"

Brandy flipped the page of the tapestry organizer covered with burgundy leather trim. She was still feeling pressured, but reasoned that there would be no harm in seeing him for lunch. "Monday sounds like a winner."

"Let me have your phone number again and I'll call

to confirm our lunch date Sunday evening." Brandy gave him her number.

"Thanks for calling. It was nice talking to you. I'll call you on Sunday."

"Okay, I look forward to hearing from you. Goodbye."

" 'Bye." They hung up.

Brandy called Simone back. When Simone picked up, Brandy repeated the conversation to her. She wasn't sure about him, but she'd give it a shot.

LaDonna's case went to trial in late July.

The bailiff said, "All rise, this court is now in session with the honorable Octavia Davis presiding . . ."

As the bailiff spoke, Brandy reassured her client that everything was going to be all right. She felt confident that she could get the judge to dismiss the case against LaDonna.

". . . the People of the State of California versus LaDonna Washington. Is the defendant here?"

"Yes, your honor." Brandy and LaDonna rose together. LaDonna looked very businesslike in a black suit, black patent leather pumps and a white blouse. Her braids were neatly pulled back in a bun. Brandy had selected this outfit for her to wear to court. She banked on the belief that if the judge saw a well-dressed, employed woman, she would have a better chance of getting off.

The judge looked over at the defense table. "You may be seated." She shuffled through several pages on the bench. "It says here, LaDonna, that you are accused of writing bad checks. Is that right?"

"Yes, your honor," LaDonna responded softly.

"How do you plead?"

LaDonna looked to Brandy for support. "Not guilty."

"Mr. Scheck, it says here that the people are asking for the maximum sentence. Is that correct?"

"Yes, your honor, we are. We owe it to the taxpayers of this state to punish offenders like Ms. Washington and put a stop to this egregious behavior." Henry Scheck was the deputy district attorney for this case.

LaDonna's body began to shake. "Ms. Curtis, did you hear what he just said about me? I'm not an evil person."

Brandy patted her arm. "Don't worry, LaDonna, he's just trying to intimidate you." She recognized Scheck's tactics as standard practice for the district attorney's office. He knew his case was weak, which was why he was attempting to accumulate as many points as possible with the judge.

"Thank you, Mr. Scheck. Ms. Curtis, what do you have to say about this matter?"

Brandy rose from her seat. She wore a houndstooth black and cream silk suit. She looked and felt extremely confident. The courtroom was like her second home. "Your honor, we are here today to ask for a dismissal of this case. While it is true that my client is accused of writing several bad checks, she did so for a good reason. At the time the checks were written, Ms. Washington was employed and had just paid her rent and car insurance. Ms. Washington thought she had enough money to cover the checks, and in reliance upon this purchased food, diapers and other sundry items for her children. She was laid off from her job the next day. Your honor, my client received a telephone call on April 29, one day after those checks were written. She was laid off with no severance pay, no bonus."

It was Mr. Scheck's turn to respond. "Ms. Washington knew exactly what she was doing. Not balancing her checkbook is no excuse for writing bad checks. The law is the law and I am personally insulted that Ms. Washington wants us to believe that she was ignorant as to the amount of money in her checking account. Ms. Washington is pathological, terminally unemployable and doesn't deserve to be a member of society." His arrogance was so overwhelming that he forgot to make his case for the court.

The judge looked at the prosecution's table. "Is that all the people have to say, Mr. Scheck?"

"Yes, your honor. There is nothing more to be said."

"Rebuttal, Ms. Curtis?" Brandy could see that the judge was not impressed with Mr. Scheck's argument.

"I'd like to make two last points before we conclude, your honor. Number one, everyone in this room is guilty of writing checks the day before they know they will receive a paycheck. In Ms. Washington's case, she wrote these checks the day after. Where is her crime? She simply thought she had enough money in her account. Number two, seeking the maximum punishment is not going to improve society. Nor will it provide Ms. Washington's children with food and other necessities. The court needs to consider Ms. Washington's record. She is currently employed as an administrative assistant at Benjamin Banneker Elementary School. She has held this position since May 15. Ms. Washington is the sole provider for her children and not a menace to society, as Mr. Scheck has attempted to paint her." Brandy paused. "It is in the court's best interest to dismiss the charges without impunity against my client, LaDonna Washington. Thank you, your honor."

"Ms. Curtis, I agree with you. Ms. Washington does not appear to be a menace to society. Though we are all guilty of over-calculating the amount of funds we have in our checking accounts, it is important that we not make this a habit. This case is hereby dismissed." Judge Davis banged her gavel on the bench.

As the bailiff called for the next case, LaDonna

hugged Brandy. "Oh, Ms. Curtis, thank you so much! You are the greatest!"

"LaDonna, you don't deserve to go to jail." This win was far more precious to Brandy than all of the cases she won for Lloyd & Lloyd.

Six

On monday morning, Brandy was a nervous wreck. She was so excited that she hadn't slept much the night before. William had called as promised, and they spoke for about an hour. Brandy found William easy to talk to. He didn't spend the whole time telling Brandy how wonderful and perfect he was. Instead, William told her that he loved jazz, his favorite color was black, and his favorite food was Italian. She, in turn, told him that her favorite time of year was spring because that was when life was at its fullest.

Brandy dressed very carefully for their first date. She wore a salmon-colored pants suit with matching low-heeled, sling-back suede pumps. There were four pearl buttons on either cuff and four larger pearls that decorated the front of her jacket. She chose the suit because it accented her caramel skin tone. Though the cut was conservative, the ensemble suggested a perfect body hidden beneath the silk. Brandy wore tear-drop pearl earrings and also let her hair down. She couldn't comb her hair to save her life and she tried her best to duplicate what her beautician had done on Saturday morning. Since Brandy was not scheduled to meet with any clients that day, her bright colored suit would not offend the office dress code.

"Brandy, girl, you look good! You have a date today

with William, don't you?" Shirley smiled and handed Brandy her messages.

"I forgot that nothing gets by you. Yes, I have a lunch date with him. He'll be here about one o'clock."

"One? Brandy, my relief is here at one. Now, I'm not going to get to meet him." Shirley looked hurt.

"Shirley, you'll meet him when we come back from lunch." Brandy laughed. She didn't know who was more excited, herself or Shirley.

One hour later, Lloyd rapped softly on Brandy's office door. "Brandy, it's Lloyd."

Brandy answered cheerfully. "Come in." Lloyd entered and sat in the chair Brandy pointed to. After he had made himself comfortable, he handed her a letter.

"I'm assigning a new client to you. I'm giving you the letter he mailed to me." The letter was short and to the point. J.D. Hamilton needed an attorney to represent him against Hamilton Insurance Company, Inc. He was a multi-millionaire, so money was not a problem. Hamilton wrote that he had heard excellent things about Lloyd & Lloyd and that he would rest easy at night knowing that they would represent him in the matter. Brandy folded the letter and set it gently on her desk.

"Brandy, the partners and I have assigned you this case. Mr. Hamilton is a very wealthy man and he is accustomed to people following his every order. I know you'll be diplomatic as well as professional once you meet him."

"Where are his attorneys, and why isn't he using them?" Brandy spoke in a controlled voice. She couldn't help sounding curt, but she was already up to her eyeballs in files and was angry that he'd assigned her another.

"For reasons unknown to us, he wants to use lawyers outside of his staff. However, that's not important."

Richard Lloyd paused. He really admired her spunk. In fact, it was why he'd fought tooth and nail to get her hired. But her attitude over the last two months had been getting progressively worse and some of the partners asked him to talk to her.

"Before I continue, Brandy, I need to ask you a question. I get the feeling that you are, for lack of a better word, unhappy. Are you?" Lloyd appeared genuinely concerned. He didn't expect Brandy to answer him truthfully. He knew discontentment when he saw it. Though she still outperformed most of the attorneys at Lloyd & Lloyd, her enthusiasm was fading more and more each day.

Brandy took a deep breath and said, "I'm not so much unhappy as I am bogged down with work." Truth was, she hated her job. She loved the law, but she hated her working conditions at Lloyd & Lloyd. The back-biting had reached an all-time high. She had heard through the office grapevine that two attorneys had been fired. Apparently they had been caught accepting work from former clients of Lloyd & Lloyd. Firm lawyers were expressly prohibited from doing this, as it detracted from the clients who retained Lloyd & Lloyd. Actually, accepting clients outside of the firm was a direct threat to Lloyd & Lloyd. While Brandy agreed that they were in the wrong, the men had received referrals to the clients by one of the partners. If that wasn't a planned firing, she didn't know what one was. She was afraid that her own neck would soon be on the chopping block, but she didn't know how to stop the tide.

"Brandy, you're one of the best woman lawyers I've ever met. You'll make partner right on time. Most importantly, Brandy, you are our best litigator." Brandy tried to smile. "Mr. Hamilton will be coming to our office today at one p.m. I've checked with your secretary. Your schedule is free."

"Today!" Brandy's voice rose an octave. "Lloyd, I'm not dressed to meet a new client."

"What are you talking about? You look great." Lloyd had caught a glimpse of Brandy in the kitchen earlier making herself a cup of coffee. Her suit was very flattering.

"Look, Lloyd, I wasn't expecting a client . . ."

"Mr. Hamilton is an impulsive and powerful client." Richard Lloyd then excused himself and walked out of her office.

"Lloyd." Brandy knew before the word slipped out of her mouth that she would have to cancel her date with William.

Brandy searched frantically for William's number. When she finally found it, she left him a message. There was no way for her to know if he would get it in time.

One o'clock rolled around and Brandy was still angry. The relief receptionist buzzed her and told her that her one p.m. appointment had arrived. Clearing her mind, she prepared for the routine meeting of a prospective client. Normally, this process was used to interview prospective clients as well as allow them to interview Lloyd & Lloyd. This situation was different. J.D. Hamilton was already a client, he just wanted to meet Brandy.

Brandy's fake smile turned into a real smile when the man on the other side of the door turned out to be not J.D. Hamilton but William.

"Hi! I didn't expect to see you today."

"What are you talking about? We have a lunch date." William smiled and gave her a peck on the cheek.

"Oh, no, you didn't get the message I left you." She couldn't believe her eyes. He was even better looking than she remembered. He wore an olive blazer and khaki pants. His cream-colored shirt was unbuttoned at the neck and a thick herringbone choker glistened underneath, and he had on a new pair of egg-shell bucks.

"Message? No, I didn't check my machine." William looked puzzled. "You look beautiful."

Brandy blushed. "Thank you. I'm really sorry, but at nine this morning I was informed that I have a new case and I have to meet the client today at one. I feel really bad about this. Can I take you to dinner to make up for this?"

"Don't worry about it, even though I *did* drive all the way across town just to meet you. I even got a haircut." William sounded serious. Brandy's face fell. William stepped toward her and caressed her right cheek. "I'm just playing. It's not your fault. I would love to have dinner with you. Call me later this evening." William hugged her and then stepped away.

"I'll call you later," Brandy said and smiled. She was rooted where she stood. William walked to the door, where he smiled and waved. "Good-bye, Brandy, I'll see you later." After he left, Brandy closed her eyes and took a deep breath. She could still smell his cologne.

Minutes later the door flew open and Jackson David Hamilton entered. He was a short, portly man who might have been very attractive in his youth with a head full of thick, curly, silver hair and a silver handlebar mustache. He wore a black coat with a white tie, white shirt, white vest, black pants and white shoes. Brandy couldn't help but smile at the man in the W.C. Fields outfit.

"Hello, missy, I'm looking for a Mr. Curtis," the man said as he blew smoke in Brandy's face. Brandy didn't flinch. She inwardly cursed Lloyd for making her counsel for the potentially troublesome.

"Mr. Curtis isn't here, but I'm Ms. Curtis." Brandy extended her hand.

J.D. Hamilton ignored her hand and walked to the receptionist's desk. "Good afternoon, sweetie, my name is Jackson David Hamilton and my attorney is B. Curtis. Go get him for me." Every word that came out of his mouth was a command. Brandy knew Richard Lloyd was right; he was accustomed to giving orders and Brandy could already sense his disapproval of a female attorney.

The relief receptionist looked embarrassed. "Excuse me, sir, but B. Curtis is standing right next to you."

J.D. turned and stared at Brandy. "This woman?" He looked at her with contempt.

Turning back to the receptionist, he said, "Missy, I don't know what kind of game you are playing, but I am a very wealthy man and a very important man. If you don't get B. Curtis right away, I'll have you fired." His tone was menacing. The relief receptionist looked as though she were about to have a stroke.

Office protocol dictated that no matter how insolent, arrogant or demanding a client was, the attorneys were supposed to remain professional and polite. Fed up with being polite, Brandy took control of the situation. "Excuse me, Mr. Hamilton, I am B. Curtis. The B. stands for Brandy. I was informed this morning by the managing partner, Richard Lloyd, that I would be handling your case. If you will come this way, I'll take you to my office." Brandy did not attempt to shake hands with him again. She went to the door which connected the lobby to the other offices and asked the relief to buzz her in. Once inside, she turned to J.D. Hamilton. "Please follow me."

He didn't move.

"Is there something wrong, Mr. Hamilton?" Brandy asked with an edge to her voice.

"Yes, Ms. Brandy, something is wrong, something is terribly wrong. I did not expect a— person like you to represent me." The menacing tone had not left his voice.

Brandy's eyes turned cold and her hand gripped the doorknob. She felt the color drain from her face. She was furious.

Just as she was about to speak again, Lloyd appeared at her side. Apparently, the relief had called him and told him what happened in the lobby. Lloyd breezed by Brandy and shook hands with J.D. Hamilton.

The sexist spoke. "Richard, I told you I wanted your best attorney to represent me, not the hired help."

Lloyd responded with equal authority, "Brandy is our best litigator, J.D."

"Why didn't you tell me that B. Curtis was a woman? I thought my attorney explained to you that I don't like working with women."

Lloyd gave J.D. his best schmooze smile and conveniently ignored his question. "J.D., follow me into my office and Brandy will bring us a cup of coffee." Lloyd shot Brandy an apologetic look. "Brandy, we won't start until you arrive." Lloyd escorted J.D. into the corridor.

Brandy felt betrayed. Lloyd had acted like nothing was wrong with the picture, and to add insult to injury she was expected to serve them coffee! There had to be a reason J.D. was assigned to be her client. Since she had made a name for herself at the firm, she was no longer assigned arbitrary cases. Lloyd was deliberate and systematic about how he divided cases between her and the other attorneys. Something was wrong. J.D. clearly did not want a female attorney. Even the relief receptionist could see that. How was she going to be able to effectively represent a client who hated her on sight? Were they setting her up to fail?

As Brandy neared Lloyd's office, she could hear J.D. Hamilton yelling at Lloyd. "What kind of operation are you running here? You know, I knew your father very well."

"J.D., listen, I could easily assign you a new attorney, but you weren't exactly in the right when you froze the corporate accounts at your insurance company. That is the reason your brother is suing you, isn't it? If you want to win big and get off with only paying attorney's fees, I suggest you stay with Brandy. But if you want to take a chance on losing the settlement and pay your brother millions of dollars, then I'll reassign you right now."

"This is against my better judgment, and I'll hold you personally responsible if I lose."

Brandy entered the office as J.D. started listing his conditions. Again he glared at Brandy. This time she glared right back. What had started out as a beautiful day was turning into a nightmare. Lloyd reached for a cup of coffee. Brandy handed him his and set J.D.'s cup on top of Lloyd's desk.

"Miss Brandy, I'll have two lumps of sugar," Hamilton said.

"My name is Ms. Curtis and the sugar is in the silver bowl on the credenza," Brandy said firmly. Her look told him that there was no way she was going to put sugar in his coffee.

Lloyd jumped to his feet and brought the sugar bowl to J.D. "Would you care for some cream?"

"No, thank you. I only want to sweeten my cafe latte, not ruin it by making it lighter." Brandy was amazed at Lloyd's ability to maintain a smile no matter what was said.

"Richard, what are her credentials?"

J.D. addressed all of his questions about Brandy to Lloyd. He acted like she wasn't sitting less than three feet from him.

"She attended law school at Georgetown Law Center.

She passed the bar on her first try and she's been with us for four years." Lloyd was beaming. Brandy sighed heavily and shifted in her seat. Before he continued, he shot her a look out of the corner of his eye. "Brandy was born and raised in Los Angeles, has one brother and no husband. J.D., she's different. Brandy is really bright and very easy to work with." Lloyd was trying his best to salvage the situation.

Horrified by what she was hearing, Brandy heard herself say through clenched teeth, "Lloyd, will you please step out into the hallway with me?"

Shocked, Lloyd stared at Brandy before turning to J.D. "We'll just be a minute."

Out in the hallway, Lloyd guided Brandy into the kitchen. "Brandy, what's come over you? You know better than to act that way in front of a client."

"Lloyd—" Brandy tried to interrupt.

"I'm not finished." Lloyd paced in front of her. "J.D. Hamilton is a man with a lot of money. *Money*, Brandy."

"Lloyd, I do not want to represent him and it's clear that he feels the same way. Mr. Hamilton is insulting, rude and sexist."

Softening a little, Lloyd responded. "Brandy, I'll talk to J.D. If you win this case, the partnership will be yours, guaranteed. Also, it will be a means of further establishing your reputation not only in this firm, but around the city. Go back to your office and I'll be there just as soon as I finish with J.D."

Brandy didn't know whether or not to believe him, but she went to her office anyway. While she sat at her desk, she flipped through her messages. One in particular caught her eye. Henry Jarvis, of Jarvis and Hawthorne, had called. He owned his own law firm and had been after her to leave Lloyd & Lloyd ever since she'd successfully litigated the Price case. The Price Corporation owned oil and petroleum which it leased to gasoline stations throughout the country. A patron had spilled gasoline all over him and subsequently burst into flames. He sued the company for negligence and damages, but Brandy successfully defended the Price Corporation. She learned that the patron had been smoking while he pumped his gas and accidentally dropped the gas pump. Gas spewed all over him and ignited on his cigarette. The negligence in the case was the patron's and the Price Corporation got off on the condition they posted larger "No Smoking" signs near the pumps. Brandy was close to accepting Jarvis' offer to work for him, but thought about how close she was to making partner at Lloyd & Lloyd. If she left now, she would have to start her journey to becoming partner all over again.

Thirty minutes later, Lloyd casually strolled into Brandy's office. In his usual polite voice, he informed her that he had straightened everything out. J.D. promised to be cooperative. His attorneys would send Brandy his file tomorrow. She thought she detected a note of finality in his voice.

"If I'm hearing you correctly, I don't have a say in this at all."

"You heard correctly."

"Also, if my ears did not deceive me, I will be representing a sexist, arrogant jerk whether I like it or not." Brandy looked straight into Lloyd's pale blue eyes. She had never seen eyes so cold before in her life.

Lloyd icily responded, "That too is correct. Brandy, we do not pay you to like the clients, we pay you to work. I thought you understood that."

"No, Lloyd, I didn't forget. I am, however, a little confused about why you are so insistent that he be my client."

"He's not your client. J.D. belongs to the firm and so do you. If there's nothing else, I will see you at the partners dinner tonight." Before Lloyd reached the door, he added, "By the way, Ms. Curtis, if you ever object to a client in front of him, the way you did today, I will personally see to it that you never work as a lawyer again."

Brandy matched his tone, "I hope you mean every word of your threat, Lloyd, because if you ever again explain away my femininity, apologizing for my gender as if it makes me less of an attorney, I will call a press conference and sue this firm for sexual discrimination."

"Brandy, I wasn't threatening you. I just want you to understand that many of our clients don't like working with women. I have to sell them on your finer points so as not to lose business." Noticing her visible anger, Lloyd continued, "There has never been an African-American partner at Lloyd & Lloyd. While I'm on your side and want to see you succeed, there are some who don't think that you're partner material." Lloyd was being sincere. "By taking this case, we can prove to them that they misjudged you. Why don't you go home and relax before dinner? You look as though you could stand a minute of calm."

Though Lloyd sounded like he meant what he said, Brandy was still upset. "I won't be at dinner tonight, Lloyd."

The edge to his voice returned. "Everyone will be there and that means you, too."

"Tonight I don't have to be anywhere I don't want to be," Brandy answered.

"If you don't attend, the other associates will feel that they too can dismiss these dinners and not attend." Lloyd's tone had softened. He knew he was about to lose this round.

Brandy found an opening. She was convinced that J.D. Hamilton would be her undoing. "I'm sure that you will be able to explain away my absence as easily as you explained away my existence." Brandy smiled tightly. She grabbed her purse and sauntered past Lloyd. It was 2:30 in the afternoon. She didn't know where she was going, but she knew she had to get the hell out of there.

Seven

By the time the elevator reached the bottom floor, Brandy had her sunglasses on and her car keys in her hand. She was so intent on reaching her car that she ran straight into Mr. Robinson. Without looking up, Brandy coldly said, "Excuse you."

"Excuse me? Excuse you, Brandy Curtis." Mr. Robinson smiled at her. "Where's the fire?"

Brandy froze in her tracks. Turning around, she was embarrassed. "I am so sorry, Mr. Robinson, I didn't see you. I'm so mad I can't see straight. But that's no excuse for being rude. I'm sorry."

Brandy looked like she needed a hug. "That's all right, I know you didn't mean it. Where are you going now?" He was concerned about her driving in this mood and wanted to delay her until she calmed down.

"I was going to get a drink, but I think it's a little early for happy hour. Actually, it doesn't really matter where I go, just as long as I get out of here before I blow the firm up."

"Those folks finally got to you, didn't they?" Mr. Robinson was no longer smiling. He could feel her pain and though he did not know the details of her anger, the indignity was always the same. He hugged her to him tightly.

"Thank you. I needed that hug." Brandy felt better. "I'll see you tomorrow."

"Okay, sweetheart." Mr. Robinson walked her to her car. "You sure look pretty today. I just know my grandson would like that suit. In fact he just left here an hour-and-a-half ago. I haven't forgotten our conversation last month, you know— I still want you to meet him."

He was doing his best to play the role of the casual matchmaker. He knew that she wasn't dating anyone and neither was his grandson. Well, he couldn't be sure about his grandson, but of the women his grandson had brought by to meet him and his wife, he had not been impressed. Brandy, on the other hand, would be perfect. She was smart, beautiful and very sweet. Her only flaw was that she worked too much.

Brandy smiled. "All right, Mr. Robinson, I won't make you any promises, but I will meet him." She knew that Mr. Robinson, like her family, wanted her married off. It would be pointless to tell him no, so she reasoned that if she at least met him, one less person would nag her about finding a man.

"You're not making any promises now, Brandy, but I bet you will as soon as you meet him." Mr. Robinson winked at her. "Take it easy this afternoon and I'll see you tomorrow."

Whatever that was supposed to mean, Brandy thought to herself.

Instead of looking for a bar, Brandy took a drive through her old neighborhood, Windsor Hills. She admired the well-kept lawns and the beautiful homes. It never ceased to amaze her how the media dubbed everything south of the Santa Monica freeway South Central. Never mind that these people worked very hard to buy and keep their homes. Never mind that these so-called ghetto residents shared the same fears of gangs, crime and drugs as their neighbors north of the dividing line.

Since the media and other authorities had tried to destroy any pride these people felt about themselves and their neighborhood, many were moving out into the suburbs. Brandy was wholeheartedly against this because she believed that once African-Americans lost their homes in the city, they would never be able to move back. Her parents told her that there was a sprinkling of white people who had moved into the neighborhood. They theorized that those long commutes from the valley had gotten old and had finally realized that this area was central to everything. The airport was fifteen minutes away, instead of an hour and fifteen minutes. Downtown was only twenty minutes away and the beach was even closer. She could hear her father Booker's voice as he complained about his new neighbors. While he generally liked everybody, he was uncomfortable about what the new residents meant. White folks had a way of driving the property value up, keeping many African-Americans that much further from achieving the American dream. In her father's eyes, the affordable housing and land promised in the suburbs was a ploy to lure black folks into townships. With blacks gone from the city and the price of homes doubling and tripling, they would be unable to leave the suburbs. And once the metro was complete, African-Americans would have limited access into the city and Soweto and Johannesburg would be in full effect.

Brandy thought about stopping by to see her parents, but she knew that if she did, she would have to visit for a while. Suddenly, she thought about how much she missed James. Whenever she would complain about a long day's work, he would come over and rub her feet. Sometimes they wouldn't even talk, but just sit and hold one another. That was one memory she cherished above all others.

Booker T. Curtis didn't think any man was good enough for his precious Brandy. He did, however, want grandchildren. When he met James, he'd instantly disliked him. He thought the younger man was arrogant and simply trying to get Brandy into bed. What he later found out was that James was a hard worker and would be a good provider for his daughter.

"Daddy, please be nice to James."

"You know I will be."

"No, I don't know that, so I'm asking you in advance to be on your best behavior."

He smiled mischievously. Raising his right hand and closing his eyes, he said, "I promise to be nice to the young man who has stolen my daughter's heart."

Brandy and her mother laughed.

"By the way, Brandy, what does he do for a living?"

"He's a stockbroker for Tyler Securities."

"A stockbroker? What kind of job is that? Doesn't he know that the market is bad?"

"I'm sure that he's well aware of that."

The doorbell rang before her father could continue. Brandy went to the door, but her mother beat her to it.

"Hi, I'm Mrs. Lena Curtis, please come in." Her mother shook hands with James.

"Hello, Mrs. Curtis. These are for you." He handed her a potted African violet. "I'm sorry we didn't have a chance to talk the day Brandy moved."

"Oh, that's quite all right. I'm glad we're meeting now. My, what lovely flowers, thank you." She looked at Brandy. "He is so thoughtful." Lena, who was a sucker for flowers, smiled a warm smile at James. It was clear that she was impressed already.

Booker stepped forward. "Booker Curtis, pleased to meet you."

James met the firm handshake with, "James Collins, sir, I hear you're a boxing fan."

"Yes, I am. I was a little boy when Joe Louis knocked out Max Schmelling and I've been sold ever since!"

"That was a little before my time, but I've been following Mike Tyson's career since he first got in the ring. His right hook is deadly."

"That's true, but the boy needs more polish." Booker was a boxing wizard. "Now take Sugar Ray Robinson. That guy— "

"Uh, I hate to break up this discussion, Daddy, but dinner is getting cold." Brandy tried to hide her shock. Her own father was obviously impressed with James, and all it had taken was the word "boxing."

"Brandy, I'm sorry, I didn't see you standing there." James hugged Brandy.

"James, honey, let me take your jacket." Lena took his jacket and hung it up in the closet.

After Booker blessed the food, a lively discussion ensued. Brandy had to admit that she learned a lot about James that night. One, he believed that a woman should only work because she wanted to and not because she had to. His own mother had raised him alone and he hated watching her work two jobs, come home to be mother and father to himself and his three siblings, put them to bed, and then start all over the next day. In addition to helping them with homework, she was a willing listener to all of their moans and groans, no matter how small. As the eldest of four, he tried to be the man of the house, but his mother wouldn't let him. She made him go to college instead of dropping out of high school and getting a job. Because of her, he

went to college on a full academic scholarship. He'd
promised her that when he finished college he would
take care of her, and he'd made good on that promise.
So far he had retired her and bought her a new house.

The second fact he kept to himself. James was commitment shy. Whenever he got close to a woman, he
invariably backed off. He didn't know why he did it,
he just did. James suspected that his parents' divorce
may have had something to do with it. There were two
women in his life that had slipped away from him. The
first, Desirée Matthews, his college sweetheart, was educated, articulate, sweet and his best friend. He was convinced that he was going to marry her after graduation.
Well, graduation came and went, then another year
came and went. By the end of the first year out of
school, James claimed that he was engrossed in his career and told Desirée that he didn't have time for a
relationship. Looking back, he had made a mistake. His
fear of commitment in that instance had cost him his
best friend.

The second woman was Michelle Parker. She was outgoing, artsy and out of control. She was more than he
could handle, but he had forced the issue of commitment in an effort to compensate for losing Desirée.
That relationship ended in a fiasco, forcing James to
realize that love took time. After false starts with a
dozen women since Michelle, he'd found Brandy. He
was determined to not run away or force the issue.

After James finished second helpings of turkey, dress-
ing, cranberry sauce, string beans and two pieces of
sweet potato pie, he and Booker went into the living
room to talk.

"Do you like him, Mama?" Brandy hoped she did.

"Brandy, he's so sweet. I can't wait for you two to get
married."

Brandy's mouth flew open. "We've only been dating for a month!"

"So?" Lena knew a good thing when she saw it.

"*Sooo*, I don't really know him."

"What do you want to know about him? I'll tell you."

Brandy was almost afraid to ask. Her mother read people like she read the paper. "Okay, Mama, tell me about his soul."

"I like his air. He has honest eyes and he loves his mother. He'll make a great husband and father. While I think he will marry you, it will probably take some time. You may even have to leave him first. He's afraid of commitment, Brandy, because he watched his parents divorce."

"You read all of that out of what he said at dinner?" Brandy decided to give James another look. Though she was in no rush to be in a relationship, she had to make sure that she spent her time wisely.

"Um-hmm. It's not always what people say, Brandy, it's usually what they don't say that tells on them."

"Well, he's not going to have to worry about commitment because I'm hardly trying to get married."

"You say that now, but we'll see what tomorrow brings." Lena hugged her daughter. "I'll get the dishes. You better go in there and save James from your father. You know that he'll have him here all night talking about boxing."

Brandy checked her hair and lipstick in the mirror above the sink. "You're right. We should be leaving."

Brandy got her coat and James' jacket out of the closet. When she walked into the living room, they were deep in conversation about the greatest, Muhammed Ali.

"So you see, son, Mike Tyson could learn something from Ali." Booker looked up and saw the coats in

Brandy's arms. "Hi, sweetie. I guess you guys are getting ready to leave."

James helped Brandy into her coat.

"Thank you, Mr. Curtis, I had a great evening. Your wife is an excellent cook," James said as he put on his jacket.

"Don't forget your plates." Lena was handing Brandy two plates of food.

"You didn't have to do that. Please don't go to any trouble on my behalf."

"It was no trouble, James, but there's going to be trouble if you don't take this food." Lena smiled, but she was serious.

James smiled. He gave her a bear hug and she kissed him on the cheek. "I enjoyed having you here for dinner. Be sure and come back and see me sometime."

"I will. Thanks again."

"And next time you come, you'll get to meet my son, Byron. He spent Thanksgiving with one of his friends from school."

"Okay, I'll look forward to meeting him."

Booker shook James' hand for the fifth time. "Call me and we'll finish our conversation."

Finally they left. "I'm sorry, James, I thought they would never let us leave."

"I had fun, Brandy. Your family is very kind. I liked them a lot."

"Actually, they are a bit over-protective."

"They're just looking after their investment." James put his arm protectively around Brandy as they crossed the street to his car.

"James, your car is wearing my favorite color, midnight blue. It's so pretty." Brandy's attention was focused on the car.

James turned her around to face her. "Not nearly as pretty as you."

* * *

Involuntarily she smiled. She had to admit, they'd had some good times together. It was already four o'clock and she needed to go home and get ready for dinner with William.

Fifteen minutes later, Brandy was home. She called the restaurant and canceled the reservation. It was a beautiful Italian restaurant nestled in the Hollywood Hills. Though she knew that William loved Italian food, she didn't feel like being around white folks tonight. She had a taste for jerk chicken. There was a little place on Crenshaw Boulevard which made the best jerk chicken in the world. Coley's was always crowded and the atmosphere was very festive. It reminded her of the trip she had taken to Martinique after she completed the bar examination.

She and Tricia had stayed at a hotel in Fort de France, the capital of Martinique. It was August and there were several festivals going on that week. They attended the Ladya martial arts festival, learned the "Zook" dance and took ferry rides on the warm waters of the blue-green Atlantic Ocean. All in all, they'd had a great time and spent lots of money in the open air markets.

Brandy went into her bedroom. Her brass bed sat in the middle of the room. When she'd moved from Fox Hills in November, she left her bed and bought a new one. Since she was a teenager, she'd wanted to live near the beach. Now that she could afford to, she'd bought a three-bedroom townhouse in Marina Del Rey. Her new place was walking distance from the sand. She loved the feel of satin, so she slept on champagne-colored satin sheets. There was a low couch against the left wall and a nightstand right next to her bed. In the right corner of the room was a brass floor lamp. Her closet had sliding mirrored doors.

The digital read-out on her answering machine told her that she had three messages. Before she hit the play button, she called Simone.

"Hello?" It was Phil's voice.

"Hi, brother-in-law. What's going on?"

"Nothing, Brandy. I hear you've got a new man. When do I get to beat— I mean, meet him?" Phil laughed.

"I do not have a new man— William is my friend. We haven't even gone out yet."

"What's the problem? When are you guys going out?"

"Tonight."

"Where are you going?"

"To Coley's on Crenshaw."

"Jamaican food? Well, don't be offended when he doesn't kiss you good-night."

"What?"

"You know Jamaicans put curry on everything. Curry breath is not a breath of fresh air. Get it, breath of fresh air?" Phil fell out laughing.

"Yeah, yeah. I get it." She couldn't help but laugh. "You're so stupid. I'll call you back." Brandy hung up.

While talking to Phil, she had undressed and settled herself into the peach and mint green couch in her bedroom. She felt a tinge of excitement as she dialed William's number. He answered on the third ring. "Hello?"

"Hi, William, it's Brandy."

"Hi, beautiful." Brandy blushed. Sensing her hesitation, William kept talking. "I hope you're not calling to cancel our dinner date."

"No, William, I'm not calling to cancel. In fact, I forgot to give you my address when we spoke earlier."

"Oh, yeah." William rummaged through a drawer. "I found paper and a pencil. What's your address?"

"4140 Via Dolce Way, #301." She had just moved to this location a few months before. "Be sure to dress casually."

"I can do that."

"Well, I'll see you when you get here."

"Okay, see you soon. 'Bye."

Brandy got up from the couch and pressed the rewind button on her answering machine. While it was rewinding, she called Simone back.

"Hel-lo." Aisha's voice.

"Hi, pumpkin."

"Hi, Auntie *Braan*dy. When are you coming to see me?"

"I'll come see you soon, sweetie. Where's your mommy?"

"She's right here."

"Hey girl," called Simone's voice. "Phil told me that you and William are going out to dinner. I thought you were going to meet him for lunch."

"We were supposed to have lunch, but my boss, Lloyd, informed me that I had to meet with a client at one, so I had to cancel my plans with William."

"I *know* you were angry."

"Angry is not even the word. Then, to make matters worse, I've got to represent this sexist, racist man. Girl, he was disgusted because I'm African-American and a woman."

"So why do they want you to represent him?"

"Lloyd said something about me being the firm's best litigator. I don't know." Brandy was getting mad all over again.

"That's stupid."

"Um-hmm, but let me finish telling you what happened. After this man gets into Lloyd's office, he asked him if I was qualified."

Simone was shocked. "What did that man think, you just spent your free time as a lawyer?"

"I don't know what he thought. He was dead set against having a female attorney, that's for sure." Brandy rolled her eyes at the ugly scene in Lloyd's office earlier that day. "Anyway, William didn't get my message and he showed up at the office at one."

"He did?"

"Yes! And he looked good!" Brandy was happy that William was cuter than she remembered. She could remember times when she'd made plans with men whom she had not seen for a long period of time. Three out of five times, she wished she had stayed home.

"What did he have on?"

She thought of his clothes. He was dressed simply, but he looked really nice. "He wore khaki pants, a cream shirt and an olive blazer."

"What were you wearing?" Simone inhaled. Brandy had great clothes, but most of them were extremely conservative.

"I had on a salmon pants suit."

"The one you bought during the holiday season?"

"Yes, that's the one."

"Good choice! How was your hair?"

"I worked a miracle and pulled it together. Now, it's standing up all over my head." Brandy walked over to the mirror. "Hold on while I change phones." She picked up her cordless phone. She needed to switch her play purse and her work purse was near the front door. "Okay, I'm back."

"What did you do to it?"

"I left work early and drove around with the top down." Brandy took her purse into her bedroom. She emptied its contents onto the bed.

"Brandy, it was cold today."

"I know, but my car has a heater in the seat. Oh yeah,

before I left work, Mr. Robinson, the doorman at my building, told me that he still wants me to meet his grandson."

"Well?"

"I told him I'd meet him. It definitely can't hurt anything." Brandy was trying to remain enthusiastic about reentering the dating world.

"Good, you need to get out and meet new people."

Brandy laid down on her bed. She didn't want to meet anyone else. "I know. I've mourned over James long enough."

"Brandy, James didn't die."

She closed her eyes. "He might as well have." Brandy thought about their dinner at The Fountain, where they would have reconciled if James had not tried to blame her for their break-up.

"You are so cold."

"Anyway, Simone, William is picking me up at six-thirty." Brandy could hear Aisha crying in the back-ground. One day, she would have her own children to tend to.

"What are you going to wear?"

"I don't know."

"Brandy, why is your TV turned up so loud?"

"That's not the TV, that's my answering machine."

"Is James still calling you?" Simone asked with a hopeful voice.

"Yep. He calls once every three weeks like clock-work." This comforted Brandy. As long as he called, he still cared.

"Are you ever going to talk to him again?"

"No, not if I can help it." Brandy's voice was upbeat, but Simone detected a note of sadness. "What time is it?"

"It's five-twenty-five."

Brandy sat up straight. "Let me get off this phone—William will be here in an hour."

"Have fun."

"I will, I'll call you tomorrow."

Brandy went into the bathroom and stared at the mop on top of her head.

Across town, William was also standing before the bathroom mirror. He was shaving. He couldn't remember the last time he had been truly excited about going to dinner with a woman. He didn't date that much anymore and he had had enough of meaningless relationships. He had not run across a woman who made him think about the future in a long time. Outside of his plans for getting his doctorate, he had not given much thought to getting married. William knew that he wanted children, he just didn't know when. Well, that was before he met Brandy. There was something about her that made him want her.

William slid on faded blue jeans, a long-sleeved denim polo shirt and a pair of black snakeskin boots. He brushed his hair, grabbed his black leather jacket and headed out the door. It was only five forty-five, but he wanted to stop and buy Brandy flowers before he went to pick her up.

James was also thinking about Brandy. He was reclining in his black leather chair. Though the sun had set an hour ago, he sat and stared through open vertical blinds at the darkness which lay beyond. His neck was tense and his eyes were sad, but he didn't bother to get up. He was overdue for a shave and a haircut. What difference did it make? he reasoned. He didn't have anyone to impress. He fingered the remote control to the TV in his hand, but didn't bother to turn it on. On Mondays she left work early. It was six o'clock. By now she would be home from work. He wanted to call, but he had already left one message for her. She wouldn't call him back. She never did, but he didn't care. He would keep calling until she talked to him. Lately, he didn't have much of an appetite and going out to clubs wasn't what it used to be. He was lonely.

James found himself singing her all-time favorite song, "All I Do," by Stevie Wonder. He laughed quietly— all he did was think of her. He watched her favorite television shows: *Living Single, Murphy Brown* and *60 Minutes*. He'd even stopped going to the movies, because for the last two years, she had been his date. Now, who would he go with? He was miserable without her. He could admit that now.

He was waging a losing battle with himself. On the one hand, he congratulated himself on not getting walked on by a woman. On the other hand, the distance he had put between himself and Brandy had cost him the best woman he'd ever had. The pain in his neck began to intensify. He reluctantly got up from his seat. Before he shut the blinds, he took one last look into the night. "Brandy . . ." He said her name aloud. There was no answer. He shut the blinds.

Brandy had changed clothes three times and fixed her hair three different ways to match each outfit. She finally settled on jeans, a hunter green turtleneck, and dark green shoe boots. Her hair fell softly on her shoulders and her make-up was very light. She wore a pair of diamond studs and a gold bracelet watch. Earlier, she'd changed the gold ring on her watch for a green one. While she waited for William, she cleaned her townhouse. It wasn't really messy, but she didn't want William to think she was a slob.

At six-thirty on the nose, William pressed the buzzer at the front of Brandy's building. Though he was standing away from the door, the security camera picked him up. Brandy could see who was at the door by turning on the TV.

After she said hello to him, she buzzed him in. Minutes later, he was standing in her doorway. William leaned down and kissed her on the cheek. Then he presented her with three white orchids and three pink tea roses surrounding one big beautiful violet.

"Where did you find these beautiful flowers this time of year?" Brandy was geniunely surprised.

"I have my sources." He smiled a mischievous smile. "Can I come in?"

"Of course, come in." Brandy could have kicked herself for not inviting him in. "Make yourself at home. I'll be right back, I need to put these flowers in a vase."

Brandy disappeared downstairs for a few minutes, giving William a chance to look around. In the living room, the carpet was mauve and the couches were mauve, white and heather gray. There were paintings by Ernie Barnes and Romaire Bearden hanging on each wall. A huge marble fireplace faced him as he sat on the couch. On the glass table in front of him lay a hardback edition of *I Dream a World, Songs of My People, Rare Air* and the latest "Law Journal." It was definitely a woman's house and though he'd seen only the one room, he knew that he would love the rest.

"Are you ready?" Brandy had her jacket in her hand.

William took it from her and helped her into it. Once they were outside, William opened the door of his Jeep for her. *So far so good,* she thought to herself.

By the time they made it to the restaurant, they were old friends. Dinner went on without a hitch. When he dropped her off, he walked her to her door. Brandy was very impressed by the fact that he didn't ask to come in. Instead, he kissed her lightly on the cheek and told her that he would call her later in the week.

Brandy had a warm feeling when she went to bed that night. He made her feel safe, but more importantly, he made her happy. She knew that this was only their first date, but the evening was perfect and for a few hours it overshadowed the anger and isolation she'd felt for the last few months. Those feelings were largely connected to her job, but some of them were rooted in her feelings about James. That night, however, she was determined to forget about both of them.

Eight

Brandy and William went to the Forum for their second date. The game was sold out. The fans were yelling and screaming. Brandy joined in the Michael Jordan chants. "If he wasn't married," she thought, "hmm, he'd be in trouble with me."

"William, are you enjoying the game?" Brandy was teasing. She knew he was trying not to show his apparent disgust at Chicago winning yet another game.

"Yes, Brandy, I'm enjoying myself."

Brandy laughed. "If you're ready to go, we can."

"No, I don't want you to miss the last quarter."

"I don't have anything to miss. The Lakers are too far behind to catch up. So, if you're ready, I'm ready."

"Unfortunately, you're right. The Lakers played so badly tonight. They've got so many injuries, it's going to be impossible for them to come back in time for the play-offs."

Just before they left, Brandy went to the ladies' room. Since the half-time crowd had gone back to their seats, she decided to buy some popcorn and candy.

She nearly died when he hugged her from behind. Brandy wanted to melt right then and there. She didn't even bother to turn around. The feel of his chest was as familiar as her own breathing. Brandy would know the feel of James' body anywhere in the world.

"I knew you'd be here tonight." He kissed her on her ear.

Her voice was breathy. "You did?" Brandy was not interested in small talk. "James, let go of me." Her heart started beating madly.

He didn't let go immediately, but instead he slid his arms slowly from around her waist. "Yes, Brandy, I know how much you love Michael Jordan." James hated to let go of her. She felt good in his arms.

"You remembered. How nice." She was nervous. This was the first time she had seen James in a month. Brandy had to fight to maintain her composure.

"I remember everything about you, Brandy." He wanted to see her beautiful brown eyes. It was in those two pools of mystery that he was lost in love.

She willed her eyes to look away, but they wouldn't. "Look, James, before you even get started, I'm here with someone." Brandy hoped her tone was hard, especially since her insides had turned to mush.

"Well, he must not be much of a man letting you come down here by yourself. I'd never let you do that."

Attitude rising in her throat, Brandy sucked her teeth. "I don't need an escort to the bathroom. And you know what? I don't owe you an explanation." Brandy started walking in the direction of her seat. She had to get away from him. It had been some time since she had seen him, and yet it felt like they had never parted. Brandy had trouble reminding herself that James was part of her past.

"I'm going to call you tonight." He hoped she wouldn't say, "No." But even if she did, he was going to call. Seeing Brandy was confirmation that he could no longer live without her. He had to get her back.

"Don't bother." She didn't mean that. Brandy really wanted to talk to him.

William was concerned about Brandy. She'd been

gone a little too long. He spotted her as he rounded the corner. "Brandy, who's that?" He was staring at James.

"Nobody."

At that moment, James came over to them and introduced himself to William.

"James Collins," he said as he extended his hand to William.

"William Johnson."

"All right, Ms. Curtis, I'll be talking with you soon." James leaned over and kissed her on the cheek. Brandy willed the pavement to open up and swallow her whole.

James walked away. There was nothing he could say or do to make her change her mind. She was not going back to him.

"Brandy, are you okay?" William was concerned.

"Yes, I'm fine."

"It's your call— do you want to go back to the game or are you ready to leave?"

Brandy didn't want William to think James had affected her so she told him that she wanted to go back inside.

Later, they stood up and made their way out of the crowded stands and out into the parking lot. They held hands the length of the walk to William's Jeep. Before William unlocked the door for Brandy, he took her in his arms and kissed her. It was a long, passionate kiss.

When they stopped kissing, Brandy's eyes were shining.

"Brandy, I see a sparkle in your eyes." William smiled at his own comment. "I really had a good time tonight. Thank you."

"I'm glad you enjoyed yourself." It was Brandy's turn to smile.

"You have a beautiful smile."

"Thank you. It's nice to know that those three years of being a brace-face weren't in vain."

"I would say they weren't." He kissed her on her nose. "Your nose is cold."

"Well, it is a little chilly out here." Brandy hoped that she didn't sound like she was complaining.

"I don't want you to turn into a Fudgesicle, so I'd better take you home."

Just before they reached her townhouse, William turned down the car radio. "Brandy, who is James?"

"Oh, he's just someone I used to know." She hoped she sounded casual.

"Well, from where I was standing, he seemed to know you very well."

Brandy did not respond. She really didn't want to get into it. There was no way she could express to William how she felt about James. It wasn't his business and she hoped he didn't press her for details. Fortunately, William proved to be as smart as he was handsome and turned the volume on the radio back up.

Nine

Shirley witnessed the most bizarre episode in the nine years that she had worked at Lloyd & Lloyd. She had returned to work to get some copies she had made. Michael needed them for Men's Night at church. She saw a light on in the secretarial pool and went to the edge of the stairs. The secretarial pool was located on the floor below the main office. There were two spiral staircases that flanked both sides of Shirley's desk. The pool was a collection of cubicles with burgundy ergonomic computer chairs, bare walls, burgundy carpet, two enormous Canon copiers, three smaller ones and rows upon rows of file cabinets. She had started down the stairs when she heard Nancy's voice. She tiptoed halfway down. She stood stock still until she recognized the man's voice. When she heard feet rapidly shuffling, Shirley tiptoed back upstairs and went home. She couldn't wait to tell Brandy.

"Brandy, you will not believe what I saw last night!"

Brandy was researching case law in the office library. The library was a comfortable room with wooden desks and chairs. The entire room was covered from the ceiling to the floor with books. "What?" She was excited. Shirley always had a funny story to tell her.

"It's Brad and Nancy." Shirley paused for effect. "Girl, something is going on between them!"

"How do you know that?" Brandy was all ears. Brad

was her arch enemy and she needed the low-down on what he was doing. They had been pitted against one another since the first day she began working at the firm.

"I saw them in the secretarial pool." Shirley giggled. "Actually, I could hear them better than I could see them."

"Shh." Brandy got up and closed the door. "How do you know it was them?"

"I recognized their voices."

If anyone would know their voices, it would be Shirley. "What were they doing?"

"I think, and I could be wrong now, but I think someone was being chased." She wanted to make sure she got her story right. "I could hear them laughing."

"Hmm." *Could Brad and Nancy be having an affair?* Brandy asked herself. That didn't sound right, but it was definitely something worth remembering. "Thanks for that tidbit, Shirley. I'll keep my eyes open."

"And so will I!"

Two months had gone by and J.D. Hamilton was still trying to tell Brandy how to practice law.

"Ms. Brandy . . ."

"Ms. Curtis."

He cleared his throat. "You were late this morning and I'm not paying you for the first hour."

"No, Mr. Hamilton, you were late this morning. I've been here since seven-thirty." They went through this twice a week every week without fail. "As far as billing is concerned, I will bill you because I was here."

"We'll see what Richard has to say about this."

"Fine." Brandy had stopped arguing with him. She wanted their relationship to be strictly professional. "I have a copy of the answer I plan to file with the court."

"I already saw it and it's garbage. Do you realize that if you pursue this strategy, not only will I lose the money, I will lose my share of the company as well!" He looked at her with contempt in his eyes.

Brandy was confused. "Mr. Hamilton, how could you have read the answer? I finished it last night on my computer at home." She stopped and thought a moment. The last time she'd seen the original draft of the answer was Friday. She had asked Nancy to make a copy of it so she could take it home. There was no way possible for J.D. to have received a copy of the answer, unless . . . Nancy had sent it to him. Why would Nancy send J.D. a copy of an incomplete draft?

He uncrossed his legs and leaned forward. "Gal, do I look like a fool to you? I received a copy of your answer via special delivery on Saturday. I am going to sue you and the firm for malpractice." He reached into his briefcase and whipped out a three-page copy.

"May I see that?" she asked. J.D. let out a disgusted sigh and threw the copy on her desk.

Brandy skimmed the answer and then set it down on her desk. Without reading any deeper, Brandy saw that someone had taken her rough draft and cut and pasted affirmative defenses from another case that was totally unrelated to J.D.'s. "Mr. Hamilton, you're right—this is garbage. I didn't write this answer. Where did you get this from again?"

"Don't act like you don't know what I'm talking about. I'll be sure to show this piece of trash to Richard. Not only are you incompetent, but you're a liar." He grunted, stood up, snatched the answer out of her hand and stormed down the hallway to Lloyd's office.

Brandy sat motionless as she watched Hamilton leave. She knew that she hadn't sent a messenger to J.D.'s house. Also, her answer had not been complete until Sunday. The only person other than herself who had access to her work was her secretary. She buzzed Nancy and asked her to come into her office immediately.

Nancy was a nondescript woman in her mid-forties. She was short and frumpy, with pasty skin. She wasn't unattractive, but because she dressed in browns and grays, there was a drabness about her. She must have sensed that she needed to add some excitement to her appearance, because about three years before she'd dyed her hair platinum blonde. The hair color only emphasized how pale she was and made her dark brown eyes look almost black. "Yes, Ms. Curtis, do you need something?" Nancy said, entering the office with a notepad.

Brandy did not invite her to sit down. "Nancy, did you print out a copy of the rough draft of J.D. Hamilton's answer and have it delivered to him via special messenger on Saturday?" Brandy's tone was flat.

"No, Ms. Curtis. You told me on Friday that you would finish it at your home." Nancy's voice was shaking.

"I did tell you that, didn't I?" It wasn't really a question, but more of a statement. "Thank you, Nancy."

Because the attorneys had so much work to do, they rarely even sharpened their own pencils. They were hired to produce and that was it. Nancy had worked for her for the past four years and nothing unusual had ever happened before. Though they had never established a close relationship, Brandy felt that Nancy was trustworthy. Or she had until that day.

There was a knock on the door and then it opened. "Hey Bran, what's up with your client? What did you do to him to make him go shouting down the hall?" Brad Stevens had a knack for showing up at the wrong time every time.

Brandy just stared at him. "How can I help you, Brad?" She did not try to hide her obvious irritation.

"Mind if I come in?" He was seated before he finished his question. "Well, I couldn't help overhearing your conversation. He hated your answer." Brad looked like a cat who had just swallowed a canary.

"Brad, tell me something. How could you have heard our conversation when these walls are separated by three inches of plywood?"

Brad's smile froze on his lips. "I was passing by your door when I heard him. He doesn't exactly whisper when he talks. Come on, Bran, you know that." His smile returned.

"Excuse me, Brad, but I have work to do." She began to shuffle papers on her desk.

"Oh Bran, don't be a spoiled sport just because your answer was less than great. If you needed help, all you had to do was ask. *Ciao*, Bran." He closed the door.

Somebody was sabotaging her. She couldn't go further with her thought because Lloyd began buzzing her.

"Yes, Lloyd."

"Please come to my office." His voice was as cool as ever.

As Brandy walked down the hallway, everyone stopped and stared. She guessed everyone had heard the altercation. David blew her a kiss, but he didn't say anything. The only person who spoke to her was Brad. "Good luck, Bran." He reached out to pat her on the shoulder. Brandy shot him a look that froze his hand in mid-air.

"My name is Brandy." She rolled her eyes at him.

Nancy handed Brandy a document when she passed her desk. When Brandy finally reached the corner office, the heavy oak door was closed. She knocked but there was no answer. Seconds later, the door flew open.

"Brandy, I am surprised at you!" Lloyd said this before she had a chance to sit down. J.D. was not there, but the other partner, Stan Cohen, was looking out the window.

Brandy felt like she was in the principal's office.

Stan turned around. He had the bogus answer in his hand. "Brandy, this is a piece of crap. This almost cost the firm a client and a malpractice suit. A first-year law student could have written a better answer than this." Normally a very calm man, Stan was highly agitated. He face had turned crimson.

"Brandy, I don't know where your mind is." This admonishment came from Lloyd. "I didn't want to have to tell Stan about your first blow-up with Mr. Hamilton, but after this, this *answer*, if that is what it's supposed to be, I had no choice. Tell me, is this some kind of sick joke?"

"There has been a mistake. That's not my answer."

Cohen barked, "Then whose answer is it?"

"If you cannot work up to Lloyd & Lloyd's standard of excellence, then maybe you should find another firm." Lloyd was all but firing her. "Brandy, rule eleven clearly spells out the sanctions for the filing of fraudulent claims and counterclaims."

"I know what the law says, Lloyd." Brandy, who was accustomed to being attacked in court, used her litigation skills to respond to Stan and Lloyd. "My duty to my client would not allow me to risk sanctions or a possible malpractice suit. I do not conduct business like that, and neither does Lloyd & Lloyd."

Cohen said, "Oh really, Ms. Curtis. I would never have known that from the answer you submitted to court!"

The wheels of the train *de saboteur* were grinding in her ear. "I don't know who or where that answer came from. I haven't filed anything with the court." Brandy fought to keep her composure. Her neck was officially on the chopping block. Her worst fear had come true.

"Lloyd, I gave Nancy a rough draft of the answer on Thursday. On Friday, I told her I would finish the answer at home, and I finished it last night. When I got to work this morning, I left the final draft with Nancy so she could prepare it for court."

"So you never filed this with the court?" Stan asked, waving the paper at her. He was not familiar with Brandy's work, though he'd heard that she was a great litigator.

"No. That copy you got from J.D. doesn't even have my signature on it. I don't know where he got that." *Why won't you believe me?* Brandy silently screamed.

"Brandy, do you have your answer with you?" Lloyd asked. He was inclined to back down and support Brandy. He didn't think she would be so careless, but if she hadn't sent it, who had?

"Yes." Brandy handed him her five-page answer and her rough draft. "Other than the first paragraph, the answer you have and my answer are completely different. My rough draft doesn't even look like this."

Stan took five minutes to skim the document which was the longest five minutes of Brandy's life. When he was finished, he passed it to Lloyd. His face was unreadable. Lloyd, who was familiar with her work, was able to read the answer quickly. "Brandy, you're right. Other than the first paragraph on the first page, these reports are different. This is the most brilliant answer I've read in a long time."

Stan was still not impressed, though his tone had softened. "Clearly, these are two different documents, but it doesn't explain how Mr. Hamilton received this first one."

"Stan, it was obviously some bizarre mix-up." Lloyd came to her defense. "Brandy, were you here Saturday?" He was trying to get to the bottom of it all.

"Yes, Lloyd. I'm here every Saturday."

"Did you send the messenger out, Brandy?"

"No, I didn't. I knew that I was meeting with J.D. this morning, so there was no need to send him the answer via delivery." Brandy, pleased that they approved of her work, now became annoyed. This was the last straw. "Like I told you before, I didn't finish the answer until Sunday evening at home."

"Thank you, Brandy. We're terribly sorry about this. I will personally get to the bottom of this," Lloyd said with authority.

"Lloyd, Stan, I don't know who did this. I hope I *never* know who would go out of his way to destroy a client's faith in my abilities. I admit that Mr. Hamilton and I have had disagreements," she added in code. "However, it would go against the oath I took when I became a barrister to deliberately sabotage my own client's case, no matter how I felt about him or her." Brandy paused, then continued, "If becoming a partner means that I will endure childish, sophomoric treatment from my colleagues, then Lloyd & Lloyd may not be the place for me." Brandy spun on her heels and walked out of Lloyd's office.

Career-wise, the last two months had been a living hell. At first only small things happened. Nancy would misplace a letter here or a document there. Nothing blatant had happened in the beginning. Even when she saw Brad winking at Nancy in the hallway, she still didn't think too much of their interaction. Truth was, she had been in and out of court on three different cases and really didn't have time to take notes about who was doing what to whom in the office. In the last three weeks, however, she began to take notice. Her files had been moved, copies destroyed, and after the incident over J.D.'s answer, she was convinced that someone was trying to get her fired. Brandy was not a paranoid person, nor was she the type to back down from a fight. She was, however, tired of fighting. In a minute, she was going to quit and then whoever was after her job could have it. Eighty, sometimes ninety hours per week, no sleep, a cut-throat work environment, and a perpetual attitude was not how she wanted to greet her twenty-ninth birthday, which was around the corner. She needed to make some important decisions. Something had to go.

William had been her one bright spot. They had grown very close in a short period of time. He was very special to her, although she didn't know what kind of relationship she wanted from him.

Brandy marveled at how small the world was. Mr. Robinson had invited her to dinner at his house the week before, planning for her to meet his grandson. When she arrived, she heard a familiar voice. She would have never guessed that William and Mr. Robinson knew each other, let alone that they were related. Dinner was a huge success and she received his family's stamp of approval. When dinner was over, William followed her back to her townhouse and they took a stroll on the beach.

Their night together reminded her of an occasion when she'd talked James into a late-night swim in the ocean. He hated the sand, but agreed to go. Brandy had had an exceptionally hellish week at work and James wanted to comfort her. That particular week, Lloyd was breathing down her neck about a client who wanted to settle his case, Nancy had been out sick, and the temporary secretary was as slow as molasses— Brandy didn't think she'd ever get any work done. On top of it all, Alma Guiterrez, an eccentric old woman, retained her counsel. Ms. Guiterrez wanted to sue her neighbor, Aubrey Calahan, for not returning her Picasso. Ms. Guiterrez had loaned Aubrey Calahan the painting because he was a real estate agent and was showing a model home to a potential buyer. When the open house was over, he refused to give it back, stating that Ms. Guiterrez had given it to him. Ms. Guiterrez insisted that he stole the valuable painting from her. It was a vicious fight and forced Brandy to do quite a bit of investigating. Brandy learned that Ms. Guiterrez had a habit of "giving" things to people and then accusing them of stealing from her. Brandy had to terminate her legal services to Ms. Guiterrez for fear of being labeled a fool in court. Oh, the things people fought about.

It had been a cool, clear night and the sky was midnight blue. James carried the blanket and corkscrew; she carried the white wine and two gold-trimmed wine flutes. He made a toast to her beauty and to their future together. They walked down to the ocean's edge and stared out into the blackness of the sea. Brandy took off her beige coverup, revealing a one-piece, midnight blue bathing suit, and made a run for the surf. She didn't anticipate the water being so cold, so her late-night swim turned into a late-night dip. The cold water sent her rushing into James' arms. He didn't bother to wrap the towel around her. Instead he held her close to him until she stopped shivering. Once she was warm, they walked over to their blanket and laid down. James popped the cork and Brandy held the glasses. Between sips of wine, they counted stars and sang love songs. James had a sexy voice like Christopher Williams'. Later, he walked her back to her place, kissed her passionately and drove off into the night. James was her knight in shining armor.

Now, between work and William, there stood James. She had not returned any of his phone calls, nor his letters . . . although a couple of times, she had attempted to call him back. Each time his answering machine picked up, she hung up. She would not allow herself to leave a message for him. He had even called her mother to apologize for the way things had ended between them. It was funny, her mother hadn't told her about it until two weeks after the fact.

"Mama, why didn't you tell me that James called you?"

Lips pursed, Lena chose her words carefully. "Would it have made a difference to you?"

"No, but you could have told me."

"Do you want to know what he said?"

"No."

"He said that he loves you and that he was sorry."

"So?" Brandy's stomach started doing flips.

"Look, I don't know what happened between you two. What I do know is that that boy still loves you and, if I'm not mistaken, you still love him, too."

"For the first time in your life, you are *wrong*. I do not love James! Mama, I am finally out from under his spell and I don't want to talk about him anymore."

"So what are you saying, Brandy?"

"I'm saying that I'm through with him."

Lena looked at her daughter. Brandy was losing weight and she had complained about her hair falling out.

"Mama, you need to get over him, too. James and I are history. I have a new man in my life."

"I know that, Brandy. I know about your new friend, William. Your father and I think he's very nice." She rubbed her hand. "It's only been three months since you and James broke up. It takes longer than that to get over someone you almost married."

"I can't believe you've taken his side!"

"I'm not taking sides!"

"Yes, you are! When are you going to let go of that memory?" Brandy was fuming.

"Okay, you're right. I'm out of this." Lena got up from the table. "I'm sure you know what you're doing."

James started calling once a week. Her brother had told her a long time ago that a woman never looked better than she did on another man's arm. She guessed that was the root of James' intensified attraction to her. By her birthday, she planned to be through with James and hopefully her job.

She revised her resumé; she needed to make a move. By doing so, she would lose her place in line for partner. *So what,* she thought to herself. The partner track and the money that came with it had finally lost its glory. At this point in her life, she'd consider taking a job selling incense at a freeway intersection if it meant that she would have peace of mind.

Ten

One Year Ago

In the beginning, James was the sweetest man alive. He used to send her cards and leave sappy messages on her machine.

Beep. "Brandy, this is the J in your joy. I was thinking about you and how much I love you. Call me when you get in." *Beep.*

"Does he always leave gumpy messages like that?" Simone laughed.

"Yes, he does. He's so sweet, Simone." Brandy hugged herself. "I just love him to death."

"What did you just say?"

"Huh?"

"Did Ms.-I-don't-want-no-man-don't-have-time-for-love-Curtis say that she's in love?"

Brandy hated it when Simone was right. She had been fighting falling in love with James. Initially she made work her excuse for not having love in her life. She ate, slept and drank the dream of becoming a partner at Lloyd & Lloyd, until James showed her the difference between coming home to cold books and coming home to a warm body. Her next excuse was time. She volunteered at Legal Aid twice a week; worked eighty hours per week at Lloyd & Lloyd; went weekly to the gym; kept a weekly hair appointment; and then,

when there was time, she slept. Her life ran like clock-
work. Brandy barely had time for herself, let alone a
significant other. When James came into her life, she
found minutes in the day and hours on the weekend to
spend with him. It had been a struggle, but well worth
the effort. Brandy quickly covered her face with her
hands so that Simone could not see her smiling. "Okay,
you got me. And before you even say it, *I'll* say it— you
were right!"

"I knew it! I knew it! Brandy's in love." Simone
jumped up and hugged Brandy. "I'm really happy for
you. James is perfect for you! When are you guys getting
married?"

"He asked me how did next year sound."

"Next year's around the corner. Oh my God, we've
got so much work to do. What month? Will it be in the
spring or the summer? July's a good month. What are
your colors? What— "

"Slow down, Simone. He hasn't even proposed yet."

Simone was exasperated. "C'mon girl, if no one else
in this world gets married, you two are getting married."

"I don't know about all that." Brandy's joy was fleet-
ing.

"What's up with the hesitation?" Simone's bubble
had just burst.

"It's nothing really. I don't know . . ."

"What?"

"Something's not right, Simone. I mean, I know that
he loves me and I believe that he wants to marry me,
but he's been talking about marriage since we met. I
wasn't interested in getting married our first year together. But almost two years have passed and while he's
still talking that talk, he hasn't asked me yet."

"Maybe he's waiting for the right moment."

"It's more than that. It's like he's withdrawing from me."

Six months before, in June, James had surprised Brandy at work.

"Hey sweetheart, what are you doing for lunch?" He kissed her softly on the lips.

"I hadn't even thought about eating." She needed to take a break and James' timing was perfect. She looked at her watch. "I can't believe it's already three o'clock."

James couldn't wait until they got married. He envisioned their life together and looked forward to the look on her face when she said, "I do." "Do you have a little time?"

She looked at the stack of papers on the edge of her desk. Technically, she didn't have time to sneeze, but since James was asking, she eagerly agreed to stop working. "I always have time for you."

They left her office and took a walk down the block. "James, where are we going?"

"Shh. Just follow me." He was nervous.

They continued walking for two blocks and finally arrived at their destination. Bavarian Jewelers. Brandy, who didn't wear much jewelry, was confused about why they had stopped there. She thought they were going to get something to eat and now she was hungry. "James, what are we doing here?"

She felt that James' palms were beginning to sweat. "I brought you here so that you could pick out your engagement ring."

Brandy had gasped. A wide smile spread across her face. That was the reaction James had been waiting for.

"I didn't expect this. I, I . . ." She was speechless. She was screaming on the inside. *An engagement ring!*

They looked through several rings. After an hour of trying on rings, she chose a one and one-half carat diamond solitaire. While she was trying on rings, James kept telling her how beautiful she was and that he couldn't wait until their wedding day. Brandy hated to leave, but she had to get back to work.

Simone interrupted Brandy's reverie. "Well, Phil took me ring shopping, what's wrong with that?"

"Nothing's wrong with going ring shopping as long as a ring is purchased. As we left the ring store, I went back to my office and he went home. I was so excited that I couldn't get any work done the rest of the day. For about a week after that, we discussed wedding plans, but then nothing happened."

"What do you mean nothing?" Simone was trying hard to understand.

"I mean, James dropped the subject. Sometimes I wonder if that day even happened."

"I still think he's waiting for the right moment."

"Simone, that was six months ago."

Simone didn't know what to say.

To further prove her point about James' indecision, Brandy gave Simone another example. "Prior to taking me ring shopping, James never acted as though he was afraid of making a commitment. Now, if his friends ask him when we're getting married, he says, 'Ah man, you know.' When his mother or my parents ask, he says, 'Just as soon as possible.' When I ask, he tells me, 'Brandy, please don't pressure me about this. We are going to get married.' He gets irritated with me. I'm afraid to bring it up."

"But . . ." James' hesitation was definitely a bad sign.

"That's just it, there are no 'buts,' but there *is* a but. Am I making sense?"

Simone looked confused. "Basically, what you're saying is that he's tripping."

"Bingo."

* * *

"James, man, I thought we were boys." Robert threw him the basketball. It was Sunday morning and they were out on the court shooting hoops.

"We are, it's just that Brandy wants to get married."

"Brandy wants to get married? I thought you were the man." Robert didn't care for Brandy. Ever since she and James started dating, James had changed. He had turned into a wimp.

"I am the man." The conviction that once would have been attached to that statement was long gone. James was whipped, and that was all there was to it.

"Well, then why are you letting her pressure you into something you don't want to do?" Another reason Robert didn't like Brandy was because she took up too much of James' time. He remembered when they used to go to clubs together, to the games, out to look for women, or stayed in to watch Monday night football. Now, James wouldn't look at another woman, wouldn't go near a club, and he was talking about getting married! He treated Brandy like she was a queen or something. It made him sick to see his boy sprung like that.

James threw the ball hard at Robert. He was actually aiming for his head. Brandy had told him a year ago that Robert didn't like her. James thought she was jealous of their friendship, but now he saw that the reverse was true.

"Rob, why don't you get off of her?" James had stepped up to Robert and they were standing toe-to-toe in the middle of the court.

Robert backed down. "Look, man, I'm not trying to start anything. It's just that in the last two years, you've changed. She's changed you and you can't even see it. You dis your boys, and you don't have time for anybody but her." He threw his arms up in disgust. "That's your woman." He started walking toward the car and over his shoulder he threw, "I would never let a woman do that to me." Robert was afraid that once James got married, he would be alone. Though he had other friends, James was his best friend.

If he had been within hitting range, James would have socked him. Robert was just mad because he couldn't find a woman to love him the way Brandy loved James.

It was late October and closing night of "Jelly's Last Jam." James was supposed to see Brandy later that evening. They were going with Simone and Phil to see the musical. After his argument with Robert on the basketball court, James didn't want to go. He knew that if he told Brandy that he wanted to cancel, he would get in trouble. He decided to take a drive, hoping it would calm him down.

James arrived home at six o'clock to a ringing phone. Brandy hadn't heard from him all day and was worried that they were going to be late for the performance.

"Honey, what are you still doing at home?"

"I just walked in the door." He was annoyed because he knew she was about to scream.

"What do you *mean* you *just* walked in the door? The play starts at seven. It's six-fifteen— you're supposed to be here already."

James took a deep breath. "Are you finished nagging me?"

"Excuse me, but it's not my fault that you're just now getting home from playing basketball with Robert. I don't see how you guys play all day long anyway."

"Do I complain when you get your hair and nails done and that takes all day? Or when you and Simone go on all-day shopping sprees?"

Brandy was quick on his heels. "You say that like I do it on your money."

"It may not be my money, but it for damn sure is my time." His normally smooth voice was cutting.

"You know what, James? You and your funky attitude can stay at home!" Click. She'd hung up.

James just looked at the receiver. It was so childish of her to hang up. He was still too tired and too pissed at Robert to care. He thought about the drive he had taken earlier. He rode with the top down on his Benz, and drove north on Pacific Coast Highway. As he passed the mountains on his right and the ocean on his left, he thought about what Robert had said. It had been a long time since he'd spent any time with his friends. It seemed that he spent all of his time with Brandy, her family, her friends and his mother. His mother loved Brandy. She also wanted him to marry her. It wasn't that he didn't want to— he was just scared. No one understood his fear. He couldn't talk to Robert because he would have encouraged James to leave Brandy. He wanted to talk to Keith, but Keith would have sided with Brandy and the last thing he wanted to hear was that he was wrong.

Sometimes he felt inadequate. Financially, he could provide for her, but he didn't know if he could give her the kind of life she deserved. He didn't grow up with a perfect life or a perfect family like Brandy's. His father left when he was ten. Their relationship never got on track after that. For this reason, he shied away from deep relationships. But that was an excuse because he liked being close to Brandy. She made him feel like a man. Despite that, he was pulling away from her. And he didn't know why he was doing it either, especially since she was all he ever thought about.

Brandy had left before James could call her back. He was being inconsiderate yet again. She had spent hours on the phone trying to get tickets to the last performance of "Jelly's Last Jam." Once she got the tickets, she turned Melrose upside down trying to find the perfect dress for what was supposed to be a romantic night out together. They had both been under a lot of stress and she wanted the evening to be perfect. Of late, James was complaining that she worked too much. She tried to accommodate him by working less on the weekends, but she didn't always have control over her schedule. James, she felt, wasn't being reasonable. She never asked him to stop working to be with her. She accepted his traveling and long hours without question. What Brandy didn't know was that James was feeling insecure and didn't know how to tell her that. He was afraid that if he admitted he was scared, she wouldn't think he was a man. His reluctance to share his fear with Brandy was causing the drama in their relationship. She was trying her best to ease the tension between them, but James wasn't helping.

She'd bought a strapless violet velvet dress, with a dangerous slit on her left leg. She wore matching violet pumps, diamond earrings that he had given her for her birthday and cognac lipstick. She thought about cutting her hair, but instead she wore it in a high French twist on her head. After all her trouble, he wouldn't get to see her.

By now she should be used to him flaking out on her. Last week they were supposed to go to dinner and the movies. James showed up one hour after the reservation was set and then didn't want to go to the movies. He just wanted to sit around her townhouse and watch cable.

Simone saw Brandy's car, but there was only one person in it. "Brandy, where is James?"

"In hell somewhere." Brandy snatched the ticket from the valet.

Simone was almost afraid to ask, but she did anyway. "What's wrong and why isn't he here?"

"I don't want to talk about it." Her tone was testy.
"Remember when we were talking about my marriage
to James?"

"Yes."

"There won't be a wedding." Brandy practically
barked at Simone. He had ruined her evening and in
turn, she prayed that she had ruined his.

A few days later, Brandy was sitting in her office
when David knocked on the door.

"Bella, I haven't seen you in a while, how have you
been?" David was smiling at her.

"I'm fine, David." Brandy was sitting behind a
mound of paperwork on her desk. Normally, her office
was immaculate. She put away her files and straightened her desk up each evening before she left. Lately,
she hadn't had the energy to clean her office. She
couldn't even remember the last time her desk or her
office didn't look like a cyclone had blown through it.

David waved his arm over her office. "You don't look
or sound fine. What's the matter?"

Brandy hesitated. She didn't feel like rehashing her
crumbling relationship with James. "I really don't want
to talk about it."

"It will make you feel better to talk about him."

"Who said anything about James?" Brandy snapped.
"I'm sorry. You didn't deserve that." Brandy moved
three disorganized files out of a chair so he could sit
down. "This may take awhile."

David wasn't going to leave until Brandy told him
what was bothering her. He hated to see her in so much
pain. "I have all the time you need."

"James is pulling away from me." Brandy felt tears
slowly roll down her face. "He's being distant and mean
to me. I don't know when we came to this, David. One

minute we were so happy and now I can't seem to do anything right." She burst into full tears and David let her cry. Through choked sobs, she said, "I don't know what to do."

"Let it all out, sweetheart." He went around to where she was seated. David took her into his arms and rocked her gently back and forth. When she was finished he handed her his handkerchief.

"Thank you." She managed a weak smile.

"Have you tried talking to him?"

"Yes, but he says that I'm being paranoid."

"Paranoid? In what way?"

"Listen. One night we had gone to the Blue Nile for dinner. James was quiet on the drive over. I asked him if everything was okay and he said everything was fine. I launched into telling him the details of my day and he seemed very disinterested . . ."

"James, you seem awfully distracted tonight, what's going on?"

"Nothing." James snapped at her. "Why are you always interrogating me? We're not in court."

Brandy stopped buttering her bread. "I wasn't interrogating you. It's just that we always share our days with one another and tonight you've barely said two words to me." She was on the defensive. "Have I done something to upset you?"

"No more than usual." He wished Brandy would get off his back. She acted like she needed a daily report of his every move.

Brandy wondered if an alien had taken over James' body. It looked like James, it walked like James, but it didn't sound like James. "Come again?" She was perplexed.

"Brandy, I am a grown man and I don't have to report to you."

"Why are you being so mean to me?" Brandy couldn't believe her ears. Where was this anger coming from? Last night everything had been fine. "What has happened in the last twenty-four hours that has caused you to be so evil?"

"Nothing. Let's just drop it and eat," James had said. "I need to wash my hands." He got up from the table and went to the men's room. When he returned, he was all smiles.

"Brandy, what movie do you want to see tonight?" James had miraculously forgotten that a few minutes ago, he'd been mad at her.

"The rest of our evening was like old times," Brandy told David. "Even when we went to my townhouse after the movie, he turned on cable and laid in my lap like he always does."

"Bella, maybe he was having a bad day."

"David." Brandy's voice grew weak again. "Having a bad day is no excuse for being evil. In any event, while we watched TV, I gave him a face and chest massage." She could picture her hands rubbing his forehead, sliding over his cheeks, the feel of soft lips and the curves of his chest. "Even his skin didn't feel right. I don't know."

David listened carefully. It sounded to him that James was tripping out on her. He might even want to break up with her, but didn't know how. Since David did not know James, he kept his opinion to himself. "You've been under a lot of pressure lately, Brandy. Maybe, maybe— "

"Maybe what? Maybe I'm going crazy? Maybe I'm just making this all up? I don't think so." Brandy disengaged herself from his embrace. "James is the one who's crazy, not me."

"*Mi dispiace,* Brandy, *so bene quanto l'hai amato.*"

"What does that mean?"

"It means that I'm sorry, Brandy, I know how much you love him."

Two weeks before New Year's Eve, Brandy thought she was through with James.

"James, I was thinking we'd have dinner and go see Everette Harp at The Strand for New Year's." The Strand was a jazz club in Redondo Beach. Brandy was excited at the prospect of spending a romantic evening with James. She hoped that their night together would bring them closer together.

He loved jazz and Everette Harp was one of his favorite saxophonists. "I'll call the ticket depot and get tickets for us."

An hour passed, and James called Brandy back. "There's been a change in plans. Robert just called. He's giving a party at his house. I figured we would go there instead."

Tugging on the telephone cord, Brandy said, "Robert called and just like that, you changed our plans?" Her head was beginning to pound.

"I was in the middle of calling when he clicked in." He knew he was wrong, but he had made up his mind. They were going to Robert's party and that was that.

Brandy bit down hard on her lip. "James, why didn't you tell Robert that you already had plans?" She was beginning to lose control. *What was wrong with him? Why didn't he want to be alone with her?*

"When he called, Brandy, I didn't have plans. It's not like I already bought the tickets." James hadn't seen a problem. "What's the big deal?"

Brandy didn't want to have an argument, but he'd started it. "James, New Year's Eve is supposed to be special. I wanted to spend some quiet time with you, alone. I have no desire to see Robert. You know how you two act when you get together." It was supposed to be a very intimate night for them, and he was talking about going to hang out with his boys. *This is so typical,* she thought to herself. *I shouldn't be surprised.* "Did you even call about the availability?"

"I really don't appreciate that snide comment." James was trying to avoid an argument, because he still wanted to be with Brandy on New Year's Eve. "It doesn't matter. I told my boy that we're going to be there and that's that." He had put his foot down. She would just have to deal with it.

Brandy had stopped pulling on the phone cord to hear herself scream, "There is no way in hell that I am spending New Year's Eve with you and Robert! You two act like children when you get together." This was further confirmation of James' distancing himself from her.

"I never make statements like that about you and your friends." He couldn't believe it! She was trying to force him to choose between them. "I was just trying to think of someplace fun to go. It's clear to me that you don't want to be around me or my friends."

Attitude in full effect, Brandy retorted, "It's not your friends *per se,* it's just you and Robert. And you are just trying to be cheap." Knowing that her next statement was going to push James over the edge, she said, "I'll buy the tickets."

"First, my friends aren't good enough for you, now I'm cheap! So, why did you even bother calling me?" James was pacing the length of his living room. "Here I am trying to make it a happy holiday and all you can do is spit venom at me! And—"

She interrupted, "*And* nothing! Did we not agree to spend New Year's Eve together? Did you not agree that you would get the tickets? Did you—"

"I've told you before, this is not a court room and I am not one of your damn witnesses!" James was trying not to yell. He didn't want Brandy to know how angry he really was.

"What it comes down to is this: you made plans with me and now you're trying to renege. It's obvious that Robert is more important to you than I am. This conversation is over. I don't have anything else to say to you." Click. Angry tears burned her cheeks. She could no longer stay in denial—their relationship was over.

New Year's Eve, Brandy spent the night alone while James hung with Robert. She'd turned the volume all the way up on her CD player and blasted all of their favorite songs. Between drinks she walked down "Memory Lane" with Minnie Riperton, read a "Tone Poem" with Teena Marie, agreed with George Duke that love had "No Rhyme And No Reason," and cried with Sade. She took comfort in knowing that her life had never been as bad as Sade's. Still in a drunken stupor when the phone rang, she asked, "Who is this?"

"It's James, who else calls you, beautiful?"

"Oh, it's you." Her head felt like somebody very heavy was sitting on it. "What time is it?"

It was 3:48 a.m. exactly. "I don't know, baby." He was wide awake and feeling guilty for spending New Year's Eve with his boys. Robert had arranged for every available freak west of the Mississippi to attend his soirée. James had tried to call Brandy to tell her to come, but some drunken fool had locked himself in the bathroom with the phone. He even thought about leaving the party to go call her, but he didn't want to look like a punk in front of his friends. "What did you do to-night?"

Sounding heavily intoxicated but clear as a bell, Brandy coolly responded, "I spent the evening by my damn self because the man who used to be my boyfriend felt that his friends were more important than me." With that she'd thrown the phone across the room.

James had immediately called her back. The line was busy. He must have tried a thousand times before he jumped in his car and went over to her place.

When he arrived at Brandy's he buzzed her ten times. When there was still no answer, he got nervous. He knew that she was not the type to do anything to herself, but he was nervous because she'd sounded very drunk, and for the most part she didn't drink.

Panicked, James used his set of keys to let himself into her apartment. All of the lights were on and it was a mess. There were CDs and magazines all over the floor and two empty champagne bottles sitting on the counter. He followed the CD trail into her bedroom and there lay Brandy, sprawled out across the bed. The window was wide open and her uncombed hair was moving in the early morning breeze. It was freezing in the room and her comforter was on the floor and her oversized t-shirt had crept up her thighs. James could never understand why women refused to sleep in pajamas. He didn't want her to catch a cold, so he pulled her t-shirt down and put her comforter on top of her. Next he closed her bedroom window. In doing this, he stepped on the telephone. Off the hook. He put the phone back together and took off his jacket.

He didn't bother to wake her. It wouldn't have done any good— she was out for the count. Instead he sat on the bed and watched her sleep. How he hated himself at that moment for not being with her that night. How could he not spend New Year's Eve with the only woman

he'd ever loved? Lately he had been making her unhappy. He was blowing the relationship and he didn't
know how to stop.

She'd looked so peaceful lying there. He longed to
be under the covers with her, his body curled around
hers. They fit together perfectly. He smoothed the hair
around her temple and he tenderly stroked her face.
He closed his eyes and allowed the guilt to consume
him. Memories fast forwarded and then rewound, reminding him of the precious moments when love was
new.

James remembered running his fingers through
Brandy's hair and trying to melt her with a dreamy
gaze. "You're beautiful."

"Thank you." She smiled. They were lying on the
floor of his house in front of a roaring fireplace. With
the firelight in the background, their bodies formed
perfect silohuettes against the bay windows in his living
room. He was stroking her from the top of her head
to the small of her back.

Kissing her lightly on her lips, he whispered, "You
kiss me very softly and your touch is very tender. Sometimes I wonder if you like to kiss at all."

Turning her full face to him, she sighed. "James, I
love kissing you." Looking into his eyes, she saw the
fire that she knew was her own. "As far as sex is concerned, I still don't see what all the hype is about."

Gently rolling her under him, he seductively whispered, "I'll show you what all the talk is about."

After they made love, James looked at Brandy. "Did
you enjoy that?"

Brandy blushed. "Yes."

"What's making you smile?"

"I've never been asked that before."

"Really?" James wanted to make sure that his lover was satisfied.

"Yes. Normally, men just roll over and go to sleep." Though he was tired, he forced himself to speak. "I would never do that to you." He stoked her arm. "Brandy, I want you to love making love with me." James prided himself on being an excellent lover, but he couldn't read Brandy. "You were so quiet when we had sex. I need you to talk to me. What do you like? Was I too fast? Was I too slow?"

"Oh, no." He was perfect. She felt silly. "James, you were the best lover I've ever had."

"I can be so much better." He began singing the chorus to "Tell Me How U Want It" by Johnny Gill: *Can you tell me how you want it? Can you tell me how you feel?* "I want to make you happy, Brandy."

"You do!" She thought of their shopping trip together; when she'd tried to teach him to cook; and their marathon video nights. Inevitably, James would fall asleep before the movie ended. Listening to him snore lightly in her ear cinched her affection for him. That's what had caused her to fall in love with him. No candlelight dinners could touch the realness of a man falling asleep blissfully in her arms. "James . . ."

"Brandy, what I'm trying to say is that I have all tonight, all tomorrow, and the next fifty years, if that's how long it will take to make you happy."

"Why is my happiness so important to you?"

"I love you, Brandy, and I want our life together to be special." He rolled on top of her and began kissing her again.

After an hour of watching her sleep, James got up and cleaned her apartment. He took his time because he wanted it to be spotless when she woke up. It was seven a.m. before Brandy finally stirred, but she didn't get up, she just moaned and rolled over.

When James finished cleaning, he went in search of food to cook for Brandy. He couldn't cook and thought about running out to buy her breakfast, but he didn't want to leave her side.

The smell of eggs and Eggo waffles overpowered her senses and made her nauseous. Brandy made a mad dash for the bathroom. After vomiting for fifteen minutes, she emerged from the bathroom hunched over and walking on weak legs. She felt a little better but her throat was parched. She thought she heard a noise in her living room. She spotted the phone on the other side of the room. She tiptoed over to it and started dialing 911 when she heard James' voice.

"Breakfast is ready, honey." James was standing in the doorway.

"James?" She turned around and headed back to her bed. "I'm not hungry."

"You'll feel better if you eat." He was concerned about her because she still looked a little green around the gills, but he was also making a peace offering.

"If you were really concerned, you would have been here last night." Her bark was definitely equal to her bite.

Nodding his head in agreement, he said, "You're right, Brandy. I should have been here last night."

Brandy slammed the bathroom door. In the bathroom she splashed cold water on her face and started getting dressed. Her mother was not expecting them until one that afternoon for New Year's dinner. She hoped James would be a man, admit he was wrong, and leave.

Meanwhile, in the kitchen, James was surveying the breakfast he had prepared for her. He was dealing with his own guilt for not being with her the night before.

Regardless of Brandy's mood, James was determined to make up for his insensitivity from the past night.

At eleven-thirty, she emerged from her room fully dressed. It was a beautiful, hot sunny day and she was tired of sitting in her room. To her dismay, James was still there on her couch waiting to talk to her. "Brandy, we really need to talk."

"We?" Brandy couldn't believe her ears— James couldn't possibly think that she really wanted to talk to him.

"Um, I meant that I . . ." he cleared his throat, "Well, I need to talk to you."

"My parents are expecting us at one o'clock. It's eleven-thirty now— you need to get dressed. Let's go."

He opened his mouth to speak.

"Let's go, James."

On the way to his house, James tried to talk to her again. "Brandy, I'm really sorry."

"Save it, James, I really don't want to hear it." She closed her eyes and turned her head away from him. There was nothing he could say to rectify the situation. He had chosen Robert over her. That was the beginning of the end. How many more times would that happen? How many more times would she have to deal with his hot and cold attitude? He was hurting her on purpose. She couldn't figure out why. All she had ever tried to do was love him. The rest of the trip, both to his house and to her parents', was made in silence.

At her parents' house, conversation was tense. There was so much tension in the air that her mother pulled her aside. "Baby, what's wrong?"

"I don't feel like getting into it right now; I'll tell you later."

After dinner James handed Brandy her jacket. "My brother is going to take me home later."

"Brandy, we really need to talk this through."

"At this point, there's nothing to talk about." She saw him to the door. Before he left, he turned and kissed her. She took a step back and glared at him.

Embarrassed, his ego kicked in. "So does this mean we're breaking up?" Brandy looked away from him. "Or better yet, counselor, should we break up?" Sarcasm dripped from his voice.

Never one to back down, she responded, "No, James, I'm not saying that. I just need some time."

James was upset and burned rubber down her parents' street. When he was gone, she felt empty. She didn't want to break up with him, she was just angry.

Eleven

*"You don't know like I do what the Lord has done for me
You know He saved me, He raised me, now I've got the
victory
Look what He's done, look what He's done for me
I'll never, shall never, forget what He's done for me"*

They were seated in the middle of the fifteenth pew in The First Church of God. It was a large church located in what the media called South Los Angeles. Brandy had joined three years ago. Simone was a member, too. While Brandy didn't attend every Sunday, she did attend at least once a month.

"Brandy, that girl can sing!" whispered William to Brandy. He seemed to be enjoying the service. She was glad that he had agreed to visit her church. He was Methodist, but her church was nondenominational and welcomed all.

The last time Brandy sat in the pews of First Church of God, James had been with her. He told her that when they were married, he would join her church, even though he was raised in the Catholic faith. Until that time, he'd attended St. Brigid's on 54th Street and Western Avenue. The church loomed peacefully on Western Avenue, despite its dank surroundings. It was an African-American Catholic church if there ever was one. There was a gospel choir, and a call and response

nteraction between the priest and the parishoners.
Brandy liked James' church because of its lively spirit.
They usually alternated between her church and his.

Returning her attention to William, she asked, "Can
you believe she's only fourteen?"

William's mouth fell open. "Really?"

Brandy nodded affirmatively.

"If she keeps singing like that she's going to give
Aretha a run for her money."

Pastor Reid was preaching the gospel from the book
of Matthew 14:27-29. "All right, Saints, if the Lord says,
'Come,' you better run to Him and ask why later."

"Brandy, the Lord told me to come to church with
you; that's why I'm here today!"

She smiled and took his hand. He had never looked
more handsome than he did that morning in church.
William wore a black/white houndstooth, light wool
jacket, black pants, a white long-sleeved shirt, a black
silk tie with a cream, green and white design on it, and
black slip-on loafers with tassels.

When church was over, they headed to a hotel in
Santa Monica for brunch. Their table was out on the
covered patio and the beach rested just beneath them.
The food was arranged on silver platters and served by
cooks with French, Spanish and Italian accents in tall
chef hats. There were spectacular ice sculptures, numerous floral arrangements and of course a pianist. The
music filtered through the speakers in the ceiling. The
pianist was a small-framed African-American man who
played from memory. William went over to talk to him
and learned that the man played four one-hour sets and
approximately fifty songs. He could sing, but he only
did this by request. William asked him to play "Misty."
He knew Brandy loved that song.

"Oh, William, you're so thoughtful." She was

touched. William had earned a lot of brownie points for that move.

"William, you've got to eat faster than that, the game's coming on at four." Brandy had finished eating ten minutes before and was anxious to see the first game of the basketball play-offs. Chicago was playing New York.

"Oh, yeah."

"I've got to get out of these clothes."

"Can I help?" William asked sheepishly.

Brandy shook her head. "Men."

"It didn't hurt to ask." He raised his hands in mock innocence.

"Look, William, the next man I lay down with will be my husband."

"Why does it have to be with your husband, why can't it be a very good friend?" He was challenging her.

She met his challenge. "It's simple. If I wait until I'm married, then I know that he didn't mind buying the cow."

William started laughing. "I can't believe you think like that. Just because a man has the milk doesn't mean that he won't buy the cow."

"Let you tell it."

"I'm serious." He took her hands in his. "I would never do you like that. I know that we haven't known each other for long, but I sense that you had a bad experience. I hope that you won't let one rotten apple spoil the rest."

"Did I ever tell you that I had a bad experience?" Brandy's tone was defensive. She took her hands out of his.

"No."

"So don't assume things you know nothing about, William." Brandy heard herself and tried to soften up. "Let's go."

"You're right, Brandy, I shouldn't have assumed anything. I'm sorry." William reached for her hands again. His gaze melted her. "It's just that in everything you don't say and every time you pull away from me, I can't help but think or assume the worst." He kissed both of her hands. "Brandy, I want to know about James. What did he do to you?"

"James doesn't matter. Let's go, William."

He stood up and looked down at her. "I will never understand why women continue to love the men who dog them, and never the ones who would give them the world if they just asked." Brandy looked into his eyes. Her two worlds were starting to converge. She knew she wasn't being fair to William, but he would never understand how painful it was to walk away from the love of her life.

They left the hotel and went to Brandy's townhouse so she could change clothes. Then they stopped at the market and picked up a couple of snacks to eat during the game.

While she was preparing their mini-buffet, she heard, *"Brandy, Brandy!* Girl, what are you doing?"

"I'm waiting for the popcorn to pop."

"Popcorn? We're not about to watch a movie, we're about to watch Ewing kick Jordan's ass."

"I can eat popcorn and watch Jordan whip your old sorry team."

"Brandy!"

"What?"

"Jordan's at the free throw line."

"Why didn't you say that? Hell, this popcorn can wait."

Brandy raced out of the kitchen. She had to admit that William was a very good housekeeper. Unlike some guys she'd dated, William washed the dishes while he was cooking. She'd thought only she did that.

Brandy entered the second bedroom, which William

had converted into a recreation room/entertainment center/office and sat down beside him on the couch. In her left hand she carried a bowl of strawberries and in her right hand, a glass of Korbel Brut.

"I thought you were making popcorn."

"It's still in the microwave, I'll get it after he shoots."

"Ooh good, he missed." William was hovering in front of the TV like it was going to get up and walk away.

"William, was your daddy a glass maker?"

"A glass maker? Hell, no. I told you he worked for the post office."

"Well, since your daddy was not a glass maker, I cannot see through you, so move out of the way." Brandy was teasing but serious because Jordan was about to shoot. "Jordan's gonna make the next free throw."

"No, he's not, New York is about to win and beat Chicago out of the finals. I bet . . ."

Brandy jumped to her feet, nearly dropping the bowl of strawberries. "He made it, I told you he would! Jordan can't be faded, unlike your Lakers. That's why they're out and New York's in. Now what were you saying about a bet?"

"Faded?"

"Yeah, faded."

"I didn't know lawyers spoke so colorfully," William teased.

"Well, I do my share in the community. I learn a lot from those kids."

"I bet Chicago doesn't make it to the finals," William said stubbornly.

"They've made it the last two years in a row. They better make it. Well, here's the deal— if they make it to the finals, you'll take me to one of the games."

William accepted the challenge. "And if they don't,

which they won't, you have to take me to watch New York play in the finals."

"In Chicago?"

"Yes. Do we have a bet?"

"Yes, we've got a bet. I haven't been to Chi-Town in a long time. I hear springtime is beautiful. I hope you have a camera." She smiled. "William, come here."

"What?"

"Not *what*— come here." He came, sat and started flipping the channels. New York had called a time-out.

"Here, open your mouth." William opened without looking and then asked, "What is this?"

"It's a strawberry." Just as he was about to bite the strawberry, Brandy put the strawberry in her mouth.

"You missed."

"Do it again." She did it again.

"You missed again."

"Okay, okay, I wasn't paying attention."

"That's no excuse, you're just slow."

"I could take that strawberry if I wanted to, but the game's back on."

"And?"

"And, I can't watch the game and play catch-the-berry with you at the same time."

"Sure you can, William. You're an intelligent man. I know you can walk and chew gum at the same time."

"Brandy, I can't hear what Magic just said. Look, there are only 43 seconds left in the game. I promise I'll talk to you when the game is over."

While he was talking, Brandy grabbed the remote control and slightly lowered the volume on the TV and increased the volume on the CD player. Then she leaned over and gave him a seductive peck on the lips.

"What are you doing?"

Brandy reached out and caressed his cheek. "I'm just looking at you."

"You're looking at me with your lips?"

"Uh-huh."

"Brandy pul-*lease,* there are only 27 seconds left and the Bulls are down."

"I thought you didn't like the Bulls."

"I never said that I didn't like the Bulls— I just don't like Michael Jordan."

"What's the difference? If you like the Bulls, you like Jordan, and if you hate Jordan, then you hate the Bulls."

"No, it's not the same. Jordan gets too much pub and there are other brothers out there who are better than him."

"That still doesn't answer my question."

"Always the lawyer. Does your brain ever quit?"

"Yes. Would you like to see?" Brandy got up and sat in William's lap. She started at his forehead and lightly ran her finger down his nose and outlined his perfect lips. Without stopping, she traveled to his chin and over his Adam's apple. When she reached the top of his chest, she slid her hand into his shirt and unbuttoned the top two buttons. Brandy leaned forward and gently kissed each eyelid closed. She was using her fingers and her lips to perfection.

As if on cue, William turned the TV off. The remote dropped to the floor and he returned her kiss. The hand that once held the remote found its way to the small of her back, while the other hand slid beneath her knees and lifted her off of him and onto the couch. Having laid her down, William closed his eyes. In the brief seconds his eyes were closed, William marveled at how happy she made him. Four months ago, they were perfect strangers, and tonight she would be his love. When he opened his eyes, Brandy was staring at him.

She reached out to him, circling his neck with her

arms. He moved at the same time, positioning himself on top of her while kissing her deeply. His tongue explored the hot depths of her mouth. Her breathing became heavy. She eased his shirt off so she could be closer to him. His skin was moist. Tiny beads of sweat had gathered on his brow and she could faintly hear a moan. Whose was it? Brandy couldn't tell.

William took her into his bedroom and laid her down on the bed. "Are you sure, Brandy?"

Not thinking, she responded, "Yes, I'm sure."

He searched her face one last time. "I'm not your husband."

"I know, you're my very good friend."

She unbuttoned his pants and slid them over his hips. He in turn took off her jeans and panties while she pulled her shirt over her head. He unhooked her bra and suckled each breast gently. Then he took his kisses downward and stopped at her navel. She ran her fingers through his hair and then pulled him forward, but before she could kiss him, he slid down and pushed her legs apart. He kissed the inside of each of her thighs and she was pleasantly surprised. He looked up at her and said, "We have all night."

She could barely contain herself. She wanted him to stop teasing her. He made his way forward into the center of her being and lingered there for a minute. She wanted to see his eyes, but could see only the top of his head. She laid her head back on the pillow and closed her eyes. A low moan escaped from her lips. When she opened her eyes, she didn't see William, she saw James. She froze. "Oh my God."

Thinking she was responding to being caressed, William didn't answer.

"William, get up. I can't go through with this. I'm sorry." Brandy was in a panic. *What was she doing?* She thought she could make love to William, but it didn't feel right. He wasn't James.

William was confused. "Brandy, are you all right?" She looked like she had seen a ghost.

She was up and looking for her clothes. "I— I'm fine. I made a mistake, William. I'm really sorry."

Moments passed, but it felt like a lifetime. Brandy was gone, William realized. What had he done wrong?

It was nine-thirty and she still wasn't home. James was pressing the buzzer in front of Brandy's complex. Her machine came on again. He'd stopped by earlier but she wasn't home. This time he left a message. "Brandy, this is James, I was in the neighborhood and decided to stop by. I really need to talk to you. Please call me. You have the number."

Brandy had a new man in her life and James was mad about it. He loved Brandy and if she would only talk to him, he would prove it to her. Before going home, James walked down to the beach. Though he hated the sand, he didn't mind watching the water. He and Brandy used to take walks along the ocean's edge. That was back before she'd moved closer to the beach and going was a treat for her. God, how he missed those days.

Taking her hand and rubbing her ring finger, James said, "Brandy, when we get married, it'll be easy for you to get used to writing Collins instead of Curtis, since our last names begin with the same letter." It was early on Sunday morning and they were lying next to each other in bed.

"Who told you I was going to change my name?" Brandy asked teasingly.

"Well, you don't have to. I just thought that it would be nice for my wife to have my name." James took the bait.

"I was thinking about hyphenating— Brandy Curtis-Collins. How does that sound?"

"It sounds okay, but Brandy Collins sounds better." Brandy didn't respond. "Sleepy-head, did you hear me?"

"I heard you." Brandy yawned. Her voice was heavy from the love they had made the night before.

James sat up in bed, causing the sheet to fall away and expose a cocoa-brown chest with slightly protruding nipples. He was glad Brandy enjoyed his body and appreciated his long limbs, broad shoulders, small waist and no facial hair. "Brandy, why can't you take my name?"

"James, don't get an attitude."

"I don't have an attitude, I just don't understand why you don't want my name."

"It's not that I don't want your name, but I don't see the point of getting into an in-depth conversation about me taking your name or keeping my own when we aren't even engaged."

"Brandy, I've told you a million times that we're going to get married."

"I'll believe it when I get my ring."

James got out of bed and went into the bathroom. He was inexplicably agitated with her. He stepped into the shower.

"Are you finished in the bathroom? I need to take a shower." Her voice was flat.

"Brandy, let's not start the day off like this." James walked over to her and took her in his arms.

"You're getting me wet."

"I love you, Brandy, even though you won't take my

name." Brandy attempted to return James' squeeze, but her effort was half-hearted. "I love you, too, James."

While Brandy was in the shower, James was in the kitchen cooking breakfast. He didn't know how to cook but Brandy loved that he tried. He knew his silences were coming between them, but how could he tell her how he felt?

When James entered the bedroom, Brandy was zipping her bag.

"Brandy, I made your favorite— burnt sausage, lumpy grits and pancakes . . . They don't really look like pancakes, but trust me, that's what they are."

Finally noticing that she was fully dressed and her bag was packed, James patted Brandy's bag. "You're not about to do laundry, are you?"

"No."

"Then what do you have in the bag?" James attempted to open it. Brandy put her hand protectively over the zipper.

"James, do you remember two weeks ago when you asked me if I wanted to break up and I told you that I needed time?"

"Yes, but what does that have to do with breakfast?" James couldn't believe his ears. "Brandy, please say that you're not about to say what I think you're going to say." He put his hand on her shoulder. She shrugged it off.

"Well, I've thought about it and I'm leaving."

"What are you leaving for?"

"We've been pulling apart and I don't know why." Her voice had started to crack. Brandy picked up her bag and tried to walk past James, who blocked the door.

"I'm not letting you leave. You're angry and I'm sorry."

"James, you don't even know what you're apologizing for, do you?"

"Brandy, please, tell me what I've done."

"How many times do I have to tell you? Look, I'll make it simple for you. We are looking at two different pictures. Mine says 'Marriage or Nothing,' yours says 'Freedom or Death.' You're afraid of commitment."

"How could I be afraid of commitment when an hour ago I told you I wanted to marry you?"

"That's just it. You *told* me you wanted to marry me. You've been saying that since we met! It's been two years already and you still haven't *asked* me to marry you. I was beginning to think something was wrong with me. Now, I see it's you. You're terrified of commitment. The funny thing is, you didn't used to be."

James tried to hug her, but she pulled back. "James, please move."

Reluctantly he moved out of the way. He knew it was pointless to try to stop her. He had done it. He had finally lost her. There was nothing he could do but watch her leave.

James fingered the ring in his pocket and then held it up to the moonlight. The princess cut refracted the white streetlight and split in a thousand different directions across the sand.

He hoped Brandy would like it.

Twelve

"Ha-choo! Ha-choo!" Brandy had caught a terrible flu virus and couldn't seem to shake it. Simone had come over to Brandy's early that morning to take care of her.

"Simone, I need to get over this flu. I've got a mandatory settlement conference coming up on the Hamilton case and I can't afford to be sick for one more minute." Brandy's attempt at mind over matter sent her into a coughing attack.

Simone watched as Brandy's frame jerked in uncontrollable spasms.

"A settlement conference? Forget about that— if you don't get better, Brandy, you're going to end up with pneumonia." Simone was furious. "Brandy, when are you going to put yourself first? You want to know what's wrong with you, it's that sweat shop you work for!"

"Simone, please don't fuss at me. My head is pounding and I can't see straight. Could you get me some water?"

Simone took the empty glass off Brandy's nightstand and headed off toward the kitchen. Brandy closed her eyes and tried to sleep. The ringing telephone startled her. When Simone didn't pick it up, she answered it.

Her voice was weak. "Hello?"

"Brandy."

"Yes?"

"It's James."

"Who? Hold on." Brandy sneezed.

"James."

"Oh, I'm sorry. I didn't recognize your voice."

"Has it been that long, Brandy?" James was hurt.

"No, it's just that I'm sick as a dog and my ears feel like someone stuck cotton in them."

"You do sound a little under the weather. Do you need anything?" She actually sounded terrible, but he didn't want to offend her.

"No, but thanks for the offer."

"Brandy, did you get any of my messages?"

"James, I can't talk about that right now."

"I know you're sick, and I know this is a bad time, but I really want to see you."

Brandy was silent. She was not in the mood. "James, I really don't want to sound mean, but I don't have anything to say to you." Simone came back into the room.

"Who is that?"

Brandy mouthed, "James."

"I deserve that. But I have something to say to you. It won't take very long."

Brandy sighed heavily. "Hold on." She put the phone down and told Simone what he'd said. Simone made a face and walked out of the room.

"Okay, James. I can't see you any time soon. I'll call you."

"Do you have my number?"

"No." Brandy tried to move, but she felt dizzy. "Why don't you call me next week?"

"Okay, I'll call you. Thank you, Brandy. I promise not to waste your time."

"Good-bye, James."

Simone walked back into the room. "What did he want?"

"He said he had something to tell me."

"Did he say what?"

"No, and it doesn't matter."

"What if he asks you to marry him?"

Brandy looked at her sister/friend cockeyed. "Simone, have you been nipping my cough syrup?"

"I'm serious. At this point he has nothing to lose and everything to gain by asking you."

Brandy thought about that. "I thought you liked William."

"I do like William. He's a really nice guy."

"He makes me happy."

"Really?" Simone asked. "I've seen the look that crosses your face whenever James' name comes up. And I can't help but wonder if you're truly over him."

"But I'm seeing William." Brandy's voice was soft but sincere.

"I know that, too. But what about James— do you still love him?"

Brandy was silent. "I don't know. Do I?"

"Only you know the answer to that question, Brandy."

Brandy rolled over and closed her eyes. A silent tear slid down her cheek. She was confused.

Exactly one week later, James called. Brandy wouldn't let James pick her up, so they agreed to meet for dinner. It was the first time he had seen her since bumping into her at the basketball game. He was still hurt that she had pulled away from his embrace, and he was still jealous about her walking away with William and not him. But most importantly, James was anxious about their meeting. The last time he'd tried to reconcile with her, the result was a disaster.

It was the middle of May and already warm. The little Thai restaurant Brandy chose was a dimly lit place that was crowded but not noisy.

"James, I'm still sick, and after dinner I'm going

straight home." She shot him a look and added,
"Alone."

"No problem." James reached out and felt her forehead and then caressed her cheek. She didn't move.
"I'm sorry. I shouldn't have done that."

She still didn't move. She just stared at him. His eyes
were so beautiful.

"Brandy, what are you thinking? I can't read you."

"It doesn't matter. What do you want, James?"

"I miss you." He hadn't realized how much he loved
her until that moment.

"Let's not confuse the issue." She was trying to be
businesslike. "I'm seeing someone . . ."

James interrupted her. "Do you love him?"

"Yes," she lied.

"Do you still love me?"

"No." She didn't blink.

"I don't believe you." *She has to be lying!* James
thought. He would die if she didn't love him.

"Well, you don't have to believe me." Brandy was
starting to regret meeting with him.

"Brandy, I'm sure that you do have feelings for him,
but your eyes tell me that you love me."

He was right, but she didn't want to admit it. "Ja— "

"Look, I know you, Brandy. You might have lost a
little weight, but other than that, your air is the same.
I love you, Brandy, and I want you to take me back."
James' voice rose a little and the people around them
turned and stared at them.

"James, please." Tears started gathering in her eyes.
She needed to compose herself. "I've got to go to the
bathroom." She stood up. James stood, too.

"Brandy, please don't leave."

"I'm just going to the bathroom." She was trapped.
There was no way she could leave now.

Brandy went to the bathroom and started crying. How

could he do this to her? Why now? She hated him. When she returned to her seat, James was paying the bill.

"Brandy, we need to go somewhere and talk."

"Okay, I guess we do need to clear the air." Brandy felt better. At least now she would be able to release her pent-up anger. She agreed to let him come to her house because she knew that if they went to his house, she might lose her resolve.

He followed her back to her townhouse. Once inside, she offered him a drink. He declined and she poured herself a glass of wine.

"James, since I want to get this over with as quickly as possible, I'll go first." She didn't miss a beat. "You don't love me. You don't know how to love me, or anyone else, for that matter, but yourself."

"I do love you."

"Let me finish. After all that we had been through, I can't believe that you treated me like that." Anger rose in Brandy's voice. She took a deep breath. "Even though I hated the way you were treating me, I still wanted to be part of your life. You don't how much I cared about you."

"I'm sorry, Brandy." James' voice was barely above a whisper. "I didn't realize I was doing that to you."

"How could you not realize it, James? I only told you over and over. Do you remember that night I called you and tried to talk to you? You listened for about five minutes and then you told me that you loved me, but you needed more time. What that translated into was that you weren't ready for a commitment with me."

"No, Brandy, that's not true. You're the only woman I've ever wanted to be with. I knew it then, I just— I guess I got scared. Forever is a long time. I wanted to be sure. I'm sure now." James took both of her hands in his. His voice was even and clear.

"You've said all this before." Brandy shook her head in disbelief. Removing her hands from his, she continued, "I can't believe we're having this conversation again."

"I'll do anything you want me to do. I know that sorry doesn't mean much right about now, but I never meant to hurt you." There was desperation in his voice and tears in his eyes.

"Leaving you was the hardest thing I've ever done in my life." Brandy stood up and walked over to the window. With her back to him, she finished speaking. "It was like losing part of me. But I had to do it. I had to think of me."

"You were right to think of yourself. I just got so afraid and my boys were talking about me and I don't know what happened."

"Your boys." She laughed a disgusted laugh. "You sold me out to save face in front of your boys!"

"No, that's not what I meant."

"You sounded real clear to me."

"No, that didn't come out right. I was wrong for listening to them. They are stupid and I won't be friends with them anymore if that's what you want."

"James, putting your friends down for me is not going to change the fact that you hurt me."

"I'm *sorry!*" He was begging. "Brandy, you're right. It wasn't their fault, it was mine. I got scared but I thought about you all the time. You've got to believe me when I tell you that I lost so much more, Brandy."

Brandy's neck snapped and her eyes narrowed. "What could you have possibly lost, James?"

"I lost my best friend."

Brandy froze. She hadn't expected him to say that. She was all prepared to continue ripping him to shreds, but he'd sucker-punched her. He'd touched her in a place that William could never reach.

"Best friend!" She let out a long sigh. "I can't believe you went there."

James got up and moved behind her. He hugged her from behind and buried his face in her hair. "Brandy, Brandy, look at me." She was afraid that her eyes would give her away, but she turned around and faced him anyway.

"Will you marry me?"

"What?" Her mouth fell open.

"I want my best friend back. I miss you." James led her back to the couch and got down on both knees in front of her. He took both of her hands in his left hand. With his right hand, he produced a diamond engagement ring. "Brandy, I've been carrying this ring around with me for the last two months." He slid the ring onto her finger. "I love you, Brandy Curtis, and I want you to be my wife. Will you marry me?" There was so much love in his eyes, Brandy couldn't hold back her tears.

Instinctively, she reached out to him. James held her tightly. He knew that if he let go, he would lose her forever. As he felt her body convulse from the tears, he rocked her gently and stroked her hair. "Oh Brandy, I love you so much." Brandy, the impenetrable fortress of pride, determination and strength had transformed into a beautiful, gentle flower right before his eyes. She had touched his soul. He would never be the same— nor she.

They separated and Brandy looked at him. "No, James, I can't marry you."

"What do you mean you *can't?*" James was truly confused.

"Okay, then, I *won't* marry you."

He had made up his mind before meeting her for dinner that he was not leaving until she said "Yes". "I'm not taking no for an answer."

"James!"

"Brandy, you love me, don't you?" He would beg if he had to.

"I— I don't know how I feel. I've got to think." She took the ring off and gave it to him. It seemed that she had waited a lifetime for James to give her an engagement ring, and that day had finally come. She'd imagined that sirens would go off and the world would smile on the day James proposed to her. And here she was, a ring on her finger, sirens going off somewhere in the background, and she was as confused as ever. "Here, take it."

"No, keep it. It's yours. Take as long as you need, just please say yes." He put the ring back on her finger.

He stood up and walked to the door. He stopped to look at her— she was staring at the ring on her finger. James closed the door behind him.

Brandy was exhausted. She wanted to go to sleep and wake up all over again. She leaned back on the couch and closed her eyes. Her thoughts were going a mile a minute. Unable to sort them out, she took a bubble bath and then got into bed. She switched her nightlight out and went to sleep.

Thirteen

It was difficult for Brandy to get up the next morning. Aside from the fact that James had drained her, she hadn't slept well the night before. Every time she closed her eyes, she saw William's face. When she did sleep she felt like she had fallen into a dream sequence where all of the action had slowed down. William was the focus of all of the dreams.

In one he was standing in front of a house she had never seen before, ringing the doorbell. He had an armful of purple mums and yellow marigolds. He was excited, waiting for Brandy to open the door. Finally the door opened, but to William's surprise Brandy was not on the other side. Though she couldn't see his face clearly, she knew it was James who'd opened the door. In another dream, she was trying to talk to William, but he wouldn't listen to her. She kept telling him she was sorry for running out on him, but he slammed the door anyway. She woke up crying.

Realizing that sleep was not forthcoming, she got up. She put on a black baseball cap and pulled it low over her eyes, threw on a sweat suit, and headed for the beach. She knew it was dangerous to walk on the beach alone, but she needed to clear her head. Not paying attention to where she was going, she ended up at the end of the mini-pier just south of her townhouse. She sat down on a concrete bench not thinking about anything in particular, and watching sailboats and eager surfers wade through the early morning surf. When she could no longer see the multicolored body suits, she focused her attention on the sea gulls, wishing life could be as easy as an early morning flight across clear blue water and white sand.

"God, I don't even know the words to express the way I feel. I remember Pastor Reid said that it was okay if we couldn't articulate our prayers. He said that You understood the words hidden in our moans and groans and accepted them as prayers." She crossed her legs. "This morning, I can't even speak, let alone moan or groan. The only thing I can do is sit and stare silently at the water—I hope You hear me."

Fourteen

"Good morning, Bran." He was smiling from ear to ear.

"I'm not in the mood, Brad." Brandy pushed past Brad and went into her office, asking Shirley and Nancy to take a message if she received any calls. She told them she was very busy and didn't want to be disturbed. The reason she wanted them to hold her calls was to avoid any calls from William or James. Slamming the office door behind her, she pulled her files out of her briefcase and went to work.

There was a light rap at the door before it opened.

"Brandy, is everything all right?" Lloyd asked, wearing what Brandy considered his fake mask of concern.

"Yes, Lloyd, I'm fine. I didn't hear you knock."

"I won't take up too much of your time, but I wanted to personally give you your evaluation. If you have any questions, my door is always open." He was trying his best to sound casual.

Brandy thought that it was odd of him to hand-deliver her evaluation, since the associates normally received a written evaluation through inter-office mail. "Thanks, Lloyd, that was nice of you to go out of your way for me."

"No problem at all. By the way, how's it going on the Hamilton settlement? You know we go to court on this on Friday."

Brandy responded, "I know the hearing is Friday—everything is under control."

Lloyd smiled at her. "That's my girl."

Brandy returned his fake smile and dropped her head back to the papers on her desk. Never one to miss a beat, Lloyd realized that he had been politely dismissed and left her office without further comment.

In the hustle and bustle of the last few weeks, she had forgotten that evaluations were coming out. They were evaluated twice a year. She expected high praise and to be ranked in the top tier of associates by the firm, as she had in previous years. Though she wasn't the happy attorney she once had been, her work had not suffered as a result of this. Instead she received lukewarm praise and an admonishment about her attitude. Lloyd even included a handwritten note which read:

May 10, 1995

Brandy,

Your performance of late has unfortunately been less than outstanding. While your actual work continues to be excellent, your work ethic has gone from exceptional to dispassionate. It appears that you are no longer interested in being a team player, and that attitude goes counter to the firm's objectives. We are confident that you will improve your behavior and your attitude and become the star player that you once were.

If you have any questions, please see me.

Lloyd

That was it. She couldn't believe her eyes. After billing crazy hours for the last four years, after sacrificing her social life, her health, her dreams and in many ways her identity, she had been kicked in the teeth.

She sat back and tried to think of what she had possibly done to receive such poor marks. Brandy worked harder and longer hours than anyone else in the firm. In the litigation department, she had expertly maneuvered more settlements than Brad or the others. When she did appear in court, her win loss ratio was 15-1. Those were great stats by even laymen's calculations! Everyone, including Lloyd, was confident that she was going to win the Hamilton case, one of the largest money cases the firm was handling. Those were things to be praised for, not cause for denigration. She racked her brain, but could only come up with good things that hadn't been mentioned.

Her educational and professional life had consisted of doing everything she was supposed to do. She went to the right schools, she wore the right clothes, her hair was cut in a professional manner, she spoke the correct lingo, she got to work early, and she left late. With the exception of the last few months, Brandy had attended every function and maintained a spot in the top tier of the firm. They'd said that she was a star on the horizon. Today, however, she was somewhere in the middle of the second tier. No longer a star, and not even in the race. For the first time in her life, she was face to face with the glass ceiling.

In a blind rage, Brandy went looking for Lloyd. She made a bee-line for his office and nearly trampled over the mail boy. When she got there, his secretary told her that he was out and would not be returning for the rest of the day. Not believing her, Brandy headed for his office. Sara, his secretary, blocked her way.

"Ms. Curtis, I already told you that Mr. Lloyd is gone for the day!"

Brandy had to think quickly. She didn't know whether or not to believe Sara. She slowed down and tried a different approach. "You're right, Sara, now that you mention it, he did tell me that he was leaving." Brandy flashed a jovial smile. "It's actually a good thing he's not here."

Sensing that Brandy was not going to run over her, Sara relaxed a little.

"I need to ask you to do me a really big favor." Brandy needed an excuse to get into Lloyd's office.

Still on guard, Sara asked, "I'll try to help you if I can."

"Last Thursday, I gave Lloyd the original pictures of the plaintiff's yacht in the Henderson case. I realized this morning that I was supposed to give him the copies. I need the originals for the deposition this afternoon." Brandy smiled sweetly. She hoped she sounded convincing. "Lloyd told me that I would find the pictures on the credenza in his office."

Sara scratched her head. Lloyd had not mentioned any pictures to her, but that wasn't unusual. Sara reached for the writing pad on her desk. "What's the name of the case?"

"Ah . . . Henderson." Brandy began talking rapidly. "Since I know what they look like, I'll just run in and get them. It'll only take a minute." She moved towards the door. Just as Sara was about to object, her telephone rang. Brandy patted Sara on her shoulder and walked into Lloyd's office.

Sara was right, Lloyd was gone. Knowing that Sara would enter Lloyd's office any minute, Brandy quickly scanned his marble desk. The silver box where he put his outgoing correspondence was stacked high, while the silver in-box was empty. She wished her desk was so neat. Nothing appeared to be out of place. As she turned to leave, she saw a crumpled piece of paper on the floor. It was a memo that was intended for the trash, but hadn't quite made it to its destination.

Brandy retrieved the paper to toss it when she saw her name. It was a note from Stan Cohen. It said, "Office not ready for black partner— evaluation should be less than great." She felt like the wind had been knocked out of her. Aware of Sara's footsteps outside the door, Brandy folded the note and stuffed it in her pocket.

"Thanks for allowing me into Lloyd's office." She attempted to breeze past Sara, but Sara stopped her.

Noticing that Brandy was empty-handed, Sara asked, "Ms. Curtis, where are the pictures?"

"Oh, they weren't on the credenza. Perhaps they're in his desk drawer." Brandy hoped Sara didn't see her hands shaking.

"Would you like me to check his desk drawers?"

"No, that won't be necessary, I'll just use the pictures that I have. Thanks for everything."

"No problem. If I see them, Ms. Curtis, I'll buzz you." Sara's demeanor was pleasant.

"Thank you, that's very kind of you." Brandy flashed another fake smile and walked slowly toward her office. She couldn't believe the contents of the note she held in her pocket. She needed to talk to David— he'd been right all along.

Just before she reached her office, she passed Nancy and Brad laughing in the hallway. When they saw her, they stopped. It was the second instance of Brad and Nancy being together. All of her sensors went off. *Are they in cahoots together against me?*

Brandy was mad and frustrated. She didn't know whether to laugh or cry. Unable to find humor in that dismal hour, she cried bitter tears.

Fifteen

When Brandy got home from work, she went to her bedroom and laid down. She had a migraine that even Excedrin couldn't help. She stared at the ceiling for half an hour and then fell into a deep sleep. About two hours later she woke up and checked her machine. No one had called.

She looked at her overflowing briefcase and thought about burning it. It was too heavy for her to pick up, so she dragged it into the living room. She pulled the pleadings on the Hamilton case out and spread them on the floor. Before sitting down to arrange the pile, she went over to the fireplace and turned on the gas. Next she pulled the gold metal drawstrings, opened the black screen, and removed the andirons. She took a matchstick out of the box and held it near the pilot. The fire caught quickly, warming her face. She walked back to the pile of papers and got down on her knees. She had picked up the first pleading and was starting to twist the papers into a wad when the phone rang. Her first thought was to ignore it, but by the third ring her trance was broken.

"Hello?" Her voice was heavy.

"Brandy, it's Simone. What's wrong with you?"

"Nothing."

"You're lying. This is Simone you're talking to, remember. What's wrong?"

Brandy felt tears brimming in her eyes. "Oh Simone, today-was-the-worst-day-of-my-life." Finally able to release her pent-up frustration, Brandy was running her words together.

"Brandy, calm down, I can't understand you."

She breathed deeply. "I got a bad evaluation at work, and James asked me to marry him." She started crying harder.

"Don't move! I'm on my way!" Simone didn't wait for a response and Brandy heard a loud click.

While she waited for Simone, she sat perfectly still and watched the flames. She thought about all of the hard work she had put into building her career. With the stroke of a pen, it had been taken away. David had told her about Sally Beers, who left the firm before she joined. Sally, like Brandy, worked in the litigation department. She was ranked in the first tier for five years in a row. At the end of her fifth year, she was taken to lunch by Richard Lloyd and Stan Cohen. Sally was elated, sure that they were taking her to a celebratory lunch. Instead, they'd told her that she was being transferred to another department. Once the transfer was settled, she would lose her seniority and her partnership eligibility. Crushed, she quit Lloyd & Lloyd rather than being reduced to perpetual associate attorney status. Brandy asked David if that had happened to any men. He'd silently shaken his head. *The glass ceiling,* Brandy murmured, *seemed to affect only women.*

After Brandy buzzed her in, Simone ran down the hall and stopped abruptly in front of her door. It was open and she could see Brandy sitting crossed-legged in front of the fireplace, tears streaming down her face. Simone went inside and closed the door. There were papers all over the floor and a roaring fire in the fireplace.

She sat down next to Brandy on the floor. She put

her arm around her sister and wiped her eyes with her hand. Simone decided to let her cry a little while longer before handing her a tissue. "Brandy, you didn't burn any documents, did you?"

Brandy blew her nose, "No, but I would've if you hadn't called." Simone breathed a sigh of relief. She didn't know what was wrong but she didn't want Brandy to get into more trouble at work.

"I couldn't really understand what you were saying over the telephone. You said something about your job evaluation, and James is going to marry somebody?" Simone was racking her brain to remember.

"I'll start with the evaluation I got from the partners today. It's so arbitrary, Simone. It doesn't even make sense."

"Where is it?" Simone already knew what it would look like. The same thing had happened to her husband. Phil had been in line for promotion on three separate occasions, and Phil had been passed up each and every time by a young white male with less experience. The first time, Phil hadn't thought too much of it. He just dug in and worked harder. By the third rejection, he'd become very disillusioned with his job. It was clear to him that an African-American man in upper management would never move beyond that point, let alone make general manager. His supervisor had offered him a special promotion, but that was code for "work on the ethnic issues." It was as though he was only qualified to excel in the colored areas and not in the mainstream.

Brandy found the evaluation and gave it to her. "I can't believe them. I gave them the best four years of my life! You know what, I *hate them!*" She was getting mad all over again. "David tried to tell me that this would happen. There has never been an African-American partner in the firm's history. In fact, I found a note that said the firm wasn't ready for a black partner, *and* that I was to be ranked lower than normal. Can you believe that? I was naive enough to believe that I would be the first."

"Who's David?"

"He works with me. David's the only person I can trust at work, outside of Shirley."

"Is he an associate?"

"No, he's a partner."

"Did he write your evaluation?"

"No. We work in different departments. David's a tax attorney; Lloyd is my supervising attorney."

"Oh." Skimming the evaluation, Simone asked, "What are you going to do?"

"I don't know." She dabbed her eyes. "I realized something today."

"What's that?"

"Now I know why disgruntled employees kill their employers."

Simone laughed. "Girl, you are so crazy. What are you really going to do?"

Brandy didn't answer right away. The mandatory settlement conference was Friday and she had other matters that were close to being resolved. She had money saved but not enough to start her own practice, unless she started it right there in her living room.

Reading her thoughts, Simone said, "My coworkers really appreciated your help during the strike. They thought you were great, Brandy."

Brandy turned around and looked at her. Simone was wearing a mischievous grin on her face. "And I know a talented attorney such as yourself would have no problem generating a clientele."

Brandy considered Simone's insinuation. For about two seconds, it sounded like the master plan. Then reality set in. She didn't know if she was ready to take on the responsiblity of running her own firm. Maybe she would leave the legal profession altogether and do something else.

"Brandy, don't knock the suggestion," Simone said to Brandy's silence. "They're openly looking for reasons to keep you from making partner." She was starting to get mad, too.

Brandy had finally calmed down. "I know, and the worst part is that they're getting a jump on discrediting me."

"Huh?"

"Normally, the glass ceiling doesn't surface until the fifth year. I've only been working there for four."

"Oh, I see." Simone sympathized with Brandy. She didn't know what to tell her other than to quit. "Why do you think they're trying to deny the partnership to you?"

"I think they're worried that women will disturb the order of the old boy network." Brandy threw her hands up. "I don't know."

Simone couldn't believe how threatened they were by women. "You said that today was the worst day of your life. What else is going on?"

Brandy stood up. "I'll be right back." She went into her room and got the ring James had given her the day before. "You were right, he asked me to marry him." Her tone was matter-of-fact.

Simone gasped when she saw the ring. If the size of the diamond was proportional to his love for her, James definitely, unequivocally loved Brandy. "It's beautiful." She handed it back to her. "Put it on."

Brandy slid the ring onto her finger the way James had. Simone stood up next to her. "What did you say to him, Brandy?"

"I told him no." Brandy felt her migraine returning. "I didn't know what else to say."

"Excuse me, but the love of your life asked you to marry him and you said *no?*" Simone gave her the one-eyed-are-you-crazy look. "What was wrong with saying yes?"

"Simone, I can't up and marry James just because he's suddenly ready for a commitment." She paced the room.

Simone was silent. She thought Brandy had been on the rebound from day one. "Did you use William?"

"What?" Brandy was shocked. "I was not using William, and I resent you even suggesting that!"

"Maybe subconsciously you were trying to get back at James and that's why you jumped so quickly with William."

"No, that's not true." She was adamant.

"Brandy, when you and James broke up, you were hurt and upset. You wouldn't go out, you started to work harder than usual. A couple of weeks went by, you met William, and then *bam!* You were sprung all over again."

Brandy went and sat down on the couch. "You don't operate like that. You take your time about everything, even small decisions like picking out dishes. I'm not trying to make you feel bad, hon, but I don't think William means as much to you as you say he does."

"*No.* Simone, you've got to believe me when I say that I was not intentionally using William. James was the furthest thing from my mind when I met William."

"When does James want an answer?"

"He told me to take my time, just not to tell him no."

"Well, he's right, take your time. May I make a suggestion?"

"Wait, there's something else I didn't tell you."

"What?" Simone was afraid to hear the worst.

"I almost slept with William."

It was Simone's turn to feel a knot in her stomach. She had to clear her throat. "You what?"

"One afternoon we were kissing and things got kind of out of control. Anyway, I couldn't go through with it. I started seeing James' face, and then I just froze." Brandy was embarrassed by the memory. "I can't see William anymore. I like him as a friend, but that's it." Brandy burst into tears. "I know I was using him, but I didn't mean to."

"Why don't you tell him the truth?"

"I can't, Simone, he'd never understand."

"Are you sure he wouldn't understand?" Tired of standing, she joined Brandy on the couch. "Now, may I make my suggestion?"

"Do I have a choice?" Brandy felt a knot growing in her stomach. Simone had an uncanny way of always being right.

"Yes. I'll keep my two cents to myself if you don't want to hear it."

"Speak, Simone." Tension, mingled with the heat of the fireplace, was running high in Brandy's living room.

"Before you make a decision, you need to get clear on how you feel about James. Also keep in mind that if you tell James no, that's it. By the same token if you tell James yes, you've got to tell William the truth."

"I know, I know, but . . ." Brandy took a breath. "He's been so patient with me and I don't think he'd take it well. He'll hate me if I tell him the truth. William will know that I was on the rebound."

Simone was speechless. "I don't know what to say, Brandy." She shook her head in dazed amazement. Brandy was in the worst of all possible situations. She had a serious decision to make.

Turning a tear-streaked face to Simone, Brandy sighed. "Simone, tell me what to do."

Simone found her purse and handed her another Kleenex. "If I could I would, but I can't."

Brandy blew her nose. "I know you can't. Thanks."

"Be sure and take all the time you need."

"I wish I had a lot of time."

Simone winced and patted her on the back. "I'll support you whether you marry James or not." Brandy hugged her. Simone was definitely true blue.

At eight o'clock that night Brandy had repacked her briefcase and headed back to work. She thought she had missed the traffic until she made a right turn onto the short street that led east to the 90 freeway. There were bikers and movie-goers fighting their way into the Marina shopping center to her left. The self-contained complex attracted people from all over the city. In one stop, she could buy groceries or jewelry, get a prescription filled, get money from the ATM, buy soul food, East Indian cuisine, or yogurt, play video games, rent movies, and buy a VCR. If that wasn't enough, she could go across the street to buy clothes, listen to jazz, eat Chinese food and roam through eight movie theatres. Brandy bypassed her local stomping crowds and entered the San Diego freeway heading north. Amazingly, traffic was light and she arrived at her office in fifteen minutes.

Lloyd & Lloyd was a typical firm in that most, if not all, of the lawyers were workaholics. Brandy didn't care who was there as long as Brad wasn't. Blessed twice that night, Brad was nowhere to be found.

As was customary, Nancy had left corrected drafts of the day's documents on her desk. She signed the first letter and flipped through the interrogatories. When she got to the last page where the signature line was, she dropped the pen. No corrections had been made.

"This needs to go out in the first mail!" She reached for the first signed letter and reviewed it closely. "I'll be here all night!"

Brandy had only planned to be there for one hour at the longest. Now she would have to go to the secretarial pool and print out her own documents.

Nancy's desk was the last one on the left. After working with the firm for ten years, her desk came with a view of the ocean. In fact, she and Brandy shared the same panoramic view of the Santa Monica mountains and the Pacific Ocean. Brandy flipped the light switch and fluorescent lights flooded the room.

"Funny," she thought, "they don't seem so bright during the daylight hours."

After turning on Nancy's computer, Brandy whipped out the letter in ten minutes. She was about to shut Nancy's computer off when something told her to look through her directory. After the nightmare with her answer a few months before, she wanted to make doubly sure that all of her documents were in order.

Ordinarily, copies of documents that were mailed out landed in the appropriate file and the copy on the hard drive was saved onto a disk. These disks were stored in the cubicle above the secretary's head. Since the Hamilton mandatory settlement conference was on Friday, Brandy scrolled the screen to that directory. Once inside of that file, she randomly checked her documents. When she reached the interrogatories she planned to take to court with her on Friday, she let out a gasp and felt her heart drop to her stomach. Page after page of responses to depositions, responses to interrogatories, and her correspondence with J.D. were either partly complete or not even begun. Her heart started racing. "This can't be happening to me!" she yelled at the screen.

She worked feverishly on at least fifteen different

documents, and in the blink of an eye three hours had passed. Then Brandy felt a hand on her shoulder, and she nearly fell out of her seat. "David, you scared me to death!"

"I'm sorry, bella, I didn't mean to frighten you." David massaged her neck. She was so tense. "What are you doing down here?"

Brandy's eyes were red and her hair was disheveled from pulling on it.

"I was working on the Hamilton case." The printer was still humming.

"Why aren't you doing that in your office?"

"I was in there earlier until I realized that Nancy was not doing her job." Brandy gestured toward the documents all around her. She stretched forward and cracked her back. When she stood, her legs felt like two blocks of cement. "My legs are killing me."

David pulled out an office chair for her.

"Thanks, but I need to walk around for a minute." When she did sit down, he resumed massaging her neck and shoulders.

"I don't understand, Brandy, I thought Nancy was the best secretary in the firm."

"She is. I mean, she was. Hell, I don't know what I mean." Brandy tried to relax and enjoy David's soft touch. "Something really strange is going on."

"I'm listening."

"In February you told me that there were people who were not too happy about me making partner two years from now."

"I did."

"You also said that the partners were the least of my worries."

"For now, anyway."

"You were right except for one thing."

"What?" He stopped what he was doing and pulled up a chair next to her.

"The foundation has been laid for not promoting me." She had transcended the rage she'd felt earlier and was extremely calm.

Sensing the direction the conversation was taking, David rose. "Let's go somewhere and talk."

"I don't care anymore."

"It's not over yet, bella."

"It's over for me— even Nancy's in on it."

David guided her upstairs to her office. He collected her things and carried her briefcase to the elevator. When they reached the parking structure, David took her hands into his hands, and asked, "Are you hungry?" Sometimes David's gentleness made her feel like a child.

"Not really." David looked deeply into her face and saw the pain written there. He was worried about her. *Poor thing*, he thought, she looked like a time bomb ready to explode.

"Are you sure?"

"Yes, David." Brandy looked at her watch. It was eleven-thirty. "Anyway, there aren't any restaurants open this time of night."

"I know of a place. Follow me."

She followed him to the Beverly Hills Café. It was an unassuming cafe on the south end of a posh street known as Restaurant Row in Beverly Hills. At that time of night it was quiet, allowing them to talk as long as they needed to.

They sat outside beneath an unlit heat lamp. David, who always wore a suit and tie, was dressed very casually that evening. He wore a seagrass madras linen shirt, oatmeal-colored pants and olive Gucci loafers. One look at the menu and repressed hunger pangs overtook Brandy. She ordered steak with sauteed shrimp, brown

rice and a glass of white Zinfandel. David sipped pep-
permint tea.

After the waiter brought Brandy her dinner salad,
she recounted the day's events, beginning with her
evaluation.

"Like I was saying in the office, David, they've already
started blackballing me." Her calm had lasted only the
fifteen minutes to the cafe. She laughed nervously. "Pun
intended."

"Tell me about the evaluation." David sat back and
laced his fingers together.

She told him about the contents of the evaluation,
and about the letter she'd found on Lloyd's floor. "In
a nutshell, he let me know that the powers that be are
very displeased with me. I really didn't deserve that."
Her voice started faltering, "And the letter I found said,
in effect, that I will not become a partner."

"Have you talked to Lloyd?"

"I tried to, but he was gone."

"I'm so sorry, I wish there was something I could do
to change things," David said sympathetically.

"Thanks anyway, but there's nothing you can do. I
still plan on talking to Lloyd, even if I have to ambush
him in the parking lot."

The waiter appeared out of nowhere and took her
plate. She was silent until he left.

"David, the last few months have been hell. I'm unhappy and I don't like it there anymore."

David gripped the table. "Bella, what are you saying?"

"I'm saying that this is the last straw. I can't take it
anymore. If they want their damn firm to remain lily-
white, then that's fine with me! I'm tired of fighting."

"What are you planning to do?"

"I don't know yet."

"Are you going to quit?"

"Well, I have a few options. I can remain at Lloyd & Lloyd and become an alcoholic or have a nervous breakdown. I hear that suicide is up among lawyers."

"You wouldn't!" David said, clutching her hand.

"David, I won't kill myself." Brandy laughed because David look worried. "It's not that serious. Anyway, my last option is to quit."

David was stunned. "If you quit, then you're giving up, Brandy." His fist slammed down on the table. "Stand up for yourself. Fight them. Don't let them do this to you!"

Brandy jumped. She'd never seen David break a sweat, let alone lose his cool. "It's not giving up in the traditional sense of the phrase. Let me see if I can explain this to you." She took a swig from her wineglass. "As an African-American, life in corporate America is very different from, say, your experience. You're white and you're a man. And that makes all the difference in the world."

"What does skin color have to do with anything?" Because he respected Brandy as a woman and colleague, he was surprised that she would use racism/sexism as an explanation for unfair treatment.

"You told me that a person of color has never assumed a partnership in this firm, and that there were others who wanted to keep it that way." Brandy felt comfortable discussing race with David, because he was her mentor.

"Right."

"Why did you tell me that?"

"I like you and I want you to beat them at their own silly game." A good heart and sincerity rang through his words. David was sweet and honest, but he just didn't understand.

She pressed him, "What is the name of the game they're playing?"

He nodded. "Ah-ha, I see now."

"Do you?" She leaned closer.

"I think so."

"What is it called?"

"The skin game." David threw his hands up. "Can it be that simple, bella?"

"Yes." Brandy paused and let David absorb the new truth. Though his face showed no decipherable emotion, she could see the helplessness he felt in his eyes. "The point I'm trying to make is that my skin color precedes everything and anything that I do. While I know that all white people are not racists, there are enough who are to cause people who look like me problems." The waiter refilled Brandy's glass. "You say that I should fight and that I should stand up for myself."

"Precisely."

"I say that I'm tired, that I'm twenty-eight years old, and I'm burned out and disillusioned. I say that staying would do myself a disservice and that in the end undescribable pain would be my reward for trying to fight a system that was not designed with me in mind." The wine was numbing her legs and her senses. She had finally started to relax. "And I think Nancy and Brad are playing a part in my demise."

"What does Nancy have to do with this?" He wasn't surprised that she mentioned Brad. Everyone knew he was jealous of her.

"I'm not sure exactly. I doubt the partners are using her or that they're even aware that she has become so remiss lately. They don't need anyone to get to me. All they have to do is continue giving me poor ratings, reduce my case load, and stop sending me to court. I think someone told Nancy to start half-assing her work."

"Who would do such a thing?" He was appalled.

"I don't know. I can't think of anyone in particular

who hates me that much . . ." Before she finished her
sentence, she knew the answer.

"Who, bella? Who is it?" David was on the edge of
his seat.

"I can't say just yet. As soon as I get proof, I'll let
you know." Brandy reached into her purse and grabbed
her wallet. When she attempted to hand David money
to pay for dinner, he waved her money away.

"It's late, David, I should go home."

Sixteen

Los Angeles was experiencing postcard weather and William wasn't going to be able to enjoy it. He had the twenty-four hour flu and couldn't go to work. As he lay hot and miserable in his bed, he thought of Brandy. They hadn't talked since Saturday and though that was only three days ago, it felt like an eternity. He'd left four messages for her and so far none of them had been returned. To quiet the rising hysteria he was feeling, he made a deal with himself. If he didn't hear from her by five o'clock, he was going to go looking for her.

At eleven-thirty the telephone rang. William was disoriented and, instead of answering the phone, he went to the door. After opening it, he realized that the phone was ringing.

He ran to the phone and was out of breath when he said, "Hello?"

"Little Billy, this is Pop. Why are you out of breath, and what took you so long to answer the phone?" Mr. Robinson was on lunch break at work. He'd planned to leave William a message, because he thought William would be at work.

"I thought someone was at the door, so I answered it."

"Why aren't you at work?"

"I've got the flu." William was rubbing sleep out of his eyes.

"That explains why you sound groggy."

"I drank some flu medicine earlier." The empty packet was on the table next to his mug.

"I can't talk long, but have you seen Brandy?" He hadn't seen her for two days and he was worried.

"No, I haven't. She's been very busy the last couple of weeks. I'm sure that I'll hear from her soon."

"Okay, that sounds good." Mr. Robinson paused. He knew Little Billy hated these questions, but he wanted great-grandchildren. "Are you two an item?"

"No, not yet." He didn't bother to tell his grandfather that he really liked Brandy. Or that he'd purchased two plane tickets to Chicago; she'd won the wager during the play-offs. William knew he'd taken a risk when he bought the tickets, because he hadn't heard from her in a while. Ever since Brandy had run out on him, he had had difficulty concentrating. He really liked her and still hoped their friendship would develop into something more.

"Really? I'm glad to see that you've come to your senses!"

"I hate to say it, but you were right. Brandy is all of the things you said she was and more. I mean, she's intelligent, beautiful, thoughtful, sensitive— I could go on and on." William could hear his grandfather's rich baritone laugh on the line. "I like her a lot."

"I'll call you later. Grandma's here and we're going to eat. Keep me posted."

"Tell her I said 'Hello'." William hung up the phone. Now fully awake, he flipped through *Ebony Man* in search of the perfect place to take Brandy. While he wasn't the richest man in the world, money would be no object for this special occasion. He was determined to make Brandy fall in love with him. He wouldn't cheapen the moment by taking her to a hole in the wall. After exhausting that magazine, he grabbed *Los Angeles Magazine* and turned to the restaurant section.

He meticulously scoured the list for thirty minutes and came up with three places. The first restaurant served Moroccan food. It was on Sunset Boulevard and served five-course meals. William had eaten there once several years before. The outside of the restaurant was white-washed and accented with bright shiny gold doors. The inside was covered with blue and gold Moroccan tile, with brass elephants positioned in different places throughout the restaurant. It was dimly lit with huge, colorful pillows, low couches, a belly dancer and a circular table. Dinner usually lasted several hours because the food was served one course at a time. The magazine used dollar signs to provide a range of prices per restaurant, and Dar Magreb had three dollar signs beside it.

Number two on his list was Georgia's on Melrose, a soul food place with the perfect ambience. It wasn't too dark or too light. The attire was casual and on almost any night, a celebrity might be sitting at the next table. The far wall was painted with a design that was accented by flood lights which reminded him of dancing shadows. Part of the restaurant spilled onto an uncovered patio; heat lamps provided warmth. Georgia's wasn't quite as expensive as Dar Magreb, but it wasn't cheap either.

Finally, his last choice was an Italian restaurant. Virgulio's was very expensive and sat on the southwest corner of La Cienega and Venice. They would definitely have to dress up, but William didn't mind; Brandy would look gorgeous in a potato sack. Atmosphere-wise, the restaurant was very dark. The only light emanated from candles in the center of each table. This provided a strategic edge for William— he imagined them leaning across the table staring into each other's eyes.

* * *

Brandy had lunch in her office. She was hungry, but she didn't want to bump into Mr. Robinson downstairs in the lobby, and she didn't feel like socializing with the other attorneys in the lunch room. She leaned back in her chair and closed her eyes. *Too bad my door doesn't have a lock,* she thought to herself. If it did she would have curled up on the floor and snoozed. Unfortunately sleep was hard to come by, so she looked around her office. In a couple of days, she was pretty sure that the office would be someone else's. She couldn't wait.

Shirley had also decided to stay inside and have lunch. She hadn't talked to Brandy in a while and wanted to know how things were going with William. She buzzed Brandy from her desk.

"Hey girl, what 'cha doing for lunch?"

"Nothing."

"Mind if I come in and get in your business?"

Brandy laughed. "Sure, why not? I'll try my best not to depress you."

"I've got to go to the refrigerator and grab my lunch. Do you want anything from the kitchen?"

"Would you bring me a packet of mint tea, a cup of hot water and a bag of cookies out of the vending machine? I'll pay you when you get here. Thanks a lot."

"No problem. I'll see you in a few."

While Brandy was clearing off one of the chairs so Shirley could sit down when she arrived with lunch, a piece of metal caught her eye. She knelt down and discovered that the shiny object was an earring. It was a gold clip-on button earring, with four tiny white rhinestones on it. Brandy never wore clip-ons unless she was going somewhere special. And if she never went anywhere special again in her life, she wouldn't wear the one she'd just found. She tossed the earring into her briefcase. "Hmm . . . I wonder who this belongs to."

"Are you talking to me?" Shirley was standing in the doorway.

"No, I was just mumbling to myself." Brandy stepped out of the way. "Have a seat."

"Girl, I feel like I haven't seen you in a month of Sundays."

"I know. It's been a long time since we've had lunch together."

Shirley's lunch consisted of a SlimFast shake, a salad and a Weight-Watchers slice of cheesecake.

"Don't eat too much, Shirley, we wouldn't want you to get fat." Brandy blew her cheeks out.

"Hah, hah, very funny." Shirley looked at her. "Wait 'til you have kids, Ms. Brandy, and you'll be begging for rabbit food."

"Shirley, I can't believe you're blaming your kids for putting weight on you."

"When you have kids, it's very hard to resist eating when they eat. You won't notice the pounds right away, because they grow on you in your sleep. Your clothes gradually start feeling tight, but you don't run out to the tailor. You just adjust. I started wearing dresses, pleated skirts, cotton tops and sweaters instead of cute little suits and tight silk blouses. I used to dress like you and then I had children."

Enjoying the light moment, Brandy found herself laughing and smiling for the first time in a long time. "You look fine to me. What does your husband say?"

Shirley cleared her throat and dropped it several octaves. "Baby, you're not the size nine I married, but I love you anyway." Shirley broke into uncontrollable laughter. "Ain't that something, Brandy?"

Brandy nodded in agreement. "Yeah, well, there was a backhanded compliment in there somewhere."

"Speaking of men, Brandy, how are the men in your life? Or should I say *the man*." Shirley raised her eyebrows.

"William is probably throwing a fit right about now because I haven't spoken to him in a while. The other man in my life, James, asked me to marry him. I told him no. In short, I'm alone in this world."

"You lost me." Suddenly Shirley's strawberry shake didn't taste so good. "So let me get this straight. You turned down a marriage proposal?"

"Yep."

"I can understand not dating William, but why did you turn James down?"

"What makes you say that about William?"

"Brandy, it was obvious you were on the rebound."

Brandy felt foolish. Everyone seemed to know that she'd never really been interested in William but her. "I do like William, but I'm afraid I'll only end up hurting him in the end."

"So what are you going to do about James?"

"I don't know yet." Brandy was trying to sound noncommittal. "I'm afraid a marriage won't work when one party isn't sure how she feels."

"Brandy, no relationship is fifty-fifty. I hate to be the one to tell you, but there is no such animal. Someone always loves more, works harder and compromises more than the other."

"Oh Shirley, that's awful. That's not what I envisioned for myself and the man I marry."

Shirley was amazed at Brandy's naiveté. "Let me tell you something my mother told me. She always said that women traditionally want the man who dogs them. The man who stands them up, the one who won't claim them in public and who often marries someone else. Her advice is that we, as women, need to be original and love the man who loves *us* and not the man we love."

Though Brandy was practical, she also believed in true love. "No disrespect to you or your mother, but that way of thinking is backward and leaves me without a choice. Hell, if that's the case, I'd have gotten married years ago when some fool, any fool, professed undying love for me."

"You can make jokes if you want to, but that's sound advice." Shirley sensed the topic coming to a close. "What about William, Brandy? Isn't he going to feel cheated?"

Brandy didn't answer.

"What about you? Don't you owe it to yourself to be happy for once? No one told James that getting scared meant he had a license to start tripping." She was making sense and Brandy knew it. Yeah, James had had no right to shut her out like that.

"Shirley, let's talk about something else. I need a favor."

"You name it." Shirley had said her piece. She crossed her fingers and hoped that Brandy would do what she suggested.

"I know you know all the gossip in the office."

Shirley smiled conspiratorially. "Who do you want to know about?"

"Is Brad still cheating on his wife?"

"Yes, and the scandalous part is that he's doing it with Nancy."

"I knew it!" Her suspicions were right on target!

"Yes, can you believe that?" Shirley made a face like she had a bad taste in her mouth.

"Now everything makes sense." Brandy thought about the bogus answer that had been delivered to J.D. months before, rearranged files, missing documents, and things Brad knew but shouldn't have known about her relationship with J.D. The only person who had access to that information was Nancy.

When Brandy had left David the night before, she'd thought long and hard about why Brad was trying to discredit her. Brad was pissed at the partners because four years had gone by and he still hadn't seen the inside of a courtroom, except to watch her. He was also mad because his evaluations were always middle of the road, and hers had been stellar. Well, they had been until yesterday. The Hamilton case was an important one for the firm. If Brandy won the case for Lloyd & Lloyd, the victory would mean a whole lot of money in legal fees and more business for the firm. Brandy would be also guaranteed a position as partner two years from now. Maybe.

"Brandy, what are you thinking about?"

"Tell me something, did Brad promise to leave his wife and marry Nancy?" Now that she knew what was going on, she was amused.

"You know he did."

Brandy sat back in her chair. "Hmm. That explains why she stopped doing her work."

"What are you talking about?"

"Nothing. Shirley, I need you to do a little investigating for me." She was relieved to know that she wasn't going crazy.

"Okay." Shirley was eager to help Brandy.

"In fifteen minutes, Nancy should be finished with lunch. I want to know what she's doing and if Brad is nearby."

"Girl, I don't have to leave the office to do that. They spend lunch in his office and then he follows her to her cubicle. I didn't think too much about it before but . . ."

"But what?"

"Well, they're always whispering and they stop whenever anyone goes near them. Brandy, you must've been really busy not to notice how Nancy throws herself at Brad."

"Yes, I have been tied up with the Hamilton case." She couldn't think of any signs that she had missed. Brad was his usual offensive self day in and day out. She had no reason to believe that he would go through so much trouble to make her lose her place in line for partner. After four years, she thought she had office politics figured out. Clearly, her lesson was just beginning.

"Before you go back to your desk, I want you to go downstairs and see what they are talking about."

When Shirley left, Brandy buzzed David. "David Gratani."

"It's me, Brandy."

"What can I do for you?" He was extremely professional.

"Are you alone?"

"No, not at all." Lloyd was sitting directly across from him.

"Just listen then. Brad and Nancy are having an affair. He's one of several who've been sabotaging me all along."

"Um-hmm." Before Lloyd could ask, David told him that Shirley was on the line.

"Shirley's spying on them right now. I'll call you when I know more."

"Please do."

Seventeen

Either his flu medicine was making him hallucinate or Brandy still hadn't called. William stood up and then sat down again, sorting it all out aloud.

"I was content just being her friend, especially after she told me that the next man she laid down with would be her husband. She clearly placed a premium on sex, and I was willing to go along with whatever she said. I can't believe I fell for that act! Sure, I wanted more but I kept my hands to myself until that day we were watching the game. She initiated intimacy and then she pulled away from me. I thought she was beginning to trust me, but obviously she doesn't. She's sending me mixed signals, and how am I supposed to react?"

Tired of the tennis match going on in his mind, William rose from the couch and in one stride grabbed the phone and dialed her work number. While the phone was ringing, he glanced at the clock on the wall. He had spent one hour muddling through reasons why she would dis him like that.

"Lloyd & Lloyd." The relief receptionist answered the phone.

"Ms. Curtis, please."

Thinking it was Shirley, Brandy picked up the phone on the first ring. She was anticipating news about Brad and Nancy, so she was expectant when she answered the phone. "Did you find out anything?"

"Yeah, I found out what kind of woman you really are."

Startled, she stammered, "Hel-lo? William?"

"Who else would it be?" He was so furious he started pacing to calm himself down.

She took a deep breath and attempted to steady her voice. "I was going to call you."

"When you have time to pencil me into your busy schedule?" His voice was infused with sarcasm. "Here I've been waiting patiently for you to call me."

"William, this is not the time nor the place."

"Oh, is this a professional relationship? I need to request an appointment in writing?"

"That's not true, I always have time for you."

"You could have fooled me!"

Wanting to avoid a scene over the telephone, she interrupted him. "Can you meet me tonight so we can talk?"

"Yep. What time, *counselor*?"

"Eight o'clock at my house."

"I'll be there." He crashed the receiver into the cradle.

Just when she thought she couldn't cry anymore, a torrential downpour started. William had never taken that tone with her before.

Brandy didn't hear David enter her office. "Why are you crying?"

"I'll tell you later." She took a tissue out of her desk drawer and wiped her eyes. "Brad has Nancy believing that he's going to marry her. I hate him. What should I do, David?"

"About who— the person who made you cry or Brad?" David recognized love tears when he saw them.

Brandy looked up at him. "David, I did a terrible thing. I used William to get over James."

"Bella, things like that happen in life. You shouldn't beat yourself up about it."

"And then my ex-boyfriend, James, asked me to marry him on Sunday. I didn't know what else to do— I panicked."

David remembered that James had pulled away from her before. He did not want to see her hurt again. He hoped she'd told him no. "Did you accept his proposal?"

"No, I didn't."

"So what's causing you so much pain?"

Brandy looked away from David. She was afraid to admit the truth. "I— "

"You're still in love with James, aren't you?"

"Is it that obvious?"

"After the way he treated you? Brandy, I held you five months ago because you said that he was tripping on you. He doesn't deserve you. Bella, why can't you see that?"

She was on the defensive. "You're right, it doesn't make any sense— I should hate him. But I don't. David, I can't help the way I feel."

"Brandy, James ruined a good thing between you two. He shouldn't be allowed to win in the end just because he's finally seen the light. It's not fair to you." Tears welled up in her eyes again. David went to her and held her as he had in January. He prayed that she wouldn't let James back into her life.

Lloyd saw that Brandy's door was ajar and walked in. He hadn't completely stepped into the office before he saw David hugging Brandy.

"Excuse me, Brandy, is something wrong?"

"Oh Lloyd, I didn't hear you."

David didn't want to release Brandy, but she gently pulled away from him. Ever since their conversation at the Beverly Hills Café the night before, he'd felt a special kinship toward Brandy; he thought she was right to be confused and outraged about her evaluation. Though they worked in different departments, he had heard only rave reviews about the star litigator. Something was definitely wrong. In any event, he was determined to keep a close eye on Lloyd.

"My secretary told me that Brandy wanted to talk to me about her evaluation. From the looks of things, now doesn't appear to be a good time," Lloyd said.

"You're right, can I talk to you about that tomorrow?" Brandy was still sniffing.

"Sure, I'm always here if you need me." Something was strange about the picture in front of him. "David, I didn't know that you knew Brandy."

"I make it a point to know all of the women in the office, especially the beautiful ones." David beamed at Brandy.

"I agree, David, Brandy is definitely beautiful." Before he left, Lloyd looked hard at Brandy. "If you aren't feeling well, you should go home. We need our star player to be alert and on her toes on Friday."

"I'm fine, really." She tried her best to smile. "I just need to splash some water on my face, that's all."

"We better not take any chances. Whatever's bothering you isn't work-related, is it? Because if it is, I'll get to the bottom of it immediately." There was conviction in his voice. A few months ago she would have been suckered in by his fake demonstration of compassion.

"No, it's not work-related. I got some bad news today."

Relieved that business was in order, Lloyd was about to excuse himself when he had an idea. "David, see to it that she goes home."

"That's a great idea, Lloyd. I was thinking the same thing myself." David winked at Lloyd as Lloyd left Brandy's office.

Brandy started clearing off her desk. She needed to talk to her mother.

"Don't put your papers away." David put his hand over hers.

"Why not? I don't want Nancy to do any snooping in my office while I'm gone."

"Has Shirley called you back with any information yet?"

"No." Brandy sat back down in her chair.

"I've got an idea."

"What?"

"Leave everything to me." David's brain was clicking. "I'm going to make Brad tell on himself."

"How do you plan to do that?"

"I don't want to get into too much detail in the office. I will say this much—tell Shirley to casually mention to Nancy that Brad is seeing another woman."

Brandy considered his strategy. "Hmm. If Nancy takes the bait, she'll get mad at Brad. Okay, I can do that, but what are you going to do about Brad? Do you think that will make Nancy tell on him?" Brandy considered one drawback. "David, what if Nancy's too embarrassed to admit to their affair?"

"I think she'll overcome her embarrassment if she thinks he's going to jilt her." David handed Brandy her briefcase. "Where are those documents you printed before we went to the Beverly Hills Café?"

"They're at my house. I wanted to complete the rest of the interrogatives at home."

"That's smart." David opened the door for her. "Does anyone else know that you changed them?"

"No, but I'm sure Nancy figured out that I was here, because the directory has a built-in clock showing the latest time and date a document was retrieved from the disk or hard drive." She checked her face in the mirror.

"Good, then she'll already be suspicious."

"Now that you mention it, I haven't seen her or Brad all day." Brandy closed her compact and walked toward the door.

"Greed always shows itself before long." Hearing that, Brandy felt a flicker of hope. She didn't know what she'd do without David there to help her.

When Brandy and David stepped outside her office, she bumped into Brad. "Going somewhere, Ms. Curtis?" He looked at her briefcase. "Hey Dave, how's it going?"

"Yes, I'm going home," Brandy replied. David smiled politely.

"Since your work is all done for Friday, I guess leaving early won't hurt anything," he said sarcastically.

She decided to feel Brad out. "What makes you say that?"

"Oh, I just know that an A-ranked attorney such as yourself has everything ready to go several days in advance." He'd been caught off guard. "Have a good day, Bran, and I'll see you tomorrow." Brad hurried down the hall.

Brandy giggled. "He's nervous."

David put his finger in front of his lips. When they reached the lobby, Shirley motioned Brandy to come to her.

"I've got a juicy tidbit for you. The two lovers had a tiff after lunch. Nancy was really mad and— "

Brandy cut her off. She didn't want to take a chance on anybody walking by and hearing Shirley. "I'm going home." She leaned down and whispered in her ear, "In a couple of hours, tell Nancy that Brad is cheating on her. You can tell David what happened with them earlier, and he'll give me the details later."

Shirley shot David a look that sliced him in two.

"You can trust him, he's on our side."

"All right, if you say so." Shirley wasn't too big on trusting just anybody. "Have a nice evening."

"I will."

In the elevator, Brandy laughed menacingly. "He has no idea who he's playing with. I hope this little game of cloak and dagger has been fun, because he's about to be blown out of the water."

Brandy reached into her briefcase. "Here, David, I found this in my office earlier. I wonder who it belongs to?" It was less of a question than a statement, because they both knew the answer.

He fingered the gold button earring, but remained silent. Brandy was right— game time was over for Brad and Nancy.

When they reached the lobby, Brandy spotted Mr. Robinson. How she needed one of his grandfatherly hugs, but she knew she wouldn't get one once he found out what she'd done to his only grandson.

"David, do you see Mr. Robinson over there?"

"Yes."

"That's William's grandfather."

"What a small world it is indeed."

"I can't talk to him until after I speak with William tonight. Please distract him while I sneak out to the garage."

"Anything for you, bella."

Brandy waited ten seconds and then followed David out of the elevator. They were standing to her right and Mr. Robinson's back was to her. She did her best to tiptoe past him, but her heels click-clacked against the marble floor anyway. Fortunately, David heard her and started laughing to cover up the noise and Mr. Robinson didn't hear her.

On the way to her parents' home in Windsor Hills, Brandy thought about William. She didn't know what she was going to say to him. While she was thinking of the right words, she glanced at the people to the right and left of her on the eastbound Santa Monica freeway. Each driver was in his own world—she could talk to herself without anyone staring at her.

"I wasn't trying to hurt him—I was just being honest about not wanting a serious relationship. He should be able to understand that, shouldn't he?" Her mind said no.

"Okay, okay, maybe I was wrong for running out on him." She chewed on that thought for a minute. "I went about it the wrong way. There's no way of getting around that. I used him."

She had to admit that to herself. All of the rationalizing in the world wasn't going to change the fact that he was hurt and mad, and rightfully so.

There were so many voices swirling in her head. Shirley—telling her that James may not be perfect for her. David—suggesting that she would be shortchanging herself if she accepted James' proposal. James, he said, had lost his chance at loving her. Simone—assuring Brandy that she would support her either way, although Brandy knew in her heart that Simone wanted James for a brother-in-law.

Finally, she reached her destination. No one was at her parents' home, so she let herself in and headed straight for the kitchen. She knew it was a long shot but she opened the refrigerator in search of food anyway. Ever since her brother had started college, her mother had all but stopped cooking. Luckily, there was one left-over smoked turkey wing, a half-eaten baked potato, greens and the sweetest cornbread in the world. She was in business.

When she finished eating, it was two o'clock. Her mother was a nurse and would be home at 3:45 p.m.; her father, a high school principal, wouldn't arrive until 4:15 p.m.

She fell into a troubled sleep on the couch in the den, waking to her mother's voice.

"Hi, sweetie, how are you?" Her mother kissed her on her cheek.

She gave her mother a dry look. "I still have my health."

"That's good." Lena knew her daughter like the back of her hand. By the tone in Brandy's voice, she was not having a very good day. "What's the matter?"

"A bad week," she said, sleep still in her voice. "Corporate America is no longer for me." Brandy rubbed her eyes.

"Why honey?"

"I'm tired of being treated like a work horse. My sole role at Lloyd & Lloyd is to produce and not complain about it. The environment is extremely competitive."

"Hasn't it always been competitive there?"

"Yes, but I thought that after all this time, they would have accepted the fact that I'm there and not going anywhere. I know just as much as they do. I have the same credentials. But none of that seems to matter. I feel like I'm constantly proving myself." Lena could feel her daughter's rage.

"Mama, I hate it there now. I used to jump out of the bed in the morning. Now, I slap the snooze on my alarm clock at least five times every day and pull the covers over my head. I used to rush to get there at seven o'clock sharp every morning just because I loved my job. I'd even stay until ten or eleven every night! Now, I stroll in at about eight, sometimes later, leave early and rarely return in the evening to finish working."

"Brandy, if you feel that way about it, quit. You can open your own firm. I was never too thrilled about you working in that big, impersonal firm in the first place. All they do is use you up and then throw you away."

"Quit? Just like that?" Though Brandy was seriously

considering this, she wanted to hear what her mother was going to say.

"Yes. You always have a home here and you'll find another job. Better yet, when you quit lolly-gagging and get married, you'll have a second income to fall back on." Lena laughed at her own joke. The look on Brandy's face froze her laughter. "Did I say something wrong?"

"Oh Mama, James asked me to marry him." Lena's face lit up. "Before you throw a party, I told him no."

"Are you going to get back together with him? Brandy, you're not making any sense. Why did you tell James no?"

"I can't allow him to come waltzing into my life because he's lonely. I'm not a doormat, Mama." Brandy snapped out of her trance.

"I know that and I'm sure that he knows that, too. But what did he say to you?"

"It doesn't matter." Her attitude was waning.

"Now, back to my original question, why didn't you accept his proposal? Is it that you don't love him anymore?"

"No, that's not it, Mama, I still love James, but I'm afraid to trust him again." Brandy's voice had grown very soft.

"I know you are, but don't you think you owe it to yourself to find out whether or not he's sincere?"

"If I do that, then I've given him a second chance."

"That's true. The alternative is that you and William forever remain friends and you let James get away."

"William likes me a lot."

"I'm glad that he likes you. Do you like him?"

"Um . . . yes."

"Do you like him enough to lose James?"

Brandy didn't answer. "That's not a fair question. There's no way I can answer that."

"If you can't answer me, what are you going to tell William when he demands an explanation?"

"I haven't figured that out yet."

"He's going to want an answer."

"I know, but he'll have to wait." Sometimes she hated talking to her mother. She had a knack for getting to the heart of matters.

"What if he doesn't want to wait, Brandy?"

"Oh, well." She rolled her eyes. She was tired of being told how to live her life.

"In that case, I hope you're prepared to lose them both."

Brandy had no idea what she was in for. William was definitely a nice man, but he wasn't going to be so nice when Brandy told him about James.

"Ultimately, the decision is yours. I love James and I want him to be my son-in-law. I know that he hurt you, but he apologized to you. It's clear that he realized his mistake and is making an effort to prove to you that he loves you. Doesn't that count for anything?"

Brandy sighed.

"I'm going to tell you one last thing and then I'll leave you alone. When your father and I were dating, I broke up with him for three months. I was so mad at him that I didn't speak to him, wouldn't go out with him, wouldn't return his phone calls. We were planning to get married and he got cold feet. Like you, I was devastated. After a short time, I started dating someone else. He was a real nice guy, but I didn't love him the way I loved your father. Anyway, to make a long story short, your father begged me to give him one more chance. Brandy, I made him promise me the moon and the stars before I'd take him back. My mother and my friends called me a fool for marrying him. They said that in two years, he would start acting up and then we'd either get a divorce or I'd be miserable. They were wrong, Brandy. Your father has never given me cause to regret taking him back. Thirty years have gone by and I love him more now than I did then." Lena hugged her tightly. "Follow your heart, Brandy."

Brandy heard her father's footsteps on the back porch. She didn't want her father to see her upset, so she went into the bathroom and washed her face.

Eighteen

When Brandy got home, she turned the ringer down on her phone and turned the volume up on her CD player. She put in one of her favorite groups, Da Influence, and listened to "For You I Sing This Song." She sang along with the first verse, "If this is all a dream, I can wait till morning comes." Hell, she wished she could wake up tomorrow and her nightmare would be over. She pressed repeat on the CD control, undressed, and turned off all the lights.

She went into the bathroom and turned on the bath water. While she waited for the tub to fill, she reached into her cabinet and pulled out three small, white candles. She arranged them in a perfect triangle on the sink. After she lit them, she turned the bathroom light out. She stepped down into the tub and within minutes was surrounded by bubbles made by the jets in her whirlpool. The Jacuzzi-like steam caused the bathroom mirror to sweat.

She sat in the tub until the jets turned cold. Two of the three candles had burned out. She wondered if the one flame was symbolic of what was to become of her. She blew it out and turned on the light. Her skin was wrinkled from sitting in the water for so long. She rubbed sesame oil on her breasts, arms, legs, feet and back, then she dried herself off. She went into her room and searched through her drawers for stretch pants and a baggy shirt. She brushed her hair into a ponytail. was 7:45 p.m., and William would be there in fiftee minutes.

Brandy was feeling nervous and needed to do som thing to keep her mind occupied. She went into th living room and sat down on the couch. She turned th TV on and after three minutes of mindlessly flippir through the channels, she turned it off. Then she wer through a stack of magazines and finally settled on *Ell* She couldn't find any articles of interest and her mir kept wandering back to the day she'd run out on Wi liam. Finally, she decided on an activity that require more concentration— alphabetizing her magazine She'd gotten to the letter "G" when William arrived.

William was so mad, he forgot that he was sick. Afte he'd hung up with Brandy, he got dressed.

"I wish Brandy would give me a chance. I've got t say something to convince her not to leave me," he tol his reflection in the mirror.

He was over his anger by the time he reache Brandy's house. He was, however, nervous, and he hes tated before he pressed the buzzer at her building. Wi liam knew that the moment his finger depressed th button, it was possibly the beginning of the end.

"Hello." She didn't bother to turn on the TV/se curity camera to see who it was. She knew it was him

He cleared his throat. "Brandy, it's me, William."

"Come on up." She buzzed him in.

Brandy greeted him at the door with a sad, "Hello. No affection was exchanged and no eye contact wa made. William lingered at the door. By his watery eye she could tell that he had a very bad cold. She wante to reach out to him, but she was afraid he would pul away from her.

Brandy looked bad—she was thin and worn out. He knew her job was extremely stressful, but she had never looked so tired before. Normally, her hair was done and she was always dressed to kill. Tonight was a whole different story. Any other time, William would have taken her into his arms and kissed the stress away. However, he was determined not to be sidetracked.

Since neither ventured to make the first move, Brandy invited him in. "Would you like some tea?" She walked toward the kitchen.

He'd thought he was going to go in with a mighty roar, but he started begging before he could stop himself. "Why are you doing this?"

She stopped in her tracks. "You're sick, William. Tea will make you feel better."

"Don't patronize me, Brandy." He was visibly hurt.

"I wasn't patronizing you, I was just being polite."

"Forget the niceties. What's going on?"

"William, please sit down."

He hesitated and then sat very stiffly on the couch.

She sat down beside him. "I'm not ready for a relationship."

"What does that mean?"

"What it means is that I like you, a lot, but I don't want anything more than a friendship." She hoped she didn't sound arrogant.

"Could you have told me that instead of leaving me hanging?" He was growing angry.

She looked at him in surprise. Wanting to avoid a confrontation, she told him what she thought he wanted to hear.

"I've been thinking about us for some time now. I know that only five months have passed, but it seems we're headed for the long haul. I told you from the beginning that I'm not used to depending on anyone.

And before I knew it, I felt myself growing closer to you."

"What's wrong with that? I thought a relationship consisted of two people who are dependent on each other." The edge had eased in his voice.

"There's nothing wrong with that, William." She relaxed a little and started rubbing his back.

"You're right, I don't get it." William leaned away from her. "Brandy, why are you staring me in the face and lying to me?"

She turned away. Her voice dropped. "I'm not lying."

"Yes you are."

He was making this harder than it had to be. She shrugged her shoulders. "I don't want to be in a relationship."

"I understand that, but did something or someone cause you to panic?" Only another man could make her leave him. "What's his name?"

Brandy's mouth fell open. "That's none of your business." *Who did William think he was?*

"It is my business, Brandy. I was really hoping things would work out between us. What did I do wrong?" He cupped her chin in his hand and turned her face to him.

"Nothing." She was starting to hate herself.

"You expect me to believe that we've been sailing along just fine and now you don't want to be with me because we're approaching some sort of permanency?" His eyes bore holes into her soul.

Brandy didn't answer. She was busted. He had seen straight through her.

"William, you've been perfect." She stroked his cheek. "This isn't about you. This is about me, how I feel and what I want."

He snatched his hand from her face. "I'm tired of

playing tit for tat, Brandy! Stop stalling. *What's his name?*"

Brandy sighed. She could hear Shirley telling her to tell him about James. "Do you remember that night we went to see the Lakers play at the Forum?"

"Yes."

"Well, when I went to the bathroom, I bumped into my ex-boyfriend, James. He introduced himself to you."

"How could I forget?" He remembered that Brandy hadn't wanted to talk about the incident on their way home.

"We dated for two years before I met you. I broke up with him in January, and for the last five months he's been calling me."

"Have you been dating us both?" Not really wanting to hear her say yes, he turned his gaze to the empty fireplace.

"No, in fact I never bothered to return any of his phone calls." Brandy started wringing her hands. "Except Sunday."

"This past Sunday?" William felt himself grow hot.

"Yes, the day before yesterday, I met him for dinner." She turned to him. "I don't know how to say this."

"Just say it." He knew what was coming.

"He— he asked." Her voice broke. "He asked me to marry him."

William looked into her eyes. "What did you say?" His hands grew sweaty. Before she could answer, he grabbed her left hand and checked her ring finger.

"I didn't accept his proposal."

William breathed a sigh of relief. "I should be glad to hear that, but somehow I'm not."

Brandy kissed his cheek and whispered in his ear. "Don't be mad."

"Don't be mad!" He jumped up from the couch. "How

can I not be mad, Brandy? You broke up with me because of him! Were you ever going to tell me the truth?"

Brandy started crying. "I'm sorry you had to find out this way. I'm so sorry." She bowed her head.

"I'm not trying to make you cry, darlin', but put yourself in my shoes. I bought plane tickets for Chicago next week. You didn't forget, did you? You won the bet, and I have the tickets."

"Oh my God, William. Chicago?"

"Yes, Brandy." William smiled. "I always make good on my bets."

This couldn't be happening to her! In all the chaos that had been going on at the office, Brandy had completely forgotten about their trip.

"I don't know what to say."

"Brandy, say you'll go with me."

Her heart was in her throat. "I can't say that."

"Why?"

"I just can't." This was definitely not the conversation she had envisioned. She thought that she would be able to make him understand that she wanted only to be friends with him. "It wouldn't be fair of me to tell you 'yes' today and then 'no' tomorrow."

William felt like such a fool. "All this time, Brandy, and you never said a word about James. Now, you're letting him come between us."

"I am not! William, you're not listening to me." Brandy wiped her tears; she was tired of crying. "I never told you about James because, when we met, I thought that part of my life was over. We had attempted to reconcile, but it didn't work out. I liked you from the moment I saw you. But, how was I supposed to know that he was going to ask me to marry him? Damn! You make it sound like I did this on purpose!"

"You used me, Brandy."

Brandy was through defending her position. She

didn't know how to make it any plainer to William that James had not come between them.

"William, you want a relationship with me, but I don't want one with you."

"So basically what you're telling me is, damn what I want?"

She hesitated. "No, that's not what I'm saying. William, we got close very quickly. I thought I was able to handle a new relationship, but what I discovered was that I wasn't ready. Even if James hadn't proposed to me, I doubt very seriously that we would have gotten together."

"That doesn't make any sense, Brandy. I should have known this was too good to be true!"

Her eyes flashed. "What's that supposed to mean?"

"You acted like you were all into me, when in fact you've been playing me all along. You never wanted me, Brandy, you just wanted to make James jealous. Well, I hope you're happy, especially since you got what you wanted." William's sarcasm was biting.

"That's not true and you know it!" Brandy stood closer to William. "I would never play a game like that with you or anyone else."

"Stop saying that." His tone was sharp. "The only thing I know is that I don't know you as well as I thought I did." William moved away from her. For a split second he hated her. "I can't believe you played me like this." He walked toward the door.

"William, I wasn't trying to hurt you. Everything started happening at once: my job, James, and now this. This isn't easy for me, can't you see that?"

"No, and I don't have to." William closed his eyes.

"You're being unreasonable."

William opened the door. "I'm leaving for Chicago on Tuesday. Since you've obviously made your choice,

I hope you have a nice life." She could feel the daggers in his voice.

"William, I'm very sorry." She felt like the rug had been snatched out from under her. He was hurt and it was all her fault. She felt terrible.

"Yeah, well, I'm sorry, too." William walked out and slammed the door behind him. She wanted to run after him, but knew that her actions would be in vain. Even if he did talk to her, she couldn't give him what he wanted.

Nineteen

Earlier on Monday, David had walked Brandy downstairs to her car. After she drove off, he went back to the elevator and headed up to the office. When he opened the door, Shirley motioned to him.

"Like I was saying earlier, they had a fight just before Nancy went back to work after lunch. I didn't hear everything, but she told Brad that she thought Brandy was on to them. She said that when she got to work this morning, the interrogatives for the Hamilton case were finished. Her asked her what was wrong with that. She told him that she always corrected her documents, not Brandy. Nancy also said that she was getting nervous and wanted out. He told her that if she stopped he would blow the whistle on her. Nancy got mad and threatened to tell his wife about them. Brad grabbed her arm and pulled her to him. He whispered something in her ear. I don't know what he said to her, but the color drained from her face."

"That's very interesting." Still, it wasn't enough to prove that Brad had masterminded the sabotage of Brandy's case and career. It did, however, explain how he knew that Brandy had finished her brief.

"David, what's really going on?" Shirley was dying to know. She couldn't stand Brad and would have loved to see him roast.

"I think I should let Brandy tell you." He blew her a kiss. "Shirley, you've been a great help."

David went straight to Brad's office. The door was open so he walked in. Brad's office was a mess. There were papers everywhere and a picture of him and his wife placed very prominently on his desk. "What a snake," David thought to himself.

"Dave, come in, come in. Have a seat." Brad was happy to see him. He knew that David was a partner and though he worked in a different department, Brad figured that he probably had influence in all the right places. "What brings you to my neck of the woods?"

"I met with Lloyd earlier and we were discussing the associates who received rave reviews. Since your name came up a few times, I thought I'd stop by and meet Lloyd & Lloyd's newest star."

Brad gave him an Alfred E. Newman smile. "Well, the competition was steep, but it looks like I finally made it over the top." He was thrilled that he was finally being recognized for the brilliant attorney that he was. All he needed was a few more days and he would be able to secure his place as partner in 1997. "Thanks for the congrats, Dave." He decided to play it modest. "I must admit I was a bit surprised."

There wasn't a modest bone in Brad's body. David could tell that Brad was enjoying having his ego stroked. Trapping him would be easier than he thought. "Surprised? Oh, Brad, those marks were well-earned."

"I guess you're right. Say, Dave, how about grabbing a brew tonight after work?"

"That sounds great, but I'm buying."

"No, this one's on me." Brad was not above brownnosing.

"If you insist." Dave got up from his chair. "I've got a lot of work to finish before we go. Call me when you're ready."

"No prob." Brad was ecstatic. He would be rubbing elbows with the rich and famous of Lloyd & Lloyd—finally. He had been busting his butt to be recognized by the powers that be. Brandy could hang it up—he was now the new star on the block.

David left his office and went to his own. Brad was a fool. He was so impressed with himself that he couldn't see straight. Unfortunately, he wasn't the only person in the office whose moral character was questionable. The whole office, in fact, was swarming with sharks. Poor Brandy had gotten caught up in the maelstrom before she'd known what hit her, but it wasn't her fault; Lloyd & Lloyd was superb at reeling in lambs for the slaughter.

Brandy, who had nothing to hide, could afford to be naive. David, on the other hand, had no such luxury. While he hated living in the closet, business was business and his private life was private. Thus, he'd learned a long time ago to be extremely cautious of how he dressed, the company he kept and how he spent his time.

He was aware that Lloyd & Lloyd was a conservative firm. That, however, did not deter him from interviewing and later accepting a position there. Lloyd & Lloyd was "the" firm as far as tax law was concerned; and he wasn't going to let office politics keep him from accomplishing his career goals.

David stayed out of office politics and kept a discreet distance from his colleagues. He subscribed to the belief that one should keep his friends close and his enemies closer. In many ways, the male contingent of the firm operated like a locker room. As a member of this elite club, he was supposed to participate in their immature and insensitive behavior. On more than one occasion, he'd defended the rights of others, which had earned him a reputation as a bleeding heart. That was fine with him, as long as it kept him out of those inane conversations.

David maintained a working relationship with everyone in the firm except Brandy. He'd had a mentor when he'd first started at Lloyd & Lloyd and he was carrying on the tradition with Brandy, even though she hadn't asked for his help. She'd become his only friend at the firm. Initially, he'd kept tabs on her through general conversations about the new associates with Lloyd. He made a point never to ask him anything directly about her. He hadn't wanted Lloyd to misconstrue his inquiries as anything other than professional. Later, he'd asked her to lunch and they became friends. Right away, he found her to be extremely personable and very ambitious. Brandy was destined to be the first African-American partner at Lloyd & Lloyd, and David looked forward to it. When he discovered that some of his colleagues weren't too happy about her future as a partner in the firm, he felt compelled to tell her immediately. That brief conversation in January had deepened their friendship.

While Brandy shared the intimate details of her life with him, he still had not shared his secret with her. David knew she wouldn't care, but somehow the subject had never come up. He wanted to be open with her, and as soon as the Hamilton case was settled, he was going to reciprocate her trust and share his secret with her.

After he and Brad had dinner, David went back to work and stayed there until eleven forty-five. He wanted to call Brandy, but it was midnight when he got home. David was frustrated. While his original opinion of Brad had not changed, Brad was smarter than he had given him credit for. David needed more time, which, unfortunately, he didn't have. The mandatory settlement conference was Friday and it was already Wednesday morning.

Having drinks with Brad had almost been a waste of time. The only thing David learned about him was that he was determined to make partner. There was nothing wrong with that. In fact, that type of tenacity would be applauded by the powers that be at any firm. Brad was definitely a self-absorbed ass and very mad that Brandy had been chosen as counsel for J.D. Hamilton. But being a sore loser still didn't prove that he was out to ruin her reputation. David, however, knew that Brad was behind that very scheme.

"This is going to be trickier than I thought," he said aloud to himself as he removed his cuff links. David rubbed his forehead.

"My only hope is Nancy." He didn't know how he was going to use her without arousing Brad's suspicions.

Twenty

Brandy closed the door behind William and turned the lights out in the living room. She wasn't sleepy, so she went into the kitchen and made a cup of tea. She sat down at the table and inhaled the steam. The hot liquid burned her hands through the glass mug. She didn't feel the pain because she was concentrating on what had happened. In many ways she felt very small. She was sad, but she knew that she had made the right decision. Her feelings for James were solid. He was the only man alive who could cause waves to wash over her when she was with him. She reminded herself to think objectively about what her future would be like with James.

"Question: Is that mystical, magical feeling James causes me enough to base a marriage on?" She directed this question to God.

Wednesday morning found Brandy asleep at the kitchen table. She woke in a state of confusion and for a minute didn't know where she was. After a couple of seconds, Brandy recognized her surroundings and let out a huge yawn. She rolled her neck from side to side and then focused on the clock on the wall. It was fifteen minutes past six in the morning. She didn't remember falling asleep, but was grateful for the slumber. She removed the black scrunchie which held her hair in a ponytail and ran her fingers along her scalp.

She picked up a notepad and went into her bedroom. She threw the notepad on the couch and hit the play button on her answering machine. William had called. He apologized for leaving her townhouse without resolving the situation, and wanted to talk to her before he left for Chicago. It was too early to return his call, though she didn't know what she would say other than what she had already told him. Her mind had not changed in the hours since his departure.

She switched the lever on the side of the telephone to "on" and crawled into bed, determined to sleep thirty more minutes. Before her head hit the pillow, she sat bolt upright, remembering something she hadn't done in a long time. She got out of bed and onto her knees. After she'd said her prayers, she slid under the covers and stared at the ceiling.

"Lord, can you save me? I feel like I'm sinking, and sinking fast. I know that You are well aware of all that has been happening in my life the last few months. I am leaving Lloyd & Lloyd on Friday. I'm considering opening my own firm, but I get chills whenever I think about branching out on my own. When I weigh my options, I see myself leaving Lloyd & Lloyd and joining another Lloyd & Lloyd with a different name. The sad reality is that, with a few exceptions, only the majority firms can afford me. The joyous reality is that money is no longer enough to hold me. Initially, quitting work and having no income scared me, but now I'm relieved and I can't wait. I figure I can live off my savings, beg food from my parents and open my own practice. Knowing that my sanity is about to return, I feel my spirit rising.

"Now for the biggie. Do I follow my heart as my mother suggests and marry passion, knowing that there's a possibility that when the sparks die, so will the marriage? I am so confused. I have gotten solicited and unsolicited advice from everybody. What I'm asking for is guidance. Sometimes I feel like Hamlet— 'To be or not to be', to love or not to love, whom to love or whom not to love— those are the questions. I've tried everything, Lord. James is in Your hands. I'm tired of worrying about it."

Brandy drifted off into a dreamless sleep talking to God. She woke to a ringing telephone.

"Hello?" She sounded wide awake, despite the fact that she had been dead to the world only minutes before.

"Buon giorno, bella!"

"David?"

"Did I wake you?"

"Yes, but that's okay. What's up?"

"I spoke to Brad yesterday."

"What did he say?" Brandy's brain switched to "on."

"He said that he didn't think you were going to win the settlement on Friday. When I asked him why, he said that you've been making a lot of mistakes lately and that he could definitely do a better job."

"Did he bother to explain that my mistakes were the result of his handiwork?" Oh, how she hated him!

"Of course not. I definitely believe that he's the mastermind behind Nancy's attempts to sabotage the Hamilton case, but I still don't have any proof. The only way to get to him is through Nancy. I was planning to talk to her today."

"She's not going to tell you anything, especially if Brad mentions to her that you two talked."

"That's true." David felt like he had just slammed into a brick wall. "We can't let them get away with this!"

"I'll talk to Nancy."

David felt as though he was the one who was being

ndermined. He started ranting, "It's people like him
who give attorneys a bad name! He doesn't deserve to
e a barrister!"

"David, calm down. Forget about Brad. He's not stupid and he's not going to voluntarily reveal his plans
to have me fired. The only way to trap Brad and Nancy
s to beat them at their own game."

"Brandy, how should I approach Nancy?"

"I'll take care of her."

"What are you going to do?"

Brandy was silent. "I have no choice but to confront
her."

"Confront her? What are you going to say to her and
how are you going to keep her from Brad?"

"After I get through with her, she'll never say another
word to him."

"Okay, what do you want me to do?"

"I appreciate your concern, but you've already done
enough. I can handle it from here."

"Bella, I want to help you!"

"I know you do and you *have* helped in more ways
than you'll ever know."

"But— "

"No buts— this is my fight."

"Bella, bella, why won't you let me help you? This is
our fight, we're in this together." David knew he was
risking his position at the firm, but he didn't care. He
was fed up with the ugliness that was going on at Lloyd
& Lloyd.

"David, please."

"*Va beneche tu insista* (if you insist)." He was crushed.

Brandy hung up the phone and went into the bathroom. She pulled the curling iron out of the cabinet,
moved the dial to seven and plugged it into the socket
before going into her office. There, she grabbed her
dictaphone out of her briefcase and an unopened pack

of micro-cassettes out of the desk drawer. She carrie
all of it into the bathroom, laying everything out o
the counter to begin setting her plan in motion.

She marked each tape one through six, even thoug
she would use only four of them, since each cassett
was sixty minutes long. She lightly touched the curlin
iron to see if it was hot enough. It was ready and s
was she. She slipped tape number one into the dict
phone and began her bogus dictation.

If all went well, she would fill two tapes before sh
arrived at work. After she gave Nancy the first two, sh
would fill two more before the morning was over. Be
tween the four tapes and arbitrary corrections, Brand
was going to keep Nancy busy the entire day. Her goa
was to keep Nancy from Brad, and in that way ensur
that Nancy would confess at the end of the day. He
plan was a long shot, but time was of the essence an
she didn't know what else to do.

Brandy arrived at Lloyd & Lloyd at 9:30 a.m. Mr
Robinson blew her a kiss as she went up the elevator
Apparently, William hadn't told him what was going or
between them. Somehow that comforted her. When sh
got upstairs, she went straight to the secretarial poo
and found Nancy sitting at her desk.

"Good morning, Ms. Curtis." Nancy gave Brandy
warm smile.

"What are you doing?" Her tone was sharp.

Nancy's smile faded. "Working on discovery for the
Sampson case."

"I want you to stop what you're doing and work or
these tapes. I've altered my strategy for the Hamilton
M.S.C. and I need this information by 11:45 a.m."
Brandy handed her the tapes labeled one and two. She

swept out of the secretarial pool and walked toward Shirley in the lobby.

"Brandy?"

Long-stemmed roses caught her attention first. "What beautiful roses!" Brandy inhaled their aroma. "Peach, my favorite. I'm sorry, Shirley, how are you?"

"I'm fine." Shirley removed the card from the roses. "Girl, I didn't recognize you with your hair down."

Brandy fingered her ringlets. "I know it's been so long since it's been done, I was beginning not to recognize myself."

"It looks good." Shirley handed the card to Brandy. "You're in an awfully good mood today. Mind letting me in on your secret?"

"Well, I'm tired of worrying about everything and everybody." She blinked and for a moment saw William's back as he'd walked away from her the night before. "Anyway, I have a feeling that today is going to be a good day." She smiled distantly. "Oh, what's this?"

Shirley smiled back. She was happy to see that Brandy was regaining some of her color. "Open it." While Brandy opened the card Shirley kept talking. "You look really good."

"Thanks. I finally got a couple of hours of deep sleep."

"I'm glad to hear it. For a minute there, Brandy, I thought I was going to have to rush you to the hospital myself. What you need is a good massage."

Brandy skimmed the card. "You're right, that's something I haven't had in a long time," she said absently.

"You've got to stop neglecting yourself."

She read the card again. "I know, Shirley. It's been so long since I had my hair done that Trent's been calling me." Brandy laughed at her own joke.

"Who are they from?" Shirley handed her the peach roses in the crystal vase.

"James."

"He sure knows how to pick them."

Brandy smiled thoughtfully. "He writes that he loves me."

Shirley was staring at her, so Brandy tried to make her face remain neutral. "Nancy is going to be very busy all day. If I get any calls, send them to me."

"Sure thing. Brandy— "

"Not a word, Shirley, not one word." Brandy waited while Shirley buzzed her into the office.

At eleven forty-five, Nancy knocked on Brandy's door. She stood in the doorway fidgeting. "Ms. Curtis, I was only able to finish one tape. I'll do the other after my lunch break."

"Nancy, you won't be having lunch today. I told you that this information is extremely important. I have two more tapes for you."

"Two more?" Nancy's eyes grew wide. "Ms. Curtis, there were several different forms on the first tape. By the time I finish the drafts on the second tape it will be almost time for me to go home. There's no way I'll be able to do four tapes in one day."

"Nancy, I insist those tapes be completed. I need these documents for Friday. *Friday*— that's less than forty-eight hours away. If you have to stay here all night long to finish them, they will get done."

"What about lunch, Ms. Curtis? I made plans."

"Cancel them." Brandy handed her the telephone.

"That won't be necessary. I can call that person from my desk."

"No, make your call from here. I need to give you some more instructions and I don't have time to wait for you to chit-chat on the phone."

Nancy hesitated and then accepted the receiver. Brandy pretended to busy herself with the stack of papers that Nancy had just given her. Nancy's hand shook as she dialed the extension.

"Hello, this is Nancy. I can't meet you today."

Brad's voice was as clear as a bell. He wanted to know why.

"I just can't." Nancy quickly hung up the phone.

"Did you type the dictation exactly as I stated it on the tape?"

"Yes."

"Then I trust that I won't find any mistakes."

"Well, there may be a few. It is a draft."

"No, I specifically left instructions for you to bring me the final copy, not a draft."

"I'm sorry, I-I thought you wanted a draft." Nancy was sweating. "Do you want me to print a final copy?"

"Not if there are going to be mistakes in it. The reason I wanted a final copy is that lately you've been lax about making the corrections I've asked you to make."

"I'm really, really sorry about that. I can get you a final copy as soon as I spell-check it."

"You haven't even spell-checked the document?" Brandy glared at Nancy very hard. "You have a long night ahead of you."

"I can do it right now if you like. It will only take a minute."

"If you haven't done that by now, Nancy, just forget it. I'll just hold onto this piece of work and show Lloyd how incompetent you are. He'll be very angry, Nancy, especially since you know the whole firm will be affected by the outcome of the Hamilton case."

"Please Ms. Curtis, let me fix it!" Panic-stricken, Nancy reached for the papers.

"Nancy, simply go back to your desk and finish the second cassette." Brandy dismissed her with a wave of her hand. It took all she had not to explode into a fit of laughter. Her week was finally starting to shape up. Now that she had Nancy on the ropes, it was just a matter of time before she moved in for the kill.

While Nancy was slaving away at her computer, Brandy was finishing dictation on tapes three and four. When she finished with those, she went into the office kitchen and bought a package of Cup O' Noodles out of the vending machine. She mumbled pleasantries to Brad and the other associates and headed back to her office.

No sooner had she sat down than the telephone rang. "Brandy, Mr. Hamilton is on the line."

"Please put him through."

Brandy braced herself for his usual tirade about her incompetence as an attorney. "Hello, Mr. Hamilton."

"Ms. Brandy, are you ready for Friday?"

"Ms. Curtis. Yes, I'm ready. I'm actually looking forward to it."

"You better be, or else."

"Or else what?"

"I already don't like you, Ms. Brandy, and if you lose this case for me, I'll sue you for as long as I have life left in me."

"Well, J.D., I see that you are your usual inspirational self this morning. Is there anything else I can help you with?"

"No." She didn't care. As soon as the judge rendered the verdict she was out of there; and Lloyd, J.D., Brad and Nancy could all go straight to hell.

She opened her soup cup, added water and sat back in her chair. She was having difficulty enjoying her soup because every time she looked at the roses, she saw James' face. She swiveled her chair so that her back would be to them, leaving her facing the wall. She swiveled back around and put the flowers on the floor. Even on the floor, she still felt them looking at her. After fifteen minutes of playing I-spy with the roses, she retrieved them from the floor and set them back on her desk.

Nancy reappeared at the door just in time to save Brandy from relapsing into her prior state of confusion. Brandy looked at her wall clock and then handed her the last two tapes in an icy silence.

"I'm sorry it took me so long, but the second tape had more forms on it than the first."

Brandy just stared at her, and Nancy practically ran out of her office.

It was three-thirty. William would be home from school and Brandy owed him a phone call and an apology. On the third ring he answered the phone.

"Hello?"

"Hi, William."

"Hello, Brandy. Did you leave last night after we talked?"

"No, the ringer was turned off on my phone."

"So you got my message?"

"Yes."

"Brandy, I wish I could see you tonight, but I have to meet with my advisor."

"I understand." She was relieved.

"I'm really sorry for walking out on you like that last night."

"You were angry— I would have done the same thing." There was no use in rehashing the situation. It was over between them, so she changed the subject. "William, I'm quitting my job on Friday. I hate it here and I've got to go."

He had a premonition that her job wasn't the only thing she was going to quit. "I hope you're happy with your decision."

"I am."

"Good-bye, Brandy. Take care of yours

"I will." She hung up the phone. *Good,* she thought, *one less thing to worry about.* Her prayers were beginning to be answered. She stood up, dusted herself off and walked to the file room. There she located the Gould and Bloom files, took them back to her office, and began working.

At six o'clock, Brandy buzzed Nancy and told her to come to her office. Next, she buzzed Shirley.

"Reception."

"Shirley, I know you're getting ready to go home, but can you do me a favor?"

"Yes."

"I need you to whisper something in Nancy's ear."

"What do you want me to say?" Shirley put her purse back in her desk drawer.

"Tell her that you heard a rumor that I know about her and Brad." She pursed her lips. "Better yet, tell her that the entire office knows about them."

Shirley giggled. "That should get her goat!"

"It just might."

Brandy hung up the speaker phone and pulled a large envelope out of her desk drawer. She put ten blank sheets of paper in it and wrote Lloyd's name on the front of it. She cleared the top of her desk off completely and then set the envelope in the middle of it. She wanted the envelope to be the first thing Nancy saw when she sat down. Next she grabbed her dictaphone and inserted a blank tape. She depressed the record button.

Nancy arrived at Brandy's office a nervous wreck. "Ms. Curtis, I finished tape number three." Her hands were shaking.

"Close the door behind you. Let me see what you've done."

Nancy stood before her and handed her the documents.

"Where is tape number four?"

"I wasn't able to get to it." Nancy was rubbing her hands together.

"Nancy, stop fidgeting and sit down." Brandy sighed. "Did you do any work at all today?"

"Yes, I did as much as I could."

"As much as you could is not good enough. I don't think you realize how serious this case is."

"I-I started feeling faint. I-I didn't have lunch and I . . ."

"I really couldn't care less about how you feel, since you obviously haven't cared about my feelings since you started your little affair with Brad."

Nancy's face turned deep pink and she began to stammer. "Affair? Uh, Ms. Curtis, I, uh . . ."

"It's all over, Nancy. It's common knowledge that you're sleeping with Brad. Since you've been with Brad, my files are unorganized, documents have been misplaced, answers were delivered to clients that I never authorized, corrections were not made on documents that I *specifically* asked you to correct— the list is endless. I'm not even going to talk about your poor performance today." Brandy got up from her chair and stormed over to where Nancy sat. "Did you really think that you could get away with sabotaging my case?"

Nancy burst into uncontrollable tears, then looked up. "Ms. Curtis, I don't under-understand."

"You're fired." Without moving her gaze from Nancy, Brandy sat down on the corner of her desk.

"But why?" Nancy jumped to her feet. "I'll stay and do tape number four! I'll stay until midnight if you want."

"Did you hear anything I just said? You have been sabotaging me all along. Here I thought I was going crazy and it's been you and your little boyfriend interfering with my case! Nancy, you watched me walk down the hallway and get chewed out by Lloyd and Stan for having an answer delivered to J.D. Hamilton, knowing full well that you had that answer sent." Brandy spoke with biting finality. "You can stay here until *hell* freezes over and I'd *never* let you continue working for me!"

Nancy nearly threw herself on her knees, *"Please!* I'll do whatever you want, just don't fire me!"

"Nancy, it's too late." Brandy picked the envelope up off the desk and shoved it under Nancy's nose. "I'm going to give Lloyd this envelope before I leave tonight. In it I have a list of things you haven't done and copies of mistakes you've made in letters that have been sent to clients on Lloyd & Lloyd stationery. I also have proof of your affair with Brad and your plan to ruin my career."

"Oh, Ms. Curtis, please don't tell Lloyd! I— it wasn't my idea. Brad made me do it! He said that you were incompetent and that he should have been counsel for J.D. Hamilton. He said that he wanted to show Lloyd that you were costing the firm money and its reputation." She was wringing her hands. "He said that you were going to lose the settlement and that as soon you did, everyone would shower him with praises, and then you'd be blackballed. He said . . . he said that he'd be the star litigator and get the big cases." She started crying hysterically.

"Calm down, Nancy."

"Ms. Curtis, I'm sorry for doing those things to you." She sat back down in the chair. "I don't know what came over me." She looked at Brandy and then quickly looked away. "He promised to leave his wife. He was lying all along, but I guess I got caught up. I see now that he was using me."

"Do you have anything in writing?" Brandy's tone was testy.

"Yes, I still have a few of the inter-office memos he sent me."

Brandy returned to her chair and handed Nancy two tissues. "Wipe your face. As soon as you pull yourself together, I want your resignation." Nancy's eyes welled up again. "I also want a complete typed account of your affair with Brad and all of the things he told you to do. Don't get cute and leave out any pertinent details because I have the truth right here in this envelope."

"Yes, Ms. Curtis. I'll do it right away."

"One more thing before you go." Brandy leaned across the desk and gave Nancy a menacing glare. "If you breathe a word of this to Brad, I will— "

"I promise, I won't tell Brad anything. You have my word."

When Nancy left, Brandy shut off her dictaphone. She was jubilant. "Got'em!" She buzzed David and told him to meet her at her car in ten minutes.

Twenty-one

Brad was getting worried. It was one-thirty and Nancy still had not arrived at work. He called her apartment, but there was no answer. He even asked his secretary if she had seen her. When he thought enough time had passed, he went to the secretarial pool. When he reached Nancy's desk, he let out a gasp. It was bare: no papers on the desktop, none in the file basket, or in the "out" basket. He asked the other secretaries but none of them had seen her since the day before. His last resort was Brandy, but she was in a meeting with Lloyd and Stan.

"Brandy, I told J.D. to meet us at Judge Tucker's office at seven forty-five tomorrow morning. We want you there at seven-thirty sharp."

"I'll be there." *And as soon as the case is settled, I start my new life without Lloyd & Lloyd!*

"We don't have to remind you how important this case is to the firm."

"No, Stan, you don't."

"If— *when* you win this settlement, we will be extremely grateful—"

"And generous with future promotions," Stan finished for Lloyd. They were dangling sugar plums in front of her, knowing full well that they would never make her a partner. She knew the outcome of the Hamilton case would not change her position in the firm, yet she was determined to win. Fortunately, she was no longer naive about her future place at Lloyd & Lloyd. In any event, Brandy was determined to go out on top.

The meeting with the partners finally ended and Brandy went back to her office. She could see Brad pacing in front of her door. "May I help you, Brad?"

He nearly jumped out of his skin. "Oh hey, Bran, I didn't see you standing there."

She pushed past him and went into her office. "What do you want?"

"I just wanted to make sure that you were all right."

"Why wouldn't I be?" she snapped.

"It's just that I haven't seen you or Nancy all day and I assumed that something must have happened to one or both of you."

"Well, here I am in living color." Brandy hated him so much she was enjoying teasing him.

"I see, and you look good. Yellow is definitely your color." She was wearing a mustard linen pants suit.

"Thank you. If you don't mind, I've got work to do." She sat down behind her desk and started reviewing her notes.

"Just one more thing— is Nancy here today?"

Brandy smiled. This was exactly the kind of midday boost she needed. "Nancy no longer works here." She smiled at him sweetly and then plunged the knife in deeper. "She resigned last night. Didn't your secretary tell you?"

His face went white. "No, I guess she forgot to mention it. I'm sorry to see her leave."

She drove the knife deeper. "Brad, I didn't realize that you and Nancy were so close."

"Uh, we're not. I mean, we weren't. I just hate to see

great support staff leave." He was silent for a moment. "Did she give a reason why she quit?"

"She didn't have to. Nancy was an at-will employee. I don't have to tell you what that means, do I?"

"No. I'll see you later, Bran— good luck tomorrow." He was in a rush to leave.

"Aren't you coming to the settlement conference tomorrow?"

"I think I'm going to sit this one out."

"I don't think you have a choice in the matter. Lloyd should be buzzing you soon with the good news."

His face fell. "Brad, you don't look so good. Do you want to sit down?"

"No, I'm fine, thanks." He backed out of the office.

Brandy got up and shut the door behind him. She needed him to be present tomorrow when she gave Lloyd the tape with Nancy's confession on it.

When Brad had left, Brandy dialed James' private line.

"James Collins."

"Hi, James, how are you?"

"Brandy?" He was surprised.

"Yes, I wanted to thank you for— "

"I'm so happy you called! Are you calling to say that you'll marry me?"

"Slow down. I'm calling to thank you for the roses. They were beautiful." She felt herself in control of the situation.

"I'm glad you like them, though there's not a flower on this earth as beautiful as you." He hoped she believed him, because he meant every word of it.

James was making her nervous. "Okay, well, I've got to get back to work." His voice sounded good in her ears.

"Brandy, I want to see you." He knew he was begging

but he didn't care. He had never loved anybody the way he loved Brandy.

"I can't see or talk to anybody until my mandatory settlement conference is over."

"When will that be?"

"Tomorrow morning."

Tomorrow seemed like a lifetime to James. "Can I see you tomorrow night?"

"No." She wanted to be absolutely certain about what she was going to do before she saw him.

"What about the day after? I'm not taking 'no' for an answer."

"We'll see." She knew that she couldn't stall him for very much longer.

"Brandy, I need to know your answer. I've been going crazy for the last four days. I can't sleep. I can't concentrate at work. I need to know, do you love me?"

He'd asked her the question she least wanted to answer. "James, please, I can't talk about that right now."

"When are you going to let me know?"

"I need more time, James." He was trying to force her hand. "In addition to getting back to you, I'll be making another very serious decision tomorrow."

"What could be more important than marrying me?"

"That came out wrong, James. Look, I'm quitting my job tomorrow right after the settlement hearing and I'm going to need a little time to get used to the idea of being unemployed."

"I'm glad you're quitting. You know I was never very fond of that firm anyway. Brandy, you should go where your talents are valued. You should open your own firm."

"I really appreciate your support— the last few months have been hell." James was stroking her in all the right places. "I've been thinking about opening my own firm . . . you've been reading my mind."

"Good, I'm glad to see that we're still in tune with one another. Brandy, if it's money you're worried about, I'll take care of you."

"No, it's more than that." She had to get off the phone with him. "I'll call you on Saturday."

"I'll wait for your call, Brandy, but I don't know how much longer I can wait for your answer."

"Good-bye, James."

"I love you, Brandy Curtis. Call me."

At five-thirty, Brandy went to Nancy's former desk and switched the computer on. She quickly typed a letter of resignation addressed to Lloyd with a carbon copy to Stan. While she had only two words for them, professional etiquette prevailed. Since she had Nancy's confession on tape and in writing, she was able to make her letter short and to the point.

She printed the letter out, signed it and stuffed it into an envelope. Brandy was also putting Lloyd & Lloyd on notice to prevent this type of treatment from happening to future African-American associates who joined the firm.

As far as Brad was concerned, he had messed with the wrong person and Brandy would do everything in her power to have him disbarred. She photocopied Nancy's letter and added an addendum to it. She addressed the letter to the California State Bar, the National Bar Association and the American Bar Association.

When she finished, she went to David's office. He wasn't there, so she left him a note with instructions to meet her in her office at ten o'clock. It was time for her to get her things.

Twenty-two

"Simone, we have to hurry, David's waiting for us." Brandy was standing in Simone's living room. They were on their way to Lloyd & Lloyd so Brandy could clean out her office.

"I'm coming!" Simone ran out with her tennis shoes in her hand. She was out of breath. "The boys finally fell asleep."

"Where's Aisha?"

Simone's daughter hated taking naps. "She's been out cold since nine o'clock."

"Ready?"

"Yes, I can put my shoes on in the car."

They pulled out of her driveway and sped west on Slauson Avenue to the 405 freeway.

"I'm proud of you." Simone squeezed her arm.

"I'm proud of me, too. I feel like a heavy burden has been lifted off my shoulders." Brandy smiled at herself in the rearview mirror. It felt good to smile. "Now all I have to do is get my hair done."

Simone laughed. Brandy had danced with the devil in the pale moonlight and lived to tell about it. "Good for you."

Brandy ran her fingers through her hair. She looked forward to a new perspective on life.

She and Simone arrived at her office just a little after ten. David was sitting in her chair. When he saw Brandy standing in the doorway, he got up and kissed her on both cheeks. "You are so beautiful. Lloyd & Lloyd has no idea what it's losing."

"Thanks, David. This is Simone."

"I recognize you from the picture on Brandy's desk. How are you doing?" He shook her hand with both of his and smiled at her warmly. "How are your children?"

"They're fine."

"Good." David let go of her hand as Brandy walked over to her file cabinet and started opening drawers. Over her shoulders, she gave orders. "David, were you able to find any boxes?"

"Yes, I have three of them."

"Great. Will you pass me one of them?" He did as she asked and handed her a black marker. She wrote "Pro Bono: Legal Aid" on the first box.

"David, will you put everything from these drawers that says 'Legal Aid' on it into this box?"

"No problem."

"Be careful, David, I don't want you to mess up your suit."

"Bella, you worry too much."

"Don't you own any sweats?" He was dressed in a dark grey pin-striped suit.

He smiled. "No."

"I should have known." She rolled her eyes in mock scorn. "Simone, I need you to take my diplomas off the walls and put them in this box."

"Alrighty." Simone picked up a box and went behind Brandy's desk. "Brandy, hand me the marker." She labeled that box "Diplomas."

In the third and final box, Brandy put her personal belongings. This included a picture of Simone and her family, her parents and her brother. In the dark crevices of her middle drawer, she found another old picture, one of her and James. She remembered that day— they had gone bike riding from Venice Beach to the Santa Monica Pier. When they reached the pier, they asked a man standing nearby to take their picture. Then they'd parked their bikes and had lunch, walking the length of the pier to buy cotton candy and snow cones afterwards. By the end of the day, they each suffered from a classic case of overindulging. She ran her fingers over James' face in the picture. She placed it gently in the box with the rest of her things.

They worked quietly, but quickly. Brandy remembered the day Simone had helped her move into her office four years before. What excitement she'd felt back then. Her own office and a view! She'd felt like George Jefferson. Where had all that enthusiasm gone?

In a strange way, Brandy was sad, but she wasn't sure why. She definitely wasn't going to miss her colleagues. Well, she would miss David, but she was only leaving the firm, not their friendship, which she was certain would endure. She for damn sure was not going to miss Lloyd or Stan. Maybe it wasn't sadness afterall.

"You're very quiet." Simone hoped that Brandy wasn't having second thoughts.

"I was just thinking." Brandy smiled. "I feel weird. It's a good weird, though."

"It's only natural that you'd feel something, Brandy. You spent four long years of your life here. Just think of it as getting out of a bad relationship— there's no reason for you to stay in it, but you miss it anyway."

Brandy hugged her. "You're absolutely right." She continued loading the boxes into the trunk of her car.

"Thanks a million, David."

"Anything for you." He kissed her cheeks. "Call me Saturday and tell me how the M.S.C. went."

"I'll do better than that. I'll call you tomorrow."

David nodded and turned to Simone. "Good night. It was nice seeing you again."

Simone leaned across Brandy and extended her hand so he could shake it. He kissed it instead. "Take care, David."

They drove off into the night. As they neared Simone's house, she had an idea. "Brandy, why don't you throw an 'I Quit My Job Party'?"

"That's a thought." Brandy entertained the idea. "We could rent out a place and have a barbecue. How does next week sound?"

"Great. Has James called you?" Simone asked.

"As a matter of fact, I spoke with him today."

"What did you tell him?"

"He wants an answer on Saturday, but I told him that he's going to have to wait." Brandy tapped her finger on the steering wheel. "Actually, I look forward to seeing him. I need to feel his air and see if — "

"And see what?"

"I'll know it when I see him." She turned into Simone's driveway. "Who knows— maybe I'll have an announcement to make at my party."

Simone's eyes lit up. "So you've decided?"

"No, but I have a feeling that my hand is about to be forced."

"By whom?"

"Mr. Impatient, who else?" Brandy laughed. "Don't tell anybody. I want it to be a surprise."

"Okay, where do you want to have the barbecue?"

Brandy was getting happier by the minute. She couldn't wait until Saturday. "Off the top of my head, I can't think of any place. I'll think of something over the weekend."

"Brandy, I'm so happy for you! But whatever you do, don't decide before you're ready."

"That's my plan."

Simone got out of the car. "Brandy, you can't lift

those boxes out of the trunk— who's going to take them into your house?"

Simone was right, there was no way she could lift the boxes. "James will be over on Saturday. I'll ask him to get them for me."

"I'm sure he won't mind." Yes! James and Brandy had finally gotten it together. "Don't forget to take your plants in tonight."

"I won't."

"Call me when you get home, so I know you made it."

"I will. Thanks for your help." Brandy backed out of her driveway and went home.

As far as Brad could tell, everything was in place for the M.S.C. There was nothing else he could do, except pray that Brandy blew the settlement.

It was seven twenty-nine and Brandy, Brad, Lloyd and Stan were standing outside of the judge's office. "Brandy, do you have your brief with you?"

"Yes." Brandy reached into her briefcase and handed him the hefty document. "Here it is."

Lloyd flipped through the brief and then passed it to Stan for his inspection. Stan handed it to Brad. "Pay close attention today, Brad. Next time we'll be standing here for you."

Brad gave him a nervous smile. "You bet. I won't miss a thing."

"Brandy, you appear to be very relaxed this morning." Lloyd couldn't put his finger on it, but she seemed almost happy.

"I feel positive that we can get opposing counsel to agree to let J.D. pay attorney fees." Brandy had to fight to retain her composure. She couldn't wait to give Lloyd the resignation letter in her briefcase.

"Let's hope so."

Brandy caught J.D.'s round body out of the corner of her eye. "Speak of the devil," she muttered to herself.

The opposing counsel had arrived. After introductions were made, they all entered the Honorable Judge Gerald Tucker's office.

Brandy passed out copies of her brief. Judge Tucker gave everyone a few minutes to look them over. As mandatory settlement conferences were formal, the judge was wearing his robe.

"Is everybody ready?"

"Yes."

"Let's begin." Judge Tucker turned to opposing counsel and asked what was the nature of his complaint.

"Your honor, we are willing to waive the criminal charges for illegally freezing the bank accounts, if Mr. Jackson Hamilton will sell his share of the company to Mr. Courtland Hamilton . . ." Jeremy Becker, Courtland Hamilton's attorney, droned on for an hour.

"Ms. Curtis, how do you respond?"

"We reject counsel's offer. Mr. Jackson Hamilton had every right to freeze the accounts of Hamilton & Hamilton Insurance Company. They were joint tenants in the account and this allowed Jackson Hamilton to act as he did." Brandy summed up her argument in thirty minutes.

"I'm going to leave and let both sides resolve this matter. I know that both of you are aware of the tremendous time and cost of a trial." The judge left the room. He wanted them to settle the case.

Brandy and Jeremy went at it for two hours. Finally Judge Tucker intervened and asked the attorneys to step outside with him, where he ripped Jeremy's argument to shreds.

"Jeremy, there is not a court or jury in the world that

would force Jackson to sell his shares. You are blowing the damages way out of proportion and, ultimately, your client runs the risk of losing the entire company to his brother. I suggest you forget about him selling and accept attorney fees."

"As for your client, Ms. Curtis, he maliciously froze accounts that he had only a fifty-percent interest in. It's a good thing I'm retired, because I would increase the attorney fees just to teach Jackson a lesson. I'm going to give you two one last opportunity to hammer out a settlement."

Brandy would not back down from her argument and eventually Jeremy Becker gave in. When the judge returned, all of the attorneys were shaking hands.

"I'm glad to see that a compromise has been reached. This case is hereby dismissed." He shook everyone's hand and excused himself.

Lloyd and Stan each gave Brandy bear hugs. "You were sensational."

Brad also gave her a squeeze. "You're quite the negotiator. I'm impressed." Inwardly, he was pissed. Now he would never get his chance to shine.

Brandy was a gracious winner, smiling at everyone. She had started collecting her paperwork when Lloyd grabbed her hand. "Look over there."

J.D. and Courtland had made up, and J.D. strode toward her. "Ms. Brandy, you did a fine job. While you all were outside arguing, we shook hands and agreed to be partners again."

Brandy couldn't believe her ears. She looked at Jeremy for an explanation. He shrugged his shoulders in disbelief. "What about the attorney's fees?"

"Don't worry, Ms. Brandy, your firm will get paid."

Brandy shook her head. All of her hard work had been for nothing.

J.D. continued, "Our company will be retaining Lloyd

& Lloyd with Ms. Brandy— I mean, Ms. *Curtis* as our exclusive counsel from this day forward."

"Done. Excellent, J.D. Brandy looks forward to working with you and your brother." Stan was thrilled. Hamilton & Hamilton Insurance Company was worth several hundred million dollars.

The Hamilton brothers left the office walking arm and arm.

"They truly deserve one another," Stan said.

Lloyd nodded in agreement. "I took the liberty of making reservations at La Dome for our victory celebration. We need to talk strategy about some upcoming cases that we'd like you to handle, Brandy."

"I'm sorry, Lloyd, I'm unavailable for lunch today, and tomorrow, and the day after that." Brandy reached into her briefcase. "I have something for you."

Lloyd was taken aback. "I don't understand."

She handed him two letters. "Once you read these, you will." She smiled smugly at him and rolled her eyes at Brad.

"What are these about?" Lloyd gripped the chair.

"The first one is my resignation, the second one is a copy of the letter that I mailed to the California Bar, American Bar and National Bar associations about misconduct on the part of your wonder boy, Bradley Stevens." Lloyd and Stan exchanged glances of confusion.

The blood had drained from Brad's face. "What did I do?"

Brandy did not dignify him with a response. She turned to Lloyd. "I have a micro-cassette that you might be interested in." She dangled the cassette in front of Brad's face and handed it to Lloyd.

Brad reached for it, but Lloyd closed his hand around the cassette.

Brad began to stutter, "But, but— "

"Be quiet!" Stan barked. Realizing Brandy's capacity to successfully win large settlements, he began to reconsider his earlier belief that Lloyd & Lloyd wasn't ready for an African-American attorney.

"Brandy, you can't resign. We need you." Lloyd was talking quickly.

"He's right!" Stan interjected. "Lloyd & Lloyd needs a partner like you to be in charge of the litigation department."

"I'm sorry. There's nothing you can say." She grabbed her briefcase and sauntered out of the room.

"Lloyd, run after her!" Stan yelled. "If she leaves, we lose the Hamilton brothers."

Lloyd trotted alongside of Brandy. "We'll double your salary."

"No, thank you."

"We'll fire Brad. We'll give you a new office."

"No."

"Name your price, Brandy. You can have anything you want, just don't quit."

Brandy ignored Lloyd and continued walking out of the building. She could not be bought. She was on top of the world and free at last.

Twenty-three

Brandy tossed her briefcase into the back seat of her car and put the top down. Her first stop was Trent's hair salon. He was waiting for her.

"Sorry I'm late, Trent."

"Actually, I'm glad you're late, my one o'clock just called and canceled."

Brandy sat down in his chair and he draped her with a cape. He undid the bun she had worn for the mandatory settlement conference.

"Ooh, Brandy, your hair feels gooky— what have you been doing to it?"

"I know it feels icky." She looked in the mirror in front of her.

"How do you want it styled today?"

"I want you to put it on the floor."

"What?"

"I want you to cut it all off." She reached into her purse and showed him pictures, one of Halle Berry and another of Toni Braxton. "I need a new attitude."

"Are you sure?"

"Um-hmm."

"You're positive?"

"Yes, just hurry up and cut it before I change my mind."

"Let me see those pictures." She handed him the

magazine cut-outs. He studied them both and then reached for his scissors.

"Ready?"

"Ready."

Thirty minutes later, Brandy looked like a new woman. "Thanks, Trent, I love it!" Her hair was shaved in the back. The front of her hair was parted down the middle and fell in velvety waves near the bottom of her ear lobes. Her new look gave her a sassy, playful air.

He stepped back and inspected his work. "This cut really brings out your features. I like it."

Brandy paid him and then left for her next destination, the nail shop. There she got her nails and toes painted in matching brown frost.

It was five forty-five when she got home. Her mother had left a message, so she called her back.

"Hi, Mama," she said as she looked around her messy room.

"Hi, baby, how are you doing?"

"I'm fine. I finally feel human." She admired her new haircut in the mirror.

"Was today your last day?"

"Yep."

"You sound good." Lena was happy that Brandy was happy. Now her daughter could get on with her life.

"I feel good. I even got a haircut."

"Oh, Lord." She hoped Brandy didn't look like a man.

"It's cute, Mama, you'll like it." Brandy loved the thought of being able to just get up and go in the morning, instead of fussing with her hair.

"All that matters is you like it."

"I'm having an 'I Quit My Job Party' on May 29th. I want you, Daddy and Byron to come. It's important, so don't forget."

"I wouldn't miss it for the world." For a minute she

thought Brandy had been going to say "wedding." That would have made her day. "Do you need any help planning it?"

"No, Simone and I have everything under control."

"Where will it be?" Lena wanted to write it all down on her calendar.

"I'm not sure yet, but I'll let you know."

"I don't have to wait two whole weeks to see you and your bald head, do I?" Lena started laughing.

"No, I'll stop by tomorrow."

"Love you."

"I love you too, Mama."

Brandy hung up the phone and changed into a pair of shorts and a t-shirt. She remembered that she hadn't eaten all day, so she went into the kitchen and inspected the contents of the refrigerator.

"Even Mother Hubbard had more in her cupboard," Brandy said to the cabinets. She opened the drawer where she kept take-out menus and chose Chin Chins', ordering shrimp with black beans, gift-wrapped chicken, and white rice.

On her way to pick up her dinner, she stopped in the Marina shopping center at the video store and picked out a movie. She was in a laughing mood, so she chose "The Best of Saturday Night Live with Eddie Murphy."

Somewhere around ten p.m., Brandy fell asleep in front of the TV. She woke up early Saturday morning and found herself sprawled out across her bed. She took a quick shower and made up her bed. The phone rang twice successively, signaling that someone was at the door.

"Yes?" Brandy wasn't expecting company.

"I have a delivery for Ms. Brandy Curtis."

"Who is it from?"

"James Collins."

"I'll be right down." She was excited and a little nervous. She couldn't even begin to guess what it might be.

When she reached the lobby, the deliveryman stood up. "Ms. Curtis?"

"Yes."

He handed her a small white box with a gold string around it. She tipped the man two dollars and walked slowly back to her door. She opened the box and squealed with delight. Underneath gold tissue paper lay four truffles from Godiva Chocolatiers. She wondered what each was filled with.

"He is so sweet!" she said out loud.

She put the truffles in the refrigerator so they wouldn't melt and called David, asking him to meet her for lunch at the Sidewalk Cafe on the Venice Beach boardwalk. Instead of taking her car, she decided to walk. She wanted to soak up some sun and get her thoughts together.

On her fifteen-minute walk down the bike path, she was nearly run over by a family on roller blades, which forced her to walk in the sand. It never ceased to amaze her that there was always a huge mass of people at Venice beach. For the most part, they didn't come for the surf. Instead, they came to people-watch, to eat, to shop and just to hang out.

Before she reached her destination, she passed bodybuilders, men playing basketball, women in string bikinis, police on bicycles, comedians, psychics, young, old, African-Americans, Caucasians, Latinos, Asians and every other ethnicity she could think of.

She'd told David to look out for her. Brandy was wearing a beige mesh tank top and a pair of shorts. She knew that she was too modest to wear the really short shorts that were so popular, so she'd opted for cut-off jeans and sandals.

She spotted David to the right of the crowd. He was

wearing a white tennis outfit, which sparkled against his olive skin. He was also wearing dark sunglasses and a sweatband around his head.

"Hi, David."

David jumped. "Bella! You startled me. I didn't see you walk up." He took his glasses off and kissed her. "How are you?"

"Wonderful." She gave him a radiant smile.

"Your hair!" He made a circle with his thumb and index finger and then kissed them. *"Belissimo!"*

She swirled around so he could see all of it. "I love it, too."

David signaled to the waiter that they were ready to be seated. "We're in luck, there's one table left in the patio."

"Good." David pulled the seat out for Brandy and she sat down. "One of my favorite pastimes is people-watching."

"Mine, too. People are beautiful to watch, especially in the summertime." The waiter reappeared with their menus, and David ordered iced tea and Brandy ordered an orange soda.

"I heard you won the settlement."

"Um-hmm." Brandy was distracted because she was studying the menu. "It went well."

"I knew it would." David put down his menu. "Whatever you wrote in your resignation letter must have been serious, because Brad was fired yesterday and Lloyd has begun proceedings to have him disbarred."

"Good, he saved me the trouble of doing it." She turned to the last page of the menu. "I think I'll have the herb chicken fingers with fries."

"That sounds good, I'll have the same." They placed their orders and continued their conversation.

"Before I forget, Shirley told me to tell you hello."

"Oh my God, I forgot to tell her good-bye. I'll call her on Monday."

"Good, she's a nice woman."

"Yes, she is."

"Are you going to open your own firm?" David was excited to hear her plans and reveal the truth about himself.

"Yes."

"You do know that start-up is going to be expensive." She let out a soft sigh. "I know."

"Do you know how much you're going to need?"

"No. I haven't looked into overhead expenses yet." She really didn't want to think about that.

"I have a proposition for you."

"I'm listening."

"Let me go in with you and help with the overhead expenses."

"What?" Brandy was stunned.

"I want to join your law firm. I have the money."

"I can't ask you to quit Lloyd & Lloyd, David."

"You're not asking, I'm offering."

"But if you leave the firm, you'll be walking away from a lot of money."

"Money isn't everything, bella." He played with his glasses. "We'll call it Brandy J. Curtis and Associates. We can specialize in litigation and tax, and—"

"David, why are you doing this?"

He spoke openly and strongly. "I have a confession to make. I am extremely attracted to you and if I liked women, I would want you as much as James and William do . . ." He trailed off as their order arrived.

"*If* you liked women?" She tried to control the surprise in her voice. She would have never suspected that David was gay.

"While I like women—" There was not one note of shame in his voice. "—I prefer men."

Brandy felt honored that he would expose something so personal to her. "Thank you for sharing that with me." She took his hand. Her tone was warm. "I don't care what your sexual preference is, David, just as long as we always remain close."

He kissed her hand. "We will, bella, I promise."

Brandy reached for a French fry. "I do have one question— what does that have to do with you leaving Lloyd & Lloyd?"

"In the seven years that I've worked there, I've never felt comfortable. No one knows that I'm gay. The problem is that I'm tired of living a lie."

Brandy took it all in. "You've given this a lot of thought, haven't you?"

"Yes, I have. I'm tired of covering my tracks and I know that if we work together, I can be myself." He took a sip of his drink. "Brandy, you're a strong woman and I admire you. I know that we'll make a good team."

"Your offer sounds very tempting." Brandy scratched her head. "I still can't believe that you'd walk away from a prestigious law firm to work for free. You know it's going to be a long time before we make any money."

"I'm aware of that."

Brandy chewed on a chicken finger. "I won't be ready for a few weeks." She smiled at him and wiped her hand on a napkin. She then extended a clean hand across the table. "Curtis & Gratani, A Law Corporation— I like the sound of that."

"Bella, you've made me so happy!" David leaned across the table and kissed her hand.

"I still think you're nuts." Brandy couldn't believe her good fortune. David was definitely a Godsend. "Waiter, bring us your best champagne! We have a partnership to seal."

* * *

Slightly tipsy from lunch, Brandy stumbled into her townhouse. David had dropped her off at home. Her head was still reeling from the sun, the food and David's generous offer. She checked her machine. Only James had called. She called him back and invited him over. She needed to see him one last time before she made her decision.

Brandy brushed her teeth and washed her face while she waited for James. She was exceptionally calm and hopeful about his visit. Finally, peace had replaced the hysteria that had dominated her soul for the last six days. God was definitely good and she was ready.

She thought back to Wednesday when William had come over. Then, she had been extremely nervous. "What a horrible day," she said to the mirror. "Shoot, that was only three days ago!" She dried her face. "What a difference a day makes."

James arrived at Brandy's thirty minutes later, and she buzzed him in. She could hear him singing in the hallway. She enjoyed hearing the sound of his voice.

She opened the door. "What are you singing?"

" 'I Want You' by Marvin Gaye." He kissed her on the cheek and handed her an armful of white roses, staring intently into her face. Something about her looked different. He couldn't put his finger on it.

She stepped aside so he could enter. He finished the line he was singing. *"I want you . . . the right way, baby . . . but I want you to want me, too."*

She closed the door. "These roses are lovely— thank you. James, you don't notice anything different about me?"

She moved directly in front of him. The top of her head reached the base of his Adam's apple.

"Hmm. I see someone is trying to give Halle Berry a run for her money." James touched her hair. "I like it."

Brandy tilted her head back and gazed deeply into his eyes. Her voice took on a seductive note. "Does Marvin's daughter know that you're singing her father's song?"

James' eyes lowered in anticipation. "No, but somehow I don't think she'd mind." He took a step closer, allowing his right index finger to lightly run the length of her collarbone. She felt herself opening up and didn't realize the flowers had slid from her hands until she stepped on one of them. "Oops."

He moved them out of the way with his foot. "They'll be there in the morning." James picked her up, took her into her bedroom and laid her down on the bed. A low moan escaped from her lips. Moments passed, but it felt like a lifetime. James started at her knees and kissed her until he reached her lips, and Brandy wrapped her legs around his back. He removed his underwear and she could feel his erect penis against the inside of her thigh. Before he entered her, he reached into the drawer of the nightstand, where she'd kept the condoms when they were together. In a matter of seconds, James had slid on the condom and entered her. As their bodies rocked back and forth, Brandy's breath caught. She wanted to scream. *Oh, how good it is to be back in his arms!* she thought to herself. Instead, she let out a loan moan and tightened her grip around his back. She never wanted to let go.

Time seemed to stop for James. Brandy felt good beneath him. No, it was better than good. It was almost spiritual. Their tempo quickened and at last he had reached it. He closed his eyes tight, threw his head back and gave a final thrust.

"Brandy!" he called out.

"James! Oh, James!" she responded.

Their screams of passion could be heard all through the townhouse. Spent and out of breath, James lay motionless on top of her. She rubbed his back and squeezed his butt.

"Brandy, please."

She started laughing. "I love you, James."

Forcing air into his lungs, he responded, "Brandy, I couldn't love you more if I tried." When he found his strength, he rolled off of her and took her left hand in his. "I'm tired of waiting, Brandy—does this mean that you will marry me?"

She pondered his question. "Before I answer, I need to know something." She faced him. "How do I know that you won't get cold feet again? How do I know that you won't leave when the thrill is gone? How do—"

He took her face between his hands. "Look baby, I'm sorry about all of that, but I promise that I'm not going anywhere. As much as I hated losing you, it showed me how empty my life would be without you. Brandy, I don't know how many times or ways I can tell you how much I need you."

"I believe you, it's just that—"

"What?" He pulled her on top of him.

As much as Brandy didn't want to know the answer, she had to ask. "Were you seeing someone else before we broke up?"

"No. Other women weren't the problem, I was."

"Why didn't you come to me, James? Why couldn't you talk to me?" It hurt to know that he had turned away from her in his time of crisis.

James saw the cloud pass over her face. "Brandy, I should have come to you, I know that now. When we were apart, all I did was think about you." James kissed her forehead.

Brandy found comfort in his words.

"Brandy, you are the love of my life. I was so stupid, I don't know what came over me." He squeezed her tightly.

"Shh. Just hold me." She laid her head on his bare chest and listened to his heartbeat. Eventually James fell asleep. While she listened to his light snores, she imagined her life with him. After a half hour of intellectualizing love, she gave up.

"Alexander O'Neal was right, love makes no sense."

Twenty-four

Simone called Brandy early Sunday morning. She had a feeling that Brandy hadn't spent her evening alone.

"Hey, what's up?"

Brandy sounded groggy. "What time is it?"

"Early."

"I should've known." Brandy pulled the comforter from the bottom of the bed and covered James. "Okay, what's on your mind?"

"I know James is over there."

She looked at the sleeping figure to her left. "You're right, he's here."

"Soo . . ."

"Yes." Brandy tried to whisper.

"Did you decide yet?" The suspense was killing Simone.

"Yes."

"Well, Brandy?"

"James is lying right here next to me, I can't tell you now."

"Huh." James rolled over and pulled her closer to him.

"Nothing, honey, go back to sleep." She rubbed his back.

"Brandy, go in the other room," Simone demanded.

Brandy tried to ease away from James, but he moved when she did. "If I move, he's going to wake up."

From her words, Simone figured out her decision.

Brandy was still whispering. "Can I have the party at your house?"

"Of course. I don't know why we didn't think of that in the first place. We'll have a pool party!"

James checked his pager while Brandy was in the shower. His office had beeped him five times. He called and found out that one of his accounts was about to close. He needed to go to New York and work out the details.

When Brandy emerged from the bathroom, he was getting dressed. "James, where are you going?"

"I've got to go to New York to close a deal." He ran into the living room and grabbed his shoes.

"What time is your flight?"

"Three p.m."

Brandy looked at the clock on the nightstand. It was twelve-thirty. "When are you coming back?"

"Wednesday." James found his keys. "I'll call you when I reach New York." He kissed her on the lips and then hurried out of the townhouse.

"Be careful!" she called after him. James didn't hear her. He was already in the hallway.

On Monday, Brandy automatically woke up at six-fifteen. She almost got up to get ready for work when she remembered that she didn't have a job to go to. A slow smile spread across her face.

"No Lloyd, no Brad, no stress, no pressure— I'm finally free to be me!" She rolled over and went back to sleep.

At noon, hunger pangs woke her. She wandered into the kitchen and then remembered that there was only truffles and left-over Chinese food in the fridge. She had no choice but to go to the grocery store.

Fortunately, the grocery store was empty and she was able to run in and out. She resisted the urge to splurge and buy unnecessary things like a garlic press. The only item she bought on a whim was a bridal magazine. Actually, that last item made Brandy the happiest. She got a warm feeling just thinking about the resurrected love in her life. She didn't realize how much strain her job had put on her emotionally until she touched the outside of the magazine. Her career had dictated her life and almost caused her to lose the one thing that meant the most to her— her inner peace. She'd learned a valuable lesson from that experience. Never ever again would she lose herself, her dignity or her pride in order to receive a paycheck. Life was too short.

Brandy made one last stop before she went home. She stopped at Triple A to get a travel magazine. Instead of one, she left with ten magazines that highlighted romantic getaways she had seen on "Lifestyles of the Rich and Famous."

When she got home she fixed angel hair pasta with shrimp and a huge salad. She would have cooked more, but she needed to eat immediately. While she ate, she caught the end of *General Hospital* and even braved *Oprah*. The topic for the day was "Women Who Put Themselves First." Brandy enjoyed the show because it focused on women who were happy, not because of the men in their lives or their professional titles, but because they'd made themselves number one in their lives. She hated to see the show end, because it was confirmation that she was moving in the right direction. Brandy watched the news and ate the truffles for dessert.

On Tuesday, Brandy lounged around her townhouse and then went to her parents' home. Her father was in the den watching cable.

"Well, there's my girl!" Brandy leaned over and he kissed her on her cheek.

"Hey, Daddy, what are you watching?"

"*Sanford and Son.*" He was reclining in his La-Z-Boy chair.

"Where's Mama?"

"Huh?"

"Mama, your wife."

"She's in the kitchen." Brandy left him to his show and went looking for her mother.

"Hi, Mama."

"You're not as bald as I thought you were going to be."

"I'm fine, thanks for asking," Brandy said with a tinge of sarcasm.

"Hi, sweetie."

Lena wiped her hands on a paper towel and then ran her fingers through Brandy's hair.

"Does that mean you like my haircut?"

"Yes, turn around." Brandy turned around slowly. "You look more sophisticated with your hair short."

"Thanks, I'm glad you approve." Brandy moved away from her. "I have something to tell you."

Lena was cleaning greens in the sink. "Should I sit down for this?"

"If you want." Brandy's eyes were sparkling. She reached into her pocket and pulled out a ring. She held it up for her mother to see.

Lena chose to remain standing. "Where did you get that?"

"James gave it to me."

"It's beautiful."

"Yes, it is. Mama—"

"I need to sit down." Lena rushed to the table and sat down quickly.

"I decided to follow my heart. I'm going to marry James."

"Oh, Brandy, I'm so happy for you!" Lena jumped up and hugged her daughter. "You're not doing this because I want you to, are you?"

"No. I prayed on it and this is the answer I got back." Brandy slid the ring onto her finger. She liked the way it felt.

"Where's my son?"

"He's in New York on business. He doesn't know yet."

"Why haven't you told him?"

"I wanted to talk to William first."

"That makes sense. You know he's going to be hurt, so don't expect him to understand."

"I won't."

Lena walked to the doorway of the den and called her husband. "Booker! Booker! Come in here for a minute."

"Oh Mama, *Sanford and Son* is still on."

"I know, sugar, just come here for a second." Lena went back to where Brandy was standing. "You know Booker and that damn TV are going to be the death of me."

Brandy laughed.

"What, baby?" Booker asked Lena.

"Our baby is getting married." Lena beamed at Brandy.

Booker forgot about his show. "Brandy, what's Mama talking about?"

"James and I are going to get married."

He was silent and his face grew serious. He walked over to Brandy and then gave her the biggest smile she had ever seen in her life. "It's about time you two quit being so silly." He squeezed her. "I'm so happy. Where is my future son-in-law?"

"He's out of town."

"When he gets back, bring him over here so that we can have a man-to-man talk."

"Oh Daddy, be nice."

"Honey, I'm always nice to your friends." He smashed his fist into his hand. "I'll be even nicer to your fiancé." He laughed a deep laugh and then ran back to his show.

It was Wednesday evening when Brandy buzzed James into the townhouse.

He came in carrying his suitcase in one hand and his briefcase in the other. He dropped his bag in the doorway and took her into his arms.

"Brandy, I took a cab over here. What have you decided?"

Brandy tried to sound casual, but couldn't repress her smile. "When is your vacation?"

"My vacation? What does that have to do with you marrying me?" His heart was pounding.

"I was thinking we could go to the Cayman Islands or Barbados for our honeymoon." Her heart was racing. She was so happy she thought she was going to burst.

"Honeymoon? Are you saying what I think you're saying?"

"Yes, James. I accept your proposal."

"You mean it?" He hugged her tightly. "I love you so much. You've made me the happiest man in the world!" He picked her up and swung her around the room. "I'm going to make you so happy, Brandy Curtis, you won't regret your decision for a minute!"

"I believe you, James, but there's one thing I forgot to mention."

The smile on his face froze. "What?"

"The name is Brandy Collins."

ENJOY THESE SPECIAL
ARABESQUE HOLIDAY ROMANCES

HOLIDAY CHEER   (0-7860-0210-7, $4.99)
by Rochelle Alers, Angela Benson,
and Shirley Hailstock

A MOTHER'S LOVE   (0-7860-0269-7, $4.99)
by Francine Craft, Bette Ford,
and Mildred Riley

SPIRIT OF THE SEASON   (0-7860-0077-5, $4.99)
by Donna Hill, Francis Ray,
and Margie Walker

A VALENTINE KISS   (0-7860-0237-9, $4.99)
by Carla Fredd, Brenda Jackson,
and Felicia Mason

Available wherever paperbacks are sold, or order direct from the Publisher. Send cover price plus 50¢ per copy for mailing and handling to Penguin USA, P.O. Box 999, c/o Dept. 17109, Bergenfield, NJ 07621. Residents of New York and Tennessee must include sales tax. DO NOT SEND CASH.